MW00927862

The

Time Keepers

A Vatican Novel

Ronald Bruce Gies

www.GiesBooks.com

Danville, California

To my family:

My ancestors, who brought us and our faith to a new land

My parents, who instilled in me both a strong faith and an unwavering objectivity

My wife, who still sees much more in me than I can believe

My children, who provide me the opportunity to pay it forward

And finally, to my wonderful pastors over the decades, who always provided such tireless examples of service to their Church.

TABLE OF CONTENTS

Preface

To believers in the Roman Catholic faith, the Church traces its origins back to the beginning...of everything. God established the Jewish people as His "chosen people" in the world He created. Jesus, the Christ, came from among them to reinvigorate humanity's relationship with its Creator. While preparing to leave the world, Jesus appointed His apostle, Peter, as the head of His Church. Peter's successors—the Popes—carry on that legacy.

During early centuries of the Church, the small Jewish sect grew into a dynamic (and sometimes targeted) institution. By the Middle Ages, as its census grew, so did its political power. Catholics looked to the Church to anoint their overlords, and as a result, the Church acquired tremendous influence with those who would be kings and queens. It managed to leverage that influence into political power, including kingdoms of its own. During those days of political and economic clout, the Church accumulated incalculable wealth, not the least of which is the greatest collection of art and antiquities that the world has ever known.

Today, the Vatican state remains a seat of power. While the Church no longer wields the overt political power that it once did, it still possesses an enormous emotional influence on world events through an estimated one billion believers. As a result of this influence, and in some ways to foster it, the Vatican has formal diplomatic relations with approximately one-hundred eighty nations.

Popes are elected as supreme head of the Church from among those most likely to be elected—the Cardinals, "the princes of the Church." In late 1958, a new Pope, John XXIII, was elected. Given his advancing age, he was thought by most to have been elected as a caretaker after the long reign of his predecessor. However, less than three months later, he called for a Council of Church leaders, known today as Vatican II. His purpose was to create the first reforms of the Church that reflected her worldwide nature, not only the Europe-centric view of Catholicism. This modern worldview was intended to be captured in major conciliar documents on the Church's mission, its liturgy, and its pastoral role in the world. Also during the first year of his papacy, he commissioned a group of nontheologians to study the topics of birth control and population and report back their recommendations. When he died after just four and a half years, a new Pope was elected from among the College of Cardinals. Paul VI augmented the membership of Pope John's commission and issued the Encyclical, *Humanae*

Vitae, which reaffirmed the Church's long-held teachings on birth control. The new Pope also presided over the conclusion of Vatican II and issued "clarifications" (*motu proprio*), which effectively put guardrails around the final documents of the historic Council. In the minds of many observers, these actions slowed the pace of the Church's movement into the new millennium.

When Pope Paul's successor was elected, he took the name John Paul I, out of respect for his two immediate predecessors; some thought this was an overt sign that he would seek to bend the direction of the Church back toward some of the openness associated with John XXIII. When John Paul died suddenly after just thirty-three days in the role, conspiracy theories ran rampant. Was he intent on moving too fast for the insular group that had just granted him the white robes? Would they ever really allow their Church to evolve faster than the slowest among them? These questions, and the conspiracy theories behind them, serve as an interesting jumping-off point for a work of fiction.

Some of the fictitious letters and speeches referenced in the body of this story are contained in the Papal Archives, found at the end of the book. You may choose to read them first or as they are referenced within the text.

When reading this novel, please remember that it is a work of fiction. Even some of the details, which could have been rendered more accurately, have been intentionally altered to highlight the true nature of this novel as a work of fiction. I believe that it's always fun to dance between historical reality and fiction as a way of engaging the mind and asking, "What if...?"

PART I—AWAKENING

Chapter One

His sleep was often restless in the early morning. Today he hovered between the familiar and joyful dream of his youth and the dramatically more serious world of his present day. Keeping his eyes closed, he could just barely hold the image of running after the family sheep, up and down the hills around his tiny village. His grandfather used to call him *piccolo pecoraio*, the little shepherd, although he was never officially responsible for the family's herd. That duty fell to his oldest brother, Carlo. There were other duties planned for this *pecoraio,* but he had loved his nonno and that scene so much that it was hard to voluntarily release it and return to the present.

The mental image of that distant past was in such contrast to the world to which his senses were now returning. It was such a simple childhood that many would label it as poverty. To him, however, things simply were the way they were, not just for his family but for everyone they knew.

Because of that, they focused on what they had and the happiness that it brought to them. Yet it was hard to look back without drawing comparisons to the opulence that awaited him as he awoke. He had achieved great success and notoriety, and with that came the trappings, he supposed; however, he never felt as much at home here as he had on that farm.

It was cold outside, he knew—not only because of the early-morning soreness that would strike a man his age, but because he could feel the fire that Claudio had begun quietly about an hour ago in his room. He opened his eyes slowly, slightly disoriented by his surroundings. The childhood memories were nothing like what his eyes were now drinking in. They were finally able to focus on the beautiful fresco above the bed; the last few years came flooding back. As a child, he'd never imagined being able to even visit a room like this, let alone to live in one of the most renowned palaces in the entire world. What a charmed life it had been, and how far had he come.

Just then, the door creaked and Abrielle emerged with his simple breakfast. She was such a sweet girl—handpicked like all of his personal staff. But a girl, no. Perhaps she was, but only in relation to him. No, by now she must be in her late forties, although he couldn't exactly recall. She still possessed the energy of youth, but also the peace that comes with maturity. He had remembered her birthday a few weeks ago, surprising her by arranging for Giuseppe to join them for breakfast. That was the first time she'd been aware of just how keenly observant he was. She and Giuseppe were so certain of their discretion, but somehow he had sensed that there was something between them. Now, as he watched her struggle to enter the room with the loaded tray, he reflected how difficult it was to convince his personal staff to accept assistance and share the workload. They all wanted to serve, in every sense of the word. He had been taught that work was meant to be shared.

"*Buongiorno, Santo Padre,*" Abrielle said as she placed the tray down. The Holy Father was the spiritual leader of over one billion Catholics, yet he could not get his personal attendants to call him by his more simple title, even when they were alone in his apartments.

"*Padre, per favore.*"

After Abrielle arranged his breakfast on the table in the corner and had fiddled with the fire for a moment or two, she quietly backed out of the room. He gave her the sweet smile of a favorite uncle, but she was still too formal to acknowledge it. He turned his eyes back to the fresco, closed them softly once again to the whisper of "piccolo pecoraio," and promised himself that this was the day. The Church, his church, would change. He would live up to his destiny as its shepherd.

Chapter Two

After eating breakfast and retiring to his private office in the Papal Apartments, Pope John XXIV watched the sunrise illuminate Saint Peter's Square. He could still remark at both the beauty of its current architecture and at the image in his mind of how this must have looked seventeen hundred years ago, when the original church was begun at this site. How funny that new structures could be so stunning and at the same time obscure something equally special. An old friend in Rome's Office of Archeology had once joked that, throughout history, humans have destroyed things—a building or a natural feature—in order to make way for something new, which they name after the thing that they destroyed in the process. Quite ironic.

With this thought still lingering in his mind, Pope John summoned his personal secretary. It always struck him as odd that within the Papal Household, they still observed the traditions of personal invitations, rather than picking up a telephone. This was, after all, the twenty-first century. At least it was outside these walls. He leaned over to the corner of his desk and pulled a narrow velvet rope. Outside his door, he could hear a small bell tinkle, and moments later a young seminarian stepped in, robed in a freshly starched black cassock. The Pope was amused that there seemed to be an infinite supply of these eager young men, huddled outside his door awaiting a dispatch. He had never been able to remember their names, and they always looked at him as though seeing him for the first time. As a result, he'd acquired the habit of addressing each as "Future Father," which they seemed to appreciate.

He greeted the young man, saying, "*Buongiorno, Padre Futuro*. Would you please ask Monsignor Hellman to join me at our usual time this morning? I should like to reestablish some old routines." What he left unsaid was that they were about to start a great many new routines as well.

The seminarian replied, "Yes, Holy Father, as you wish." He then backed out of the room as quietly as he had arrived.

As Pope John heard the door close, he imagined who would walk in the door next if he were to pull the velvet cord again. How many times would he have to pull it before there would be no one left to answer? More to the point, how could there be a shortage of vocations to the priesthood if there were so many excess seminarians lying around the Vatican, just waiting for the velvet cord to instigate the tiny bell?

It had not yet been a month since a minor transient stroke had put him in bed for several weeks, and these meetings with his Papal Secretary had not yet regained their former regularity. But after undergoing countless tests and performing a regimen of light physical therapy, he had decided that it was time to get back to work. The work of the Church must continue, or there was no reason for him to occupy the Throne of Saint Peter.

This next meeting, he knew, would allow him to set a revolutionary process in motion—a process that he had waited for in his church for more than two decades, but a process that scared him nonetheless. This meeting could be the point of no return. By announcing his intentions to Monsignor Hellman, he was making public his plans to remake the Roman Catholic Church. That would at once test his secretary's position on the topic and, depending upon that position, potentially alert others in the Curia about his intentions. He wasn't sure he was ready for those confrontations. Monsignor Hellman was of an age and background that suggested he might be the ideal evangelist for the improvements he planned; and yet, he knew that his secretary kept the company of some of the more conservative members of the Church's hierarchy.

As the seminarian approached the suite of offices known inside the Apostolic Palace as "The Threshold"—the place across which anyone wishing access to the Pope must cross— he recalled the one other time he had made this journey. Twenty-seven days earlier, on the day that Pope John had suffered his stroke, it was he who had been sent to notify Monsignor Hellman. Today the trip would bring him full circle, notifying the Papal Secretary that His Holiness wished to resume their normal schedule.

Entering the outer office, he noticed Monsignor Hellman hovering over his own secretary's desk, reviewing some correspondence. Officially known as *Officium Sancti Petri*, or the Office of Saint Peter, the Papal Secretary's offices were responsible in part for reviewing the thousands of daily communications sent to the Pope. It then redirected them to the numerous departments that managed the business of the Church. Correspondence of a personal nature, however, was always reviewed by the Papal Secretary personally. There were very, very few exceptions in which items would reach His Holiness without first having been reviewed by Monsignor Hellman.

Upon seeing young Francis Hennessey, the Monsignor smiled and set his work aside. Walking over to the young seminarian, he greeted him by name. Unlike the Pope, Monsignor Hellman made it his business to know the names of everyone in the Apostolic Palace, especially in the Papal Apartments. The fact that he and the seminarian in this case shared the same name made his task somewhat easier today.

"Francis, how nice to see you. Does your visit mean that I can begin my day with a bit of good news?"

"Yes, Monsignor, His Holiness wishes to resume your regular meetings this morning." Young Francis was a bit overwhelmed to be on such familiar terms with someone of Monsignor Hellman's stature.

Francis Hellman looked at his watch and realized that he had only eighteen minutes to prepare for this first meeting; he asked, "Were there any specific instructions regarding today's agenda?"

"No, Monsignor, but if it is worth mentioning, I would share that His Holiness seemed quite relaxed and in good spirits."

"Very well then, thank you for bringing me the good news." He was thinking less about the mood of the Pontiff than he was making a mental note that young Francis Hennessey seemed to be unaware of the normal bounds of

Vatican etiquette: one should never volunteer personal information about the Pope. His lax protocol might prove useful down the road.

Finding himself alone again, Monsignor Hellman thought about how he should prepare for his meeting. Certainly, Pope John wouldn't feel up to the typically exhaustive review of correspondence and requests. Perhaps a simple overview of the events of the last few weeks, along with a plan to renew their meetings and ease him back into a normal schedule. It had felt strange to him, just how little access he'd had recently. Although intimate by the standards of most business relationships, his relationship with the Pope would never have been described as much more than "cordial." Since the stroke, he had been asked by the papal physician and some senior members of the Curia, the Pope's cabinet, to curtail their time together and let the Pontiff recuperate. Now it appeared that things might be getting back to normal.

It was certainly extraordinary that a guy from Cleveland would think that it's "normal" to be serving at the foot of the Throne of Saint Peter and living in the Eternal City. To most people in the world, especially Roman Catholics, he was a man of power and prestige. In his own mind, however, he was just a guy who had happened into the vocation of the priesthood, without really thinking much about the day-to-day job of a priest. It quickly became obvious, to both him and to his Bishop, that he was not cut out for pastoral duties in a parish. He was, however, quite bright and had a flair for administrative details. His Bishop had arranged for him to attend the Pontifical Lateran University in Rome, where he had excelled at his studies and found himself a niche within the Church. Because this particular university is led by one of the Pope's right-hand men, young Father Hellman received early and special notice by the Papal Household. "It's better to be lucky than good," a friend had said to him on his return for a visit to the United States; and young Francis Hellman could never quite shake that phrase. "Why can't I be both?" he thought.

Monsignor Hellman found himself thinking back to a day almost three years ago, only a few days after Pope John had ceased to be Franco Cardinal Calliendo of Sardinia. On that fateful day, only in his early forties, he had accepted his own appointment as Papal Secretary. The appointment capped off a whirlwind courtship of sorts, but oddly enough, one that had never included the newly appointed Pontiff. It seemed that from inauspicious beginnings, Father Hellman's entire rise through the clergy could be described as a whirlwind.

As a young parish priest, he'd found himself being counseled personally by his former rector at the seminary. Father Merrick had recently been moved into the Chancery Office of the Diocese of Cleveland, with responsibility for clerical personnel. It seemed that after only a couple of years in his first parish placement, Francis Hellman had already established a reputation for awkwardness. Where his friends could be inspirational preachers, he couldn't stop using note cards. Where his friends naturally gravitated toward roles in parish life—leading youth groups, facilitating bible studies, or even visiting hospitals—Francis Hellman was too self-conscious.

Into that void stepped Father Merrick, a generation ahead, who had himself found a key mentor in his younger days. He seemed to understand that Francis might not fit the typical mold, and for the first time, that was okay. In fact, Joe Merrick actually thought that this young priest might have a higher calling. He found him a role in the Chancery Office, helping to coordinate the business side of the diocese, and Francis quickly found his place. Within five years, he wouldn't just be working alongside Father Merrick, he would be working *for* Bishop Merrick, who had been made Bishop and appointed Coadjutor (Bishop-in-waiting) for the entire diocese.

With the advancement of Bishop Merrick came the opportunity for Francis Hellman to begin his real education into the clubby-ness that existed behind the curtain of the Church. He noted that his new boss had a very important mentor, the prior Bishop of Cleveland and current Cardinal Archbishop of Boston, John Cardinal Welty. He also learned that there were basically two paths to becoming a senior cleric—administrative roles within a diocese, which created opportunities for establishing credentials as an able manager; or administrative roles within the Vatican, which created opportunities for building relationships at the "holding company." Most of the new Bishoprics were doled out by the Vatican based upon the advice of the leadership in that country. At the Vatican itself, where there could be a theoretically unlimited number of Bishops and Cardinals, one carefully cultivated a brand that would mark one as worthy of higher office. It never really struck him as ironic that the Bishops (the first teachers) of the Church didn't necessarily have to be good pastors. In fact, being a good preacher and counselor often sidetracked the ambitious, because the demands of working with a local congregation left little time for working on your brand outside of your parish.

So when Cardinal Welty invited Father Francis to dinner three years ago, on the eve of the Conclave to elect a new

Pontiff, he wasn't completely surprised. During the previous five years, he had been making his mark in Rome, working on his brand. Bishop Merrick had arranged for Francis to attend the Pontifical University in Rome, investing in him and marking him as one with a special talent. During the last few years, he had assumed a faculty appointment at the same university and had begun to work as a staff member on low-level Vatican commissions.

Francis had come to think of Cardinal Welty as his "clerical grandfather," in a manner of speaking. When he first left for Rome, the Cardinal had called to wish him well in his studies and to extend an offer to assist Francis as he acclimated to the Roman lifestyle. On the somewhat rare occasions that the Cardinal visited Rome, he always seemed to make time in his schedule to meet with him. Sometimes it was just a quick cup of coffee, but when he received his licentiate from the university, they went out for a celebratory dinner. But in the rumor mill that is the Vatican, John Welty knew that he was creating a buzz around Francis, marking him as part of his family.

By the time Cardinal Welty was visiting Rome to elect a new Pontiff, he felt that Francis was ready for his next step. The dinner began easily enough, for Francis and the Cardinal had established a bit of a rapport over the years, as much as was possible in such relationships. As their main courses were being cleared, however, the conversation turned serious, with a hint of intimacy that hadn't existed before. Francis had always expected to be treated as no more than a minor lord in the presence of a prince of the royal household. Now the Cardinal looked at him, through him really, as if trying to assess his ultimate potential. For the rest of the evening, they discussed views on the direction of the Church and the roles that succeeding generations have to the "blessed continuity." Francis felt at times as though it was a quiz and at times as though he was being brought behind the curtain. He was suddenly aware that they had been seated alone, with no one permitted at the adjacent tables. During their entire conversation, Father Hellman was continually reminded of the statements he'd heard for decades about this man with whom he was having this very private meal. "He is certain to become the first American Pope," was what people regularly said about John Cardinal Welty. From the time he was elevated from the humble diocese of Cleveland, Ohio, to run one of the most important Catholic regions in North America at a relatively young age, people had been talking. "Why would they move him to Boston so young?" and "Isn't it time that the United States (or the Western Hemisphere for that matter) be represented at the Vatican?" In time, it became dogma in the American Catholic Church that it was time for an American to sit at the Throne of Saint Peter, and further that that man should be Cardinal Welty.

By the time their final coffee arrived, it was clear that these rumors were not outside the earshot of the Cardinal himself, for he was speaking very directly about his future. Perhaps it was just the caffeine in the strong Italian coffee, but Father Hellman felt the world spinning a bit out of control. The trepidation that had always accompanied his quick rise through the Church was being dwarfed by the potential outcome of this conversation.

"You must have heard the rumors over the years that I was on the short list of possible successors to Saint Peter," confided the Cardinal.

"Well, of course, everyone considers you eminently qualified."

"Interesting choice of words," observed the Cardinal with a chuckle, as *Your Eminence* is the customary way of addressing a member of the College of Cardinals. "I trust that this outcome wouldn't surprise or disappoint you personally."

"Without a doubt, Your Eminence, it would be a great joy to see you rise to become our Supreme Pontiff, especially given the special privilege that I feel in having come to know you over these years."

"Should I assume the Throne of Saint Peter, it will be very important for me to be surrounded closely by people who I feel are looking out for my best interests. In such times, personal loyalty can be very important. As you have come to learn over the last few years, the Vatican is a political as well as a spiritual place. There are some who would be disappointed if I, well, any American actually, were to wear the Papal Tiara."

"I understand. I find it very unfortunate—"

"Be that as it may," he said, cutting off the young priest in mid-sentence, "would it surprise you that a great number of the Cardinals in the College have called me over the last few days, inquiring about my interest in the chair?"

"That's wonderful news, Your Eminence." Father Hellman was feeling a little chastised about his earlier informality and cautious about offering his opinions.

"In preparation for that possibility, I came to Rome quickly, in order to discuss what might be the next steps. While it may seem undignified to some, there are practical considerations."

"Yes, Eminence."

"Should I become the next to wear the crown, it is my choice that you should become my personal secretary. Bishop Merrick and I agree that we have provided you with the adequate training and connections to serve effectively in that role."

"I'm overwhelmed, Your Eminence."

"In order to finish polishing your credentials, we began the process some months ago of working with His Holiness on an appointment for you, *Apostolic protonotaries de numero*." Francis knew that this meant he would receive the title Monsignor. "You were to have certain new duties close to the Papal Household. Now, with His Holiness' passing, while the appointment has already been completed, the role will be held in abeyance until a new Pontiff takes his place. Should that be me, you will take the role of Papal Secretary instead."

"I am even more overwhelmed, Your Eminence."

"Well, Monsignor, our meal has concluded and I still have some jetlag from which to recover."

"Your Eminence, at the risk of overstaying my welcome…" The newly minted Monsignor Hellman paused for a moment for permission to continue. "It has always seemed an unworthy honor to have enjoyed your counsel and courtesies over the years. If there is any way in which I may serve the Church and you in particular, I would always be most grateful."

Without another word being said, they both rose from the table and shared a friendly and gentle handshake. Monsignor Hellman watched as the Cardinal left the room. The thought occurred to him that the next time they spoke, he might be addressing him as *Your Holiness.*

Chapter Three

Snapping back to reality, Monsignor Hellman quickly packed his satchel with the most urgent correspondence that needed His Holiness's attention. He knew the earnestness with which Pope John looked at his office and instinctively knew that he would want to get back to work far more quickly than his physicians would recommend.

The contrast between the assumptions in his conversation with Cardinal Welty three years ago and the reality of the role he now held was striking to him. In fact, that contrast filled him with renewed trepidation. The events surrounding the election of John XXIV and the recent events surrounding his illness were causing Monsignor Hellman to feel concern about the role he played in the life of the Church.

The day following the breaking of the Conclave, when the Cardinals had finished the work of electing Franco Cardinal Calliendo to be the next Pontiff of the Roman Catholic Church, Cardinal Welty had summoned Francis to meet with him for a midmorning cup of coffee. It had been less than a week since their dinner, but when they met, Cardinal Welty spontaneously and immediately expressed his belief that the Holy Spirit had correctly guided the College in electing a very thoughtful cleric—one who had also spent most of his life in pastoral duties. Without breaking the seal of the Conclave, he shared that his heart was warmed by the sentiments expressed by the other Cardinals about his role as a pillar of the Church. In fact, Cardinal Welty had been one of the first to be granted a private audience with the new Pope John. It was during that audience that Cardinal Welty had pledged his loyalty and offered Monsignor Hellman to the new Pontiff as his personal secretary.

Francis Hellman asked about the personal loyalty that a Pope must feel from his secretary, almost parroting the words the Cardinal had used a week earlier. Even before the words came out of his mouth, Francis recognized the political elegance of the offer. It was an offer of loyalty, which demanded the reciprocation of trust, where the Pope felt bound to accept and thereby show his trust in the Cardinal. As Cardinal Welty finished his coffee and rose from the table, he thanked Francis for his expressions of loyalty to him, and thereby to the Church; and it struck Francis that nowhere in the statement did he mention loyalty to the new Pope.

More recently, Francis had first called Cardinal Welty on the occasion of the Pope's suspected stroke. One of his duties was communication with the College, especially in the event of any important happenings in the Vatican. By virtue of Francis's appointment, Cardinal Welty was always the first-among-equals when it came to hearing about such important happenings. What struck him at the time as odd was not the ease with which he was able to reach the Cardinal directly, but his reaction to the news of the Pope's illness. It was almost as if there was no real surprise, as the Cardinal inquired primarily about the usual administrative details. After a dozen such conversations, with each of the most senior prelates, Francis had shaken that odd feeling. Until now.

Now, as Monsignor Francis Hellman left his office for the Papal Apartments, he did so with both a purpose on his mind and a weight on his heart. He didn't even notice the priceless frescoes and wall hangings that he passed in the Palace. Actually, it had become all too common for Francis and his compatriots to take for granted the beautiful history encapsulated in these buildings. As with all people, familiar surroundings tend to fade in our minds; and at the Vatican, even the weight of everyday duties is sufficient to distract the most thoughtful souls.

As he neared the suite of rooms on the top floor of the Apostolic Palace, Francis passed Abrielle in the hallway. He mused that over the past three years she had brought such a breath of fresh air to the Papal Apartments. The small touches of gentleness that she brought to an otherwise very officious environment had been most welcome in Francis's life; the mere sight of her soothed his mind somewhat.

As one of the few persons who had permission to enter the Pope's study unannounced, Monsignor Hellman didn't draw much attention from the attendant outside the door. He knocked, waited a few seconds, and entered the door slowly. Greeting Pope John, he tried to keep his eyes bright and the mood businesslike, though he was very conscious of the recent separation and the lingering concerns over the Pope's health.

"Buongiorno, Santo Padre."

"Buongiorno, Monsignori," replied Pope John as he rose to greet Francis. "I am so glad to see you, as much as for what it represents as for your thoughtful indulgence. I am very anxious to resume our former schedule, now that I am back to full health."

"With respect, Holy Father, I do not think that your physician, nor the Curia, would agree completely with your assessment of 'full health.' We are all still very concerned with the sudden onset of your stroke, however minor."

"Fortunately, I feel quite fully recovered. So much so that I have raised my doubts with the physicians that it could possibly be as serious as a stroke. I have taken to calling it a *spell.* Nevertheless, the work of Holy Mother Church must continue. The greatest gift of my life has been this role and the chance to serve Her."

"Yes, Holy Father. I have brought the most urgent of the correspondence for your attention. If you desire to work through more still, I can quickly have the next satchel sent for."

"That is all very considerate of you, Francis. You have truly become a very trusted counselor and companion, and I've missed our time together these last few weeks. You understand that, up to a point, and for a time, I needed to listen to my medical advisors over my spiritual and administrative advisors. But rather than correspondence, I should like to focus on some more pressing issues…not pressing in the sense of having recently surfaced, but pressing in the sense that time can no longer stand by and wait for a resolution."

"Yes, Holy Father. As you wish."

"I should like to see the Church become more traditional in its practices."

"Yes, Holy Father. It does appear that, after the initial burst of unrest following Vatican II, the Church has found Her way back to greater tradition."

"I fear you misunderstand me, Francis. I want to see the Church become more traditional—not medieval, but a tradition that goes much farther back. I fear that much of our Church's clerical leadership longs for the Church in her 'glory days' of political power. It is my opinion that it was during that medieval period in our history when we sacrificed our passion for prestige."

"How do you mean, Holiness?"

"We need to find our true place in the world. We need to regain hold of the spirit, the Holy Spirit, that attracted so many followers during those early centuries. Service is what attracted those first members. They understood that service to each other was what Jesus taught…to humbly serve each other as His Father intended. To treat each other as His Father's children. To be His hands in the world, focused only on doing His work."

Believing that the Pope was speaking largely metaphorically, Francis quickly signaled his concurrence. "Yes, Holy Father. We must be an example of service to the world, so that people everywhere can take up that example and, in turn, serve each other."

"So you see that our role needs to become more tangible. Our Church needs to impress the world with our commitment to service. We need to remake the Church as the service bureau of the Lord on earth. And the senior clergy must lead by example if our actions are to be sufficiently impressive.

"I should like to begin by drawing up a list of retirees," continued Pope John. And I need your help to think about the possible criteria that we should apply. The Curia will insist that we apply an even hand, or they will do everything in their power to discredit the plan. And make no mistake, Monsignor, while I occupy the Chair of Saint Peter, I am not the only one with resources and influence in Holy Mother Church."

"Holiness? I think I missed a step in the plan. Do you mean to shrink the staff of the Vatican? If so, what would be the purpose, and how does that contribute to making the Church a better example in the world? I suppose that we could save some expenses here and there and redeploy them to our missionary work. Perhaps we could help some of the more successful orders to expand to new countries."

"Francis." It was rare for the Pontiff to call him by his Christian name, but it came across as fatherly. "You still don't understand; and perhaps that's my fault. Perhaps I'm still fearful about speaking plainly on this topic. For that, I'm going to need your prayers, for courage.

"Francis, I'm not talking about retirees among the lay staff of the Vatican. I'm talking about retirements among the senior members of the College, among the Curia. If we are going to remake the Church, it's going to require excitement for our original mission, which I am not sure exists among many of my brother Bishops. Do you imagine that many of them would like their worlds turned upside down, their apostolates?

"No, I think not," the Pope continued. "It would be better that a great number of my brothers be given the opportunity to step aside, encouraged even, to make way for a new generation. We need a generation that's ready for a new apostolate, one of pure service, close to the people they serve. Francis, does this sound like an undertaking that you support? Is this an undertaking that you will share with me?"

"Holy Father, I cannot claim to fully understand what you are planning or asking of me, but I have pledged my service to you and to the Church. If this is something that you wish, something that the College wishes, then of course you have my effort at your disposal."

"Please understand, Francis, this may not be something that the College wishes. It is time for Peter's successor to lead in a way that he hasn't in centuries. But this time, we're going to lead back to the basics. We're going to lead back to the original, simple message of our Lord. You will need to prepare yourself for the anger of some, and you will need to help me to navigate some difficult conversations. Are you ready for that challenge?"

"Yes, Holiness." Francis said this with all the conviction he could muster in his voice. He suddenly felt that odd feeling of disloyalty return. He suddenly realized that this was what he was placed in his position for.

Francis Hellman understood that this was a critical juncture, one at which he needed to assure the Pope of his allegiance. It would be important for him to remain in this position long enough to help Pope John understand the error of this path. Monsignor Hellman understood how the Curia and the College would react, and he could not abandon the whole Church for the temporary whims of a single Pontiff, especially one who was grappling with a recent brush with death. He must play an integral role in the planning, so that he could help maintain continuity during the negotiations to come.

"It would be my pleasure to help you to fashion your plans," he reiterated. But at the same time he couldn't help thinking how unfair it was of Pope John to put him on the spot like this, to spring this plan on him.

For the remainder of the meeting, they ignored the correspondence that had accumulated during the Pontiff's illness. They spoke only of the general outline of Pope John's plan. When they broke, they agreed to reconvene later that afternoon. Monsignor Francis Hellman, acolyte of John Cardinal Welty, had only a few hours to develop the criteria for dismantling the College of Cardinals as it was currently constructed. He couldn't fathom the position in which he now found himself.

Once he was alone in his study, Pope John reached again for the velvet rope. Now it was time to speak with one of his oldest friends and confidants, Monsignor Antonio Donatello. The Pope was sure that Antonio would be pleased to see him; but more importantly, the Pontiff needed strength for the journey he was about to begin.

Chapter Four

Pope John returned to his private rooms after dispatching yet another young seminarian to invite Monsignor Donatello to his study. He knew that it would take at least an hour for his old friend to receive the invitation and return, even if he had nothing to do and was found easily. If he knew his old friend, however, neither of those things would hold true.

"Perhaps I need more time to recuperate," he thought to himself. As he slumped into his favorite chair, with his mind off in another place, he let slip out loud, "This is going to be a tough road."

"Pardon me, Your Holiness?" Abrielle stood upright from behind the bed, where she was finishing tucking in the fine silk sheets. She had heard the Pontiff enter and assumed he was addressing her. "I didn't expect to see you back here this time of day. I apologize for the intrusion."

"Nonsense, dear girl. I hadn't expected to be here either. I was just feeling a little taxed after my meeting with

Monsignor Hellman. This was my first real working session since I fell ill, and I will admit to being somewhat surprised how tired I feel right now. I was thinking of taking a bit of rest here, after which I've invited Monsignor Donatello along for a walk in the garden."

"I see. Perhaps Your Holiness should keep a light schedule for a while, rather than pushing yourself too hard," she answered, knowing exactly how he would react to such a suggestion. It had only been four days since he'd been allowed out of bed by his physician, and already he was planning formal meetings. It was one of the things that Abrielle secretly admired about this man, although she would never encourage him to push too hard.

"I appreciate your concern, Abrielle; but as you know, there is much work to be done. In fact, there is much more to be done than even I might have suspected when I took this role. Now that Our Lord has seen fit to shake me into action, I will not let Him down. Although," he added, almost whispering to himself, "I am not completely confident that I am up to the task."

"Holy Father, I know that I am not a well-educated person and not particularly wise in the ways of the outside world, but I do know the character of people. I have also worked around the Vatican for much of my adult life. I believe you to be a very special person, unique even compared to others who serve the Church.

"I am confident," she continued, "that whatever you put your mind to you can accomplish. I can assure you of my personal support, humble as it may be, for as long as you choose to lead the Church."

Clearly touched, by both her words and her promise of fidelity, the Pontiff said, "Thank you, dear child. It is because of your humility that your words mean all the more to me."

"It was so special of you to have remembered my birthday. I cannot believe that you would also go out of your way to invite Giuseppe to join us for our celebration." A faint smile came to her lips as she mentioned his name.

"I thought that might please you." Pope John reciprocated with a broad smile. "You didn't think that I knew of your fondness for each other, did you?"

They sat quietly for a while, sharing a rare moment of connection, one that doesn't typically exist in such relationships. Abrielle was perhaps more grateful than anyone in the world that Bishop Franco Calliendo was now Pope John. Not only was her selection to serve him a wonderful moment vocationally, but she had grown quite fond of him personally over the last few years. Now he was taking such a personal interest in her and playing the role of matchmaker, creating a connection that she would have never imagined.

Giuseppe Guidice was Inspector General of *Corpo della Gendarmeria dello Stato della Città del Vaticano*, the Gendarme of Vatican City, commonly referred to as the Vatican Police. More than just a bureaucrat in the Vatican, Giuseppe had known Pope John since he was himself a child, when Monsignor Calliendo was the pastor of his local parish church. Their paths had crossed on a variety of occasions, culminating in the election of Cardinal Calliendo to the role of Pope. Giuseppe frequently told people that the first time he met Pope John XXIV after the conclave, the only thing he could think to say was, "Are you following me?" While not technically responsible for the protection of the Pope—that duty falls to the more famous Swiss Guard—the Vatican Police is responsible for all normal police duties throughout Vatican City.

Some time ago, Giuseppe had been visiting the Pope's study with his mother, who was visiting Rome. It was during that visit that he had first noticed Abrielle; and having seen the spark, his mother reminded him that he was still unmarried and living a disreputable life. The thought crossed his mind, only for a moment, however, to point out to his mother the important position he held as the leader of the Vatican Police. Then he thought better of it.

The die had been cast, however; and he used the resources at his disposal to investigate all of the details of this lady working in the Papal Household…but only to confirm the safety of the Pope, he rationalized to himself. In the course of that investigation, he learned her phone number, that she was widowed, and that she was likely not seeing anyone. Since then, he had been courting Abrielle Russo, although initially without her complete awareness. Then as their relationship progressed, he learned that he deserved to take the time to appreciate life. He learned how much he missed the feminine influences of his youth. He learned that Italian women are very good for the male ego.

Abrielle, for her part, learned that she could love again. It had been over a dozen years since her husband Pietro had died, leaving her alone. After that trauma, she threw herself into her work, serving in various domestic capacities within Vatican City. Her most recent role was as Chief Housekeeper at Casa di Santa Marta, the luxury hotel built for Cardinals attending conclaves. It was there that she met Cardinal Calliendo, and from there he recruited her as his personal housekeeper in the Papal Apartments. From a vocational perspective, it was a step down—she would be making beds again—but there was no better job in the world in her mind. Giuseppe was very sweet icing on the cake.

Pope John broke the silence. "I am very happy to see you find each other. I have known Giuseppe so long that I sometimes forget how passionate he used to be…about everything. He seems to be a regaining a bit of that joy with you in his life. Now if we could only get him back to church on a more regular basis."

Abrielle chuckled. "Yes, Holy Father, I agree. But each person walks the journey in their own way. Oh, look who I am telling about spiritual growth. Forgive me. All I mean is that the funny thing about Giuseppe is that he speaks of his youth in such a happy manner, and it was so intertwined with the Church. But religion doesn't seem to inspire him today. It's almost as if he sees so much of *the Church* these days that he doesn't believe in church."

Pope John got up from his chair and walked to the window, overlooking St. Peter's square. He had long ago figured out how to stand so that he could observe the crowds without being seen. His face began to take on a forlorn appearance.

"Holy Father, can I ask what weighs on you? What's so important that you would risk your health?"

"It's Giuseppe…well, not him, per se, but all of those who don't believe in church. Unfortunately, I think this condition is contagious and is spreading like an epidemic. I am concerned that the Church is failing to inspire, failing to connect with the people. There is nothing that I wouldn't risk to change that, including my life."

"I know it's sad, but what can one man do to change the tide, even the Pope?"

"We Bishops, as leaders of the Church, are allowing ourselves to become too insulated from the real lives of the people who make up the Church. The only reason for us to exist is to inspire others to see God, to look for opportunities to serve; if our lives aren't an exemplar of how rewarding service is, then we've failed."

"It seems that you are somewhat unique in that sentiment. I believe that most of your brother Bishops see their role as to inspire by virtue of their dress and manner. There is a certain regal-ness to their manner and a detachment from those souls in their care. Perhaps they feel it's their job to uphold the dignity of the Church by always looking and acting impeccably, to make the Church special by *being* special themselves."

As Abrielle said this, the Pope noted an unconscious distaste cross her face. He wished to explore the depths of that reaction. "While I understand that there is a certain logic to that, when I look around, I don't see that this plan works the way they intend. Have you been disappointed in your dealings with clergy? You have the ear of your Holy Father: what would you like to see changed?"

"Oh, I'm sure that my opinion is insignificant in the grand scheme of things. You are much better prepared to answer that question than I am."

"Quite the contrary," the Pope said. "It is precisely you and Giuseppe that I want to make sure the Church reaches. Where have you been let down? Where could a priest have done a better job of inspiring you?"

"Holy Father, I'm not looking for inspiration. I suppose when I was a child, I was awed by the gold and the silk vestments. Then I grew up, and I wanted to believe that my priests were, you know, better than me." Abrielle sat down in an antique, straight-backed chair, looking every bit as uncomfortable as the chair probably felt. "I wanted to believe that they would look out for me. When I first arrived in Rome, I was disappointed. As I moved into the Vatican to work, a more general disappointment began to creep into my mind." She looked up and across the room at Pope John, who had turned from the window and was listening very intently to her. This caused her to feel very self-conscious, and she stood up from her chair, realizing how informal their interaction had become. "But you, Holy Father, have created a new inspiration in me."

"That's very kind," he answered, not quite fully believing the flattery. "It sounds as though you've had the same experience that I've feared. I'm concerned that we are seeking to inspire by virtue of our prestige, rather than taking the time to provide a personal witness and connect. I've worried about this for years and, I suppose, even become a bit self-conscious as a result. I've come to believe that the Church needs to change, to find a new way to inspire. We all need to know our Heavenly Father and to understand his deep love for us. If Holy Mother Church can't do that, what good is it?"

"What are you saying, Holy Father?"

"What I'm saying is that there is no greater good for me to risk everything for, my health, even my life. I'm saying that our Church needs to change; and I've come to believe that it may take a remaking of the College and the Curia to force that change. Today, I've set in motion some things that I've only hinted at to a few people in my life. Before this week is out, I will have set in motion one of the most abrupt changes in the complexion of the Church since its founding. I was cautious for decades about expressing my opinions, even as I became a Bishop and then a member of the College. Concern was always on my mind that this was more about my own vanity than the good of the Church. Even during the last three years, I've done everything that I could imagine to push the thoughts from my mind—I've confessed them, offered mass to exorcise them, even shared them with a handful of people, hoping they could reinforce that harboring these thoughts is unproductive. Yet always, they creep back in. While recuperating, I took the opposite tact. I nurtured the thoughts and ran them out to their natural conclusions. In the end, they felt more correct than ever."

"Well, if I may continue in my boldness, I believe in your vision. More importantly, I know you to be a good man. Perhaps your natural humility couldn't grow comfortable with the magnitude of the task the Lord has called you to." Now it was Abrielle who moved slowly over to the window. She immediately noticed the crowds straining to determine if the figure in the window was the man she was speaking with. For a moment, she was reminded that she was having a conversation about the future of the Roman Catholic Church with the Successor to Saint Peter. But when she turned back, she remembered that it was just a man standing there—a man with concerns and self-doubt, just like every man. Glancing back out at the square, she felt his burden. "How can a single man bear such a weight?" She said, without even realizing she was speaking aloud.

"I don't," he replied. "I bear it with the support of the entire Communion of Saints and with the kind embrace of my Creator."

"I have always been amazed at how the Church has managed to endure through the centuries, almost in spite of who occupies the Throne of Saint Peter." She knew that he would understand, that she was starting to understand, this was not about him. "I've often assumed that God would run out of patience one day and found another church. But then again, if He hasn't done it yet, I suppose He can put up with a lot of disappointment." She thought he was smirking. "I just mean, some pretty dubious characters have occupied this Palace, and I'm just trying to say that at least your vision is well-intentioned."

"Yes, but there is a reason that these 'dubious characters,' as you call them, occupied this Palace. All institutions of humans are human institutions, and rarely do they remain pure for long. This vision I have of a more purposeful Church will not set well with many of my brother Bishops. Another trait of human institutions is that they are self-perpetuating. We tend to invite people like ourselves into the club. By default, that makes institutions hard to change. I suppose that's why they elected an old man—to keep the chair warm for a while until one of the young guard had distinguished himself and could bring stability and a long rule."

"But, Holy Father, you are one of us. We have all known that. You are a pastor, not a Pope. We know that the newspapers wrote about you as a 'caretaker,' but that's not how we see you. We see our pastor. Now you've survived your illness renewed. You only need to lead the Church and it will follow."

"Abrielle, you're quite good for an old man beset by doubts. Enough about me, it is too long without really getting to know you."

"There's not much to tell, really. You know that I grew up in a suburb not far from here. You know that I attended Catholic school. What you don't know is that I was forced to leave school halfway through Upper Secondary. My father died rather young, and I needed to earn money to help my mother provide for my little brothers."

"That was very noble of you. What did you sacrifice to take care of your family and to be with me now?"

"I wanted to be a nurse, like my mother. It felt like a sacrifice at times, not to be able to wear the prestige of that vocation. But I always tried to be the best I could at whatever job I did." She was quick to add, "And for the last three years, I have found real bliss in the service to your household."

"Tell me about your brothers."

She smiled with pride. "They are both so smart. Luca came to university in Rome and fell in love with the Eternal City. He had always been strong in mathematics and studied architecture. He lives not far from my apartment, and I see him most weekends. Macario was the more pensive one; he studied philosophy. He considered the seminary…although I talked him out of it." Abrielle went to the corner of the room, poured a glass of water for the Pontiff, and carried it to him, gesturing for him to sit back down.

"Why in the world would you do that?" He tried to not to sound confrontational, but he couldn't deny that he was a little hurt by the comment.

She returned to her straight-backed chair, which was where she felt she belonged at the moment. "I came to Rome on the invitation of my pastor, when he moved to the city for a new post. I had been working as a housekeeper for a number of years at the time. In addition to having worked for a very wealthy family with demanding habits, I had served as a part-time sacristan at the parish. My pastor knew how fastidious I was and that I was a diligent worker. He also knew my family, my father when he was alive, and he knew that I didn't make much money out in the suburbs."

"It sounds like a great blessing at just the right time."

"He also knew that I was single, and I suppose beautiful, back in those days." Pope John furrowed his brow, but didn't look overly surprised, and she continued. "While serving dinner one night, he invited me to join him at the table. Periodically, we would dine together; I suppose because of the loneliness that we both felt having moved to such a bustling city. He started talking about the Church in its glory days. He intimated that Bishops, as he was certain to be one day, were frequently family men. I began to get uncomfortable, seeing where the conversation was headed. He suggested that it could be that way for us, very discreetly of course. I was so surprised, more than you appear to be actually, that such corruptions could still exist. It struck me as a medieval way of thinking. It shook my faith in the Church for a time. It was during this period that my brother confided his interest in the priesthood, and I did everything in my power, short of telling him that story, to convince him not to enter the seminary."

"That's a terrible experience for a young woman to go through," he said, barely above a whisper. "I trust that your other experiences since then have convinced you that this is not common."

"Well, I met my future husband very quickly after that evening, found a job elsewhere in the Vatican, and never looked back. And yes, while it is true that I have not had that same experience again, there are many forms of corruption that ego can foster. I have seen many forms."

"Does this person still work here?"

Abrielle hesitated and looked away.

"Wait—I don't think I want to know. It's just that I'm not sure who to trust. Such big things must happen; equally big forces most certainly will wish to challenge the direction that I am looking to set."

"Holy Father," she waited until he looked her way, "you can trust me." He smiled and she continued. "There are others close to you, and surely you know that you can trust them. My own Giuseppe, whom you've known since he was a child—he loves you like a favorite uncle."

"Yes, indeed. This is one of the many reasons I am so grateful that you have found each other. I know how beautiful you both are, down deep in your souls. And yes, I am very grateful for having your strength close-by."

"And Monsignor Antonio; he seems to have a special place in your heart. I can't honestly remember you ever mentioning how you know each other, but his influence on you is so obvious."

Chuckling, the Pope said, "Oh, how is that?"

"You always seem so relaxed and energized after your chats. It's unfortunate that they are so seldom."

"Funny you should say that. Before I came back here to rest, I sent for Antonio. We are past due for a chat, given everything that I must sort out."

Chapter Five

Abrielle stayed a little longer, poured the Pontiff another glass of water, and promised to alert him when his old friend Antonio Donatello arrived. The Pontiff, feeling his age along with the lagging effects of his illness, lay down to rest his eyes. He found that special place in the hills of his hometown, which he had occupied when he woke earlier in the morning, and quickly settled in for a nap.

Ninety minutes later, Abrielle let the door creak when she entered to check on him. She was always protective and, perhaps now that they'd had their chat earlier in the day, she would always be a little more so. Whenever he did anything unexpected, like this late morning nap, she worried a little more than necessary. As the door creaked, as she knew it would, he stirred. Abrielle was grateful and regretful at the same time. Nonetheless, she'd promised to let him know when his guest arrived.

"Your Holiness, Monsignor Donatello is waiting in your study. Should I fix him some lunch and tell him that you will join him after? I know he would understand if you would like a little more rest."

"No, dear girl, I should very much like to join Antonio for lunch. Would you please set it up for us on the terrace?" The terrace to which Pope John referred was a lovely and secluded place on the roof of the Apostolic Palace. With some delicate and ancient masonry columns, it offered a quiet refuge literally a stone's throw and fifty feet above Saint Peter's square. But by virtue of the design, it was an unusually intimate place where he seldom entertained guests. The brickwork was softened by scattered topiary that lent an earthy connection to the terrace. All in all, it was a unique place among the vast public rooms and elaborate gardens of the Vatican.

When Pope John arrived on the terrace, he found Monsignor Antonio Donatello sitting at a small bistro table, set for just the two of them. On a side cart was a modest buffet of fruit, cheese, sliced tomatoes, and a variety of breads. Included among the luncheon menu was always *pistoccu*, a dry bread of his childhood, made by the shepherds because it could be carried for days without spoiling.

As the Pope's red slippers crunched the pea gravel underfoot, Antonio turned and rose to greet him. "Dear Holy Father, how wonderful to get your invitation and now even better to see you up and about."

"And you, dear Antonio, you are a sight for old and tired eyes. But listen to me: I sound like I'm fishing for pity. I am actually much better than I appear. I am quite enjoying getting back to some old routines."

"Then how is it that you have time for me?"

Pope John smiled and said somewhat cryptically, "Because I am also learning to take time for what matters."

"Well, I gratefully accept the invitation. There were such dire rumors of your health after your stroke. And this is such a lovely place to enjoy some time together. The fresh air must be a wonderful blessing to you after being cooped up in your apartments for so many weeks."

The Pontiff motioned for his friend to sit back down and walked to the side cart. After surveying the fare, he assembled his own mini buffet on a plate. It appeared to Antonio that his old friend Father Calliendo didn't want to risk missing a single morsel of his childhood.

"Well, Monsignor, the fresh air is a blessing, and it's such a lovely day for me to share this peaceful spot with a close friend. While it was a nuisance to be confined to my rooms, I never lost hope that my recovery would be swift."

"Based upon the rumors, your recovery seems remarkable."

"Don't get too carried away. I'm sure the rumors of my illness were greatly exaggerated outside these walls…even within these walls for that matter. I've been trying to get my doctors to stop referring to it as a stroke. There is no clear evidence of one, and moreover I'm not at all convinced that that's what it was."

"News of no stroke is perhaps better than news of a miraculous recovery from one. If it's possible, I believe that the faithful felt even more drawn to you when they thought you were ill and in need of their prayers."

Pope John had worked to keep Antonio out of the spotlight since his ascension to the papacy. He knew instinctively that the attention could prevent them from having quiet conversations such as these, without someone or another feeling insulted by exclusion. Of course, everyone knew of their old connections, but most suspected that their infrequent meetings were simply the Pontiff's way of keeping connected to his past. By most Vatican standards, if Antonio had a significant role to play, even informally within the Church, Pope John would have made his status known by including him in formal events. Even more telling, he would have included him in the informal events, thereby heightening his status as part of the inner circle.

Antonio went on. "I admit that I sometimes regret that I don't get to spend more time in your company, working alongside you. I'm jealous of the legions of priests who get to serve you in your current role. But by virtue of my anonymity, I can assure you that the faithful you serve have come to love you deeply. They suffered at the thought of your illness, and they will be heartened to hear of your complete recovery."

"Antonio, your perspective is so important to me and always has been. I am grateful that you are close enough to regular Catholics that you can relay their true sentiments to me. I fear that if you lived and worked in the Vatican, you would find a separation that would make that impossible. Similarly, if I had brought you in to work alongside me, I would lose some of this perspective that I require so much."

Antonio appeared as though he was putting it all together for the first time. He had a special role, one that demanded he remain uncorrupted by the daily life inside the Curia.

Pope John continued, "I hope you understand that my decision wasn't to *exclude* you, it was to *preserve* you. In fact, this is the moment that I need you for. There are things that I need to do, things that require a clear mind and untainted motives, and you will have to play that role for me."

Pope John let this all sink in while they enjoyed their light lunch, leaving Monsignor Donatello unclear about exactly what was to come.

Having nourished himself, the Pontiff continued, "I'm sorry to cut short our personal time, but it's important that we get to the point that I asked you here to discuss. By now you have grown accustomed to being my confidant and knowing that I rely on you to help me think through key matters. I have long known you, Antonio, as someone of unique vision, someone I can work with to stretch ideas and see beyond the horizon. Now that role will almost certainly become more public; and while I will rely on you all the more, it will become harder for you to insulate your thoughts from the buzzing of activity around you."

"I understand, Your Holiness. As always, I am here to serve the Church and you."

The Pontiff looked around the terrace as if taking it all in for the first time. "Our Lord went away to a special place when he knew it was time to prepare for his public ministry. In some ways, this will be that special place for you. I am asking you to take on an enormous burden, and it's one that I probably haven't fully prepared you for. One day, you may look back at this terrace and see the parallels."

Antonio nodded thoughtfully.

"I am ready to make a move to remake the Church, and I have announced my intentions to Monsignor Hellman. I believe that the Lord has grown impatient with my endless excuses and lack of courage, and I have come to believe that he just gave me some quiet time to consider all that might be done. None of my beliefs are going to be news to you, although there are precious few people to whom I have ever confided them. It is only fair, as you helped shape a great many of them."

"Excuse me, Your Holiness. What exactly did you share with Monsignor Hellman? While he is your private secretary, he is also very much a part of the fabric of the Curia. If you pull on one thread, doesn't the whole fabric feel it?"

Pope John chuckled and picked at the last pieces of his bread.

"Holiness, what exactly do *we* seek to accomplish?" Antonio emphasized the word *we*, confirming his allegiance, even as he was unclear of the direction. "Over the years, we have discussed a great many 'catholic churches.' You have always seemed intellectually curious about why Holy Mother

Church is what she is…and always somewhat more than curious about how different she might look if one thing or another about Her history were different. But how can I possibly help you as, without false modesty, a pretty obscure cleric?"

The Pontiff pressed on, glad to be finally engaged in the heart of the matter. "I have come to believe, Antonio, that this is the time for the Church to remake Herself. As I mentioned, Our Lord has given me the time, over these last few weeks, to reconsider all my prior concerns on the matter: my ego, the risks to the Church, the likely opposition of the Curia, and other issues. Outweighing all of that, however, is the real good that the Church could do in the lives of people."

"You don't mean to imply that the Church isn't doing real good in people's lives today?"

"Of course not, but I do think that the emphasis is off and the role we play can be wrongheaded. In some ways, I believe we do well in spite of ourselves. If we could just get out of our own way, the results could be unimaginable. Through this discernment process, the Holy Spirit has assured me that my motives are pure…enough. I have also come to trust that in spite of what I do, Holy Mother Church will withstand any mistakes I might make along the way. If the history of the Church doesn't tell us that, it tells us nothing.

She is resilient in the face of many mistakes and faulty leaders. And finally, the Spirit has assured me that It can work wonders in the Curia, no matter how I might be biased to write them off."

"What exactly does this remaking look like? With all respect to the Throne of Saint Peter, our Pontiff is still just one man. There are others who certainly have a stake, and more than a passing interest, in what you are looking to do. Do you propose to convene a Council of the Church Fathers to create a plan?"

Enjoying the probing questions and smiling warmly, Pope John stood and said, "We have now reversed roles. The Holy Spirit whispered to my heart that you were ready to play this role for me. Come, let's take a walk in the gardens."

Pope John led Antonio down the stairs, where they entered his private elevator for the final three floors to a corridor that led to the San Damaso Courtyard. Antonio continued to follow his friend across the asphalt, in silence. They followed a small tunnel through the adjacent building and emerged into a much smaller courtyard. Antonio had never had a reason to be here before and wondered if anyone did, other than His Holiness. After ducking through a small bustling building to their left, they emerged into what appeared to be an alleyway. Pope John stopped rather abruptly and turned to Antonio, wondering if he was listening closely. Then recognition crossed Antonio's face, there were probably thousands of people not ten feet away; for on the other side of the wall was Saint Peter's Square. Antonio had always thought the name strange for an area that is shaped more like the keyway in a lock.

Pope John chuckled again. He always found it amusing that he could stand so close to the visitors and they were completely unaware, because of the way Vatican City was laid out.

As they turned so that they could hear the crowds over their shoulders, Antonio realized they were looking at a small side door, which certainly led to the Sistine Chapel. When he had first moved to Rome, one of his first weekend excursions had been the public tour, and he was amazed at the beauty and extravagance. Now standing here, he didn't realize that Pope John wasn't just admiring the simple façade, he was buying time.

The primary responsibility for the personal safety of the Pope fell to the Swiss Guard. Early in Pope John's papacy, the Colonel of the Guard had visited him in his study. Having quickly come to know Pope John as a very gregarious man of the people, he implored the new Pontiff to allow the Guard a special indulgence. This indulgence was not of a religious nature; in fact, the Colonel of the Guard wanted the Pontiff to wear a special tracking device that would allow the Guard to know where he was at all times. Once he agreed, they deployed a system within Vatican City that would allow them to locate him within nine inches of accuracy. In exchange for this intrusion, the Guard agreed to loosen the cordon of personal guards around His Holiness until he ventured near public areas. Over time, Pope John had learned to give his watchers sufficient time to close in.

Today, Pope John was going to visit the Sistine Chapel with his friend Antonio. The Swiss Guard had come to expect this once or twice a month, while the Pope was in residence. Usually, a pause of no more than twenty or thirty seconds was required to ensure the guards had unobtrusively moved into the Chapel and surveyed the tourists. They had all agreed early on that so long as these visits remained unpredictable the true risk was quite low.

Just as suddenly as they had stopped, Pope John began to lead the way again, saying "I am about to share with you one of the most beautiful things about my life today, Antonio."

As Pope John opened the door, an unusual light source entered the Chapel, causing the throng of tourists to turn toward it. When he stepped into the hall, a collective gasp could be heard. Jaws fell open, wives tugged on their husband's elbows, and nuns crossed themselves. No one approached His Holiness, they absorbed him. He could see tears glistening in the eyes of some of the older folks. It was at moments like this that Franco Calliendo, parish priest from rural Sardinia, realized both how blessed he was and how much responsibility he had. With his recent decisions, he also realized how valuable his life could become if he was willing to give it over to a great cause.

They walked slowly through the Sistine Chapel, Pope John XXIV wanting to give the visitors a chance to see the chapel in its true context. It's not a museum or an art gallery, although it could be easily mistaken for either. It's a place of worship, built in the heart of the Church's seat of power, by a renowned artist in service to the leader of the Church at that time. Few people in the modern world would ever catch site of a Pontiff strolling through the space. He wasn't there to reinforce his ego and accept adulation; he was there to connect with real people. He met as many eyes as he could. He didn't perform the customary blessing, but rather shook hands with those who now had mustered the courage to approach. He kept moving, rather than create the impression that this was becoming a formal audience; these people were now part of his day, in his place.

In Loving Memory of

Robert L. Fedroff, Sr.

September 28, 1929
August 6, 2017

*Lord, make me an instrument
of your peace
Where there is hatred...let me sow love
Where there is injury...pardon.
Where there is doubt...faith.
Where there is despair...hope.
Where there is darkness...light.
Where there is sadness...joy.
O Divine Master, grant that I may not
so much seek
To be consoled...as to console,
To be understood...as to understand,
To be loved...as to love, for
It is in giving...that we receive
It is in pardoning, that we are pardoned
It is in dying...that we are born to
eternal life.* St. Francis

John W. Keffer Funeral Home, Inc.
York, Pennsylvania

When they reached the far end of the chapel, beyond the ropes of the tour, he couldn't help but stop and turn to look past Antonio. He took one step back and, raising his right hand, imparted his blessing on the group. Pope John turned around again, already missing that group of real people, and led Antonio outside the chapel.

Back in the sunlight, the pair crossed the Via del Governatorato, headed past the Vatican post office and toward the monument to Saint Peter. They veered to the right, toward the less-structured Old Gardens, now almost 750 years old. As they neared the monument, Pope John spoke to Antonio for the first time since they had entered the chapel.

"What did you think?"

Antonio looked over with a smile on his face, "A remarkable experience. I think that it was more moving for me even than for the unsuspecting crowd."

The Pontiff looked up to the statue of Saint Peter. "And what I know is that it was more moving for me than for all of you. It's impossible to explain the feeling, just as it was impossible for me to prepare for it the first time. To walk through that chapel; standing in the stead of Saint Peter as the Vicar of Christ on earth; to look His people in the eyes and touch them; to be the one who can give them that connection is an awesome gift. Our task, dear Antonio, is to bring that connection to more of His people. Our mistake in the past has been to think that it's the awe that inspires them, the ceilings of Signore Buonarroti, when in fact it's the personal connection."

When they arrived at the Old Gardens, they found a path and their pace slowed even more. The Pope started up right where he had left off on the terrace. "Getting back to our earlier conversation, Antonio, do you see that we have now reversed our roles?" As his friend shook his head, Pope John continued on, "Now it is I who talk of growth and change, and you who come back to me with practicalities and caution."

"Do you recall the paper that you wrote in the seminary? The rector brought you to my attention because he was afraid that you were a subversive." At this they both laughed, but the Pope continued on, "It brought you to my attention and began a fruitful discussion that has continued for more than two decades."

"Yes, Holy Father, I recall the paper well. You were very indulgent with me and my 'subversive' views. It's actually funny that you mention it; I brought a copy with me and was going to ask you to autograph it for me later. It was the first project we ever discussed. How is it that you remember?"

At that question, the Pontiff grew somewhat pensive. "I don't want this to go to your head Antonio, but in some ways the course of my life has been dictated by that paper. It touched me deeply. You're so modest, it probably never occurred to you to wonder why I don't have the same relationship with every young priest that I come across."

Antonio was somewhat incredulous. "But you grilled me mercilessly about that paper."

"As you do to me kindly now. Do you see the role reversal?"

"What did you mean when you said the course of your life was dictated by the paper? It was a paper about poverty."

The Pope quoted from memory:

The Church and Poverty, by Antonio Donatello, Seminarian: The Church must decide what role it means to play in the lives of the world's poor. It cannot continue on its present course of saying, "Go, I wish you well; keep warm and well fed." I agree with James, if the Church "does nothing about his physical needs, what good is it?"

And Antonio, I agree with you. All my pushing and prodding wasn't to dissuade you from your views, it was to probe their depths. It was to determine, as I did early on, if you could help me probe the depths of my own thoughts on the matter. I made the personal decision during those first conversations that I would always remain in pastoral life and avoid any role that would separate me from direct, personal contact with God's people. Ironically, had I not remained a relatively obscure Cardinal, it's unlikely my brothers in the College would have elected me to this role. My apparent lack of ambition made me the ideal candidate in their eyes. What they didn't realize is that I'm not devoid of ambition, just the kind that they subscribe to."

"Begging your indulgence, but my paper was still just about *how do we feed the poor*? What does that have to do with remaking the whole Church? I was just trying to argue for the church to sell a few paintings and invest in family farms."

"Do you recall, after our first few meetings on your essay, that I started pushing you to think beyond the obvious solutions? I tried to guide you to some of the solutions that had occupied my thinking for some time. Remember, you were still quite a young man, no matter how brilliant and passionate."

"I recall you taking me down some tangents, or so I thought, about the nature of pastoral care and the apostolate of the clergy."

"Antonio, didn't it occur to you that the Bishop doesn't usually have private tutoring sessions with each of his seminarians? Your thinking was crisp, but you needed some help to integrate the thinking. I had watched as the Church moved its best and brightest into roles that took them increasingly away from the body of believers; and then we wondered why our evangelization was weak and we couldn't adequately impact the lives of those believers. It's sort of like always promoting the best teacher to be principal and wondering why students aren't continually excelling."

"That is an interesting analogy, but after all these years, I still don't see all the connections."

"I believe that this is the same mindset that trips up the Church's leadership time and time again. It's this sense that the best among us must be elevated; that they must then issue doctrine and dogma for the regular folks to follow. We then comfort ourselves with the rationalization that the believers are inspired by the majesty of the Church, by its possessions and opulence. We act as if the Church is ennobled by wrapping its leaders in silk and making them less than accessible. How many Cardinals do you know of who grew up as obscure Bishops rather than as administrators and theologians? How many Bishops take the time to lead a parish bible study or fill in for an ailing pastor on Sunday? We just don't get our hands dirty anymore, so to speak."

"So, you saw a connection between the Church's accumulation of wealth and power and its distance from its pastoral mission? You want to encourage the College to refocus more on the people? Well, that certainly can't be a bad thing. Who would resist that?"

"Antonio, I've been pushing these arguments, in my own mind and regularly in retreats, since those early days. Whenever I dared to utter them out loud, I found very few people willing to entertain them. The ideas themselves were viewed as institutional heresy."

"I understand. It's hard to think about the Pope without the opulence. For anyone raised a Catholic, it's hard to think about Cardinals as regular men. Even our Popes take on new names when they take office, as though they become different people."

"After a few years, I realized that you were the only one 'subversive' enough to engage in a serious debate on these topics. Obviously I didn't give you a very coherent vision of what was in my mind; but nonetheless, you were instrumental in helping me to shape these beliefs. That's why I kept you close all those years—even during that period when you were the most dreadful secretary that a Bishop ever had."

Antonio laughed, knowing the truth of it. "And that's why you called me here to be Papal Confessor? It was an unlikely choice for a new Pontiff, to be sure."

"I wanted you close, even if in the shadows somewhat."

"But then why have our conversations been so infrequent over these last few years?"

"We'll get into that more later. For now, you can chalk it up largely to my cowardice. When I was first elected, I made some overtures to the Cardinals, which were beaten back quite strongly. They didn't expect the old Cardinal from an outpost diocese to start proposing such wild notions. That wasn't why they had elected me."

Antonio was so captivated by the conversation that he failed to notice that Pope John had led him back toward the Papal Apartments. They skirted the outside of the Sistine Chapel this time. His head was spinning, flying back to those early conversations, which he had thought were just logic exercises. It was almost inconceivable to think that he had been helping to shape a Pope…and the future of his Church.

The two men continued in silence again for a while. Pope John wished to let Antonio digest all that he had just said; and Antonio was reconciling in his mind a whole new vision of himself. They made their way back through the courtyards to the Pope's private elevator. Somehow, everything looked different to Antonio. He saw this place and its history through the eyes of someone who was not a mere visitor to a museum—he now felt as though he belonged. He felt at ease in a way he hadn't on any previous visit.

Once back in the Pope's study, they found some tea arranged on the edge of the Pope's desk. As Pope John poured tea for his guest, he imagined Abrielle watching in the courtyard for them to be sure it was ready as soon as they arrived. Then he imagined that she'd bribed the Swiss Guard to give her access to the tracking device he wore. This thought brought a smile to his lips.

Monsignor Antonio Donatello reached into the satchel he'd left here a couple of hours ago and pulled out a copy of his old paper, *The Church and Poverty*. "Holy Father, you see I really did bring a copy. Would you sign it for me? For as long as I live, it will bring me happy memories of our discussions."

Pope John walked around his desk and opened the top middle drawer. Antonio was stunned to see him pull out a very well-worn copy of the same paper. "Antonio, I will autograph yours, if you autograph mine. No matter what happens, this copy will remain in the Papal Archives forever."

The two men exchanged copies of Antonio's paper and dedicated them carefully, taking the time to find just the right words. After the solemn ceremony, they sank into a pair of comfortable leather club chairs across from each other.

"So, my dear Monsignori, let's start off by lightly framing the issue. What's right with Holy Mother Church?"

Antonio choked slightly on his tea and returned the cup to the saucer. "Well, I'm certainly glad that we're going to ease our way back into the conversation." He paused thoughtfully. "The Church holds a sacred trust; it maintains the continuity between humanity and its Creator. It also responds daily to the truth and vision revealed by Jesus Christ by making the sacraments available to the faithful."

"Very well. We are defining the Church as an institution then?"

"Not entirely. The Church is all the good people, committed to serving each other, and thereby serving the wishes of their Creator."

"Excellent, please continue. What else is right with the Church?"

"It is the godly men and women who commit their lives in service to God's people and bring more souls to know him."

"You mention people, lay and religious, who serve each other to become the Lord's hands in the world. And what do men of my ilk contribute to the mission of the Church? Does the hierarchy of the Church contribute to that mission?"

"Of course, Holy Father. Without the hierarchy, there'd be no order to the Church. The Bishops serve as the first teachers of the faith. They instruct the faithful on the teachings of the Lord and remind us how much He loves us."

"And that role helps to maintain order and continuity. Doesn't that imply a very static existence? Couldn't we just write it all down in a rule book and call it a day?"

"No, certainly not. Vatican II showed us that the Church Fathers can help to re-envision the Church through the lens of a changing world. Rather than allow the intellectual equivalent of mob rule, the Institutional Church creates a thoughtful approach to that evolution. It balances continuity with the march of time."

"So the *Institutional Church*, as you call me, can help to keep the *Real Church*, as I'll call it, centered on what matters."

"Holy Father, I certainly meant no offense."

"Oh, don't be so skittish Antonio. Out there, you will need to pay due deference to the Vicar of Christ. In here, I need someone who will spar with me a bit."

"Very well," said Antonio, only slightly reassured.

"Now, perhaps as important as what we're *doing*, what does the outside world *think* about Holy Mother Church? What impression do we give when they look our way?"

"I think the world sees the prestige of the Church. I think they see it as the fulfillment of the wishes of Christ, to bring the Good News to the whole world. The Church has the power to do a lot of good in the world."

"Ah, *power,* yes. The Church has been a powerful institution for many centuries. Is that a good thing?"

"Well it can't be a bad thing, can it? I mean, weakness can't accomplish anything."

"No, perhaps not weakness; but meekness can certainly be a blessing. In my experience, those with power tend to spend an inordinate amount of energy defending their power. They will often find ways to associate themselves with the greater goals or institutions, so that an attack on them becomes synonymous with an attack on the institution."

"Certainly so, in many cases."

"Would you argue, Antonio, that this is not the case in the history of our Church?"

"No, our history is like most; it has its blemishes as well as its radiance. But it's still standing. It would be illogical to argue that Christ instituted the Church, abandoned it because of some bad episodes, and yet it still thrives. I believe that the Christian Church is still blessed by God, who continuously hopes for its unity and renewal."

"I agree. But here is what I think the world sees. We seek to provide charity; and the world sees opulence. We speak of continuity and our connection to history; and the world sees corruption and power grabs. We have patroned the greatest artists throughout history to tell the story of God; and the world sees greed and accumulation. We dedicate our lives to the service of God's people; and the world often sees esoteric theology. And when I say, 'the world,' I sadly include the Catholic world. I think we are failing them Antonio, failing to inspire them."

"Holy Father, you can't possibly be this pessimistic. What conclusions do you draw from all of this?"

"I don't necessarily draw any conclusions, but this all causes me to look around for more edifying circumstances. Isn't the mission of the Church really being lived out every day at its lowest levels, while sometimes my Institutional Church gets in the way? Shouldn't we provide leadership by exercising moral authority on important issues?"

"And so it does, Holiness. The Church speaks out on injustice in the world and shines a light on those who truly abuse their power."

"Yes, the Church speaks, but does it do so with moral authority?" The Pope set his cup of tea down, leaned forward in his chair, and rubbed his eyes for a moment, while his guest sat quietly and observed some anguish cross his face. "Antonio, I fear that our instinct for self-preservation has cost us some of that moral authority. Look at the abuse scandals around the world. What I'm describing is playing out right now, with horrible fallout for our children…the Lord's children, Antonio. Some of my brother Bishops believe that they can justify any actions in defense of Holy Mother Church; and then they make themselves synonymous with Her. Rather than take responsibility for anything, they act like any secular corporate chieftain and hide the scandals they uncover. They excuse it as defending the reputation of the Church; but they ignore the disastrous consequences of those decisions."

After a moment, Pope John sat upright again. Antonio started, "I will not argue with that. But those same flawed men do provide stability to the Church. They represent the Church's teaching authority. That magisterium helps the Church react in a measured way to the volatile changes in the world."

"You say the Church's teaching authority responds in a measured way, but that's not entirely consistent with our history, is it? You'll recall from your history books the date Feb 23, 1616. That was the date that the Church's foremost theologians, on instructions from the Holy Office, came to a learned and scriptural conclusion that the Sun revolved around the Earth. What came next was more than three hundred fifty years of Holy Mother Church arrogantly and incorrectly declaring that its conclusions on scripture were unassailable. At the dawn of that conclusion, the Church imprisoned a man named Galileo Galilei, a man that the rest of the world and history itself would declare to be singularly correct on the topic. I would say that our form of introspection often leads to insularity. Our respect for Scripture can become a club…more than a shield. We need to focus on our work, not our thoughts. We need to be the continuing example of Christ and not worry so much about staking out territory and control."

"Holy Father, you're starting to sound hopelessly pessimistic again. What does all this imply to you, and how can so much change possibly be accomplished?"

"Great questions. I'm actually not pessimistic because I believe that I finally understand how all this fits together, and I believe that there is a solution. My cowardice, of which I spoke earlier, came when I had the observations and no conviction to support them. As soon as I tried to discuss my thoughts with my brother Cardinals, they shook my confidence and left me to believe I was alone. It was only during my recuperation that I had the time to truly discern whether my ideas were true. The Lord convinced me that they were His ideas, not mine, and from that moment I needed no more courage of my own."

"You speak of solutions…"

"Yes." The Pope was now animated and began walking around the study. "Let's play a little game, shall we?" Not waiting for an answer, Pope John pressed on. "There are three themes that I believe build on one another. The first is *to support the laity in its apostolates to serve each other*. Now you tell me what you think of that idea."

Antonio was happy to play this game. "Strong roles for the laity have become the standard condition in many countries around the world. Sometimes it is in response to the shortage of clergy, sometimes because of an upwelling of the Spirit. Vatican II created some interesting dynamics in this area, along with some tensions. I think that the Church could stand for some clarifications on the role of the laity. There are many diverse ministries in which the laity are driving the Church today, and this is a wonderful beginning; but there are always clashes possible between the clergy and the laity."

"Precisely. You have seen the same thing I have. If all believers make up the Church, then how could there ever be a conflict between the clergy, who serve, and the community of believers who are served? The relationship seems quite straightforward. Although it isn't, is it? Because we teach our brother priests that they are in charge. We train them to lead, more than to serve. It's a matter of emphasis."

"That's too logical to be correct," Antonio admitted with a grin.

"This leads us to the second theme: *leading by serving.* What do you think of that notion?"

"With respect, it sounds a bit naive and simplistic."

"That doesn't sound like a respectful response." The Pontiff waited a second before turning to Antonio with a smile.

"What I mean is, the Word tells us, 'There are different kinds of gifts, but the same spirit. There are different kinds of service, but the same Lord.' I don't think we can assume every member of the Church is born to lead."

"I'm not talking about administration—any monkey can do that. We need to reconnect the leadership of the Church to the core mission of the Church. Some of our most senior clerics have never served in a parish; they have never held regular pastoral duties. Shouldn't the leaders of the Church be the best pastors, not the most intellectual theologians?" Pope John realized that his voice was rising. "I know that I'm a little too passionate about this, and more than a little biased; but if we lead by example and lead by serving, the paradox is that we will inspire the laity to lead and serve each other. That, my old friend, is the Second Commandment of Christ."

"I see, but does that imply that the Cardinals need to go find a job in a parish? I don't think that would go over too well."

"Wonderful idea! We'll need to set that one aside, because it might come in handy. But I didn't originally mean to retrain the old theologians to be people persons. I meant quite the opposite: that our leaders should come from the ranks of the best pastors. That's whose skills should be prized. Your comment, however, brings forth another scripture, 'His winnowing fork is in his hand, and he will clear his threshing floor, gathering his wheat into the barn and burning up the chaff with unquenchable fire.' There is a time when, for the fulfillment of the harvest, the floor must be cleared of the chaff."

"Again, may I remind you, Your Holiness, you are only the Pope. There is a limit to what you can do by yourself."

"If the College consisted of two good pastors for every theologian, the odds would tip in my favor. And the College is as big as the sitting Pontiff believes it needs to be."

Antonio considered that his old sparring partner had thought about this a great deal.

"But I don't want to get too far into the details. To follow on our themes of supporting the laity in their ministry and leading them to success by our example, I believe the last step is a tangible act of our commitment. The final theme is to *demonstrate the irrelevance of possessions*. Our things are pointless, except to the extent that they are put in service to our mission. I'm sure that Our Lord will excuse me for paraphrasing, but why would a man gather up wheat into his barn if his community was starving?" As Pope John retook his seat, he asked, "What do you make of that one?"

"We have always taught that the faithful should be generous with their time, their talent, and their treasure. We have done a horrible job in the developed world of motivating people to respect tithing. I suppose there is a lot we could do to teach better on that subject."

"Antonio, you missed the mark. This isn't about teaching; this is about leading by example. My friend, this is my starting point. While the themes flow logically to this point, I arrived at them by solving them in reverse. This is your paper!"

"So you meant it? You really want to sell the Vatican treasures and feed the poor?"

"Well, it would be impractical to try to sell it all." He chuckled again, this time because he had turned all these ideas over in his head so many times. "The Director of the Vatican Museum assures me that what you can see on the grounds is dwarfed by what you cannot. He tells me that our holdings represent enough to drown the world market in art and antiquities for decades. We'd crush the market."

"So what then?"

"The question is, how much is enough versus how much good could be done? Did you know the global art market amounts to sixty billion dollars a year? There is no argument that, in measured steps and with sufficient planning, we could reap billions each year, without changing the dynamics of the market. To use the thesis of your paper, we could then create sustainability programs that would feed entire communities for generations. It's somewhat shocking, frankly, that we don't do it already."

"I'm a little older and less subversive now. Scripture says, 'The poor will always be with us.'"

The Pontiff leaned forward and touched Antonio's knee. "Don't give in. I need you for this. What good is a Renoir on the wall if there are literally hundreds of families that one painting could save from unbearable suffering and dejection for generations? How can those families possibly see that their Creator loves them if they can't stop worrying long enough to see Him? If we respect life, Antonio, we need to do anything we can to protect it; and what we're talking about now isn't even that much. We just have to be willing to have fewer pictures on the wall."

The two men sat in silence for a few minutes, looking at the bottoms of their teacups. The implications, now that it had all been said aloud, were awesome. Clearly, the Pope had thought this through in some detail; and even more clearly, he had found an inner fire.

Antonio broke the silence. "I seem to recall your first homily after your election, and then the Papal Tour that you took to America. There were a few instances, in hindsight, where I now realize you were playing around with these ideas. If I recall, your words created a bit of a stir, but you denied that was your intent. Were you just testing the waters?"

"That seems so long ago. Yes, there is much to catch you up on, now that we are bound together to this task. But right now, I need some rest and I must beg your pardon."

Antonio bounded out of his chair so quickly he surprised himself. "I'm sorry, Your Holiness, you must be exhausted: the lunch, the walk, this very animated conversation."

"Nonsense. I have looked forward to this conversation for so long. I'll admit that, since being elected, I feared that you might be too humble to really believe how much you mean to me."

The Pope stepped forward to embrace Antonio, something he hadn't done since they arrived in Rome three years ago. It was the embrace of two brothers who share more history than anyone around them.

"We will be able to work together now, Antonio. You will be my secret weapon."

PART II—PATHS CROSS

Chapter Six

Two years before Pope John's eventful meeting with his friend Monsignor Antonio Donatello, the Vatican had been bustling with preparations for the Pope's first major tour abroad. He was going to America, and the entourage was almost as elaborate as the expectations.

After rising about an hour before sunrise, Pope John ventured down the hall to his private chapel in the Papal Apartments. The room is simple by Vatican standards, with a floor covered with large tiles of heavily veined marble and walls of simple stone; this is why the Pontiff enjoyed it so much. The only real adornment in the room is a bright, stained glass ceiling depicting angels and scenes from the history of the Church. He liked to begin his day early, and by saying mass at this time of day he would be saying his final prayers just as the ceiling was illuminated by the morning sun. Generally, only a few people joined him for his daily mass, including a seminarian who served as his sacristan and a handful of nuns who ran the Papal Household.

During the course of this particular celebration of the mass, the Pope's mind kept drifting to his impending trip. He kept his homily focused entirely on the scriptures of the day, but during his prayers he asked the Lord to help him reconnect with the world of believers. After only a year, he was already feeling himself disconnecting from "real Catholics," and he was starting to become concerned that this state was irreversible. He had asked his Papal Secretary, Monsignor Hellman, to begin preparations six months ago, and now the trip was finally a reality. Of course, that was about as impulsive as a Pope could be, he supposed. There were events to be planned on the other end, warnings to be given to visited dioceses, and, of course, security to be arranged. But he was impatient, because he was feeling dragged down by the reality of the administrative burden he had assumed. Some Popes throughout history must have accepted status as figureheads, he supposed, but John XXIV knew that there was work to be done and he would abdicate the role before he abdicated that responsibility.

After concluding the mass and wishing everyone a good day, he took a quick stroll around the Palace. He noted that this place still felt oddly foreign to him after a year in residence. The formality, the new faces, the routine were all so unsettling still. He longed for the upcoming tour, in part because he knew that the strangers in the crowds in America would feel more like his people than the others with whom he shared this Palace.

Realizing the time, he rushed into the dining room in the Papal Apartments to find his old friend Monsignor Antonio Donatello waiting patiently. "My apologies, Antonio, for running late." As Antonio rose to meet the Pontiff, he said, "No, please sit and begin eating. I will grab a plate from the kitchen and join you momentarily. I'm sure that they are keeping a plate for me."

Upon returning, Antonio greeted him, "It's so wonderful to see you and so kind of you to invite me to breakfast. I'm sure the last-minute plans are all-consuming."

"Yes, they are; but I didn't want to go away without saying goodbye. It feels like we haven't spent any time together recently. Frankly, that is one of the reasons I'm looking so forward to this trip. Life is so hectic within the Palace walls that I'm starting to feel disconnected from real things."

"That's funny, because I would think that your job—if I can call it that—would give you a strong sense of being in the center of it all."

"The problem is the lack of contact with regular people. I fear that if I stay here too much longer I will no longer recognize the Church I pledged to serve. It will be wonderful to be out among the believers—and non-believers—and feel their energy."

"That does sound energizing. I would ask Your Holiness once again to please allow me to accompany you."

"Antonio, I wish I could bring you along, but I feel as though I must keep you out of the limelight. I need someone who isn't tainted by the prestige. It takes a massive effort for me to get out and see people. Because of that, the smallest thing that I do takes on the aura of something special. I want you to try as hard as you can to remember me as Father Franco. If you followed me around for a month, you might start to believe some of the press about me, and then I'd lose your objectivity forever."

"I understand, Holy Father."

"Father Franco, please." The Pope smiled at his old friend.

"Never again!"

"Antonio, I am so grateful that you agreed to leave your parish and join me in Rome. You don't understand how much I appreciate the simple sound of your accent. I really want us to be friends always, in the way a Pope and a Monsignor typically cannot."

The two men enjoyed the rest of their breakfast, reminiscing about their time together in Sardinia. Antonio caught his old friend up on his new parish, in the suburbs of Rome; and he even shared what he recently heard about Series A—the major leagues of Italian soccer.

Leaving the Papal Apartments, Antonio was still a bit surprised by his own jealousy. He had left his comfortable life to move to Rome, where he was being asked to serve as Papal Confessor. He naturally assumed that he would have unusual and special access to His Holiness—after all, he knew the man better than any of them. In actuality, however, he saw very little of his old friend and mentor. On days like this, he really felt his condition as an outsider.

After their breakfast, the Pope strode quickly over to his study, where he found Monsignor Hellman waiting. "Good morning, Monsignor."

"Good morning, Holy Father. The energy in the Palace is quite high this morning."

"Well, it should be. This little excursion you planned takes a small army to pull off."

A little concerned, Monsignor Hellman asked, "I trust that you have found the preparations acceptable, Holiness?"

"Absolutely, Francis. I was only joking. I am quite excited about the tour and am grateful for all the effort it takes to make it happen. I recognize that this is new for us both. I am hopeful that, in time, we can do more of these journeys with increasingly less fuss."

"If you don't mind, I should like to review the agenda one final time."

"Please proceed."

"The tour has technically begun, for as you may realize, the Swiss Guard has been meeting with the American Secret Service on a regular basis for months and a small contingent has recently taken up residence in Washington."

"Yes, I heard from our Nuncio in America that he doesn't recognize the Embassy for all the additional bodies rushing around."

"They are quite confident that security is well in hand and will only be playing a supporting role for the balance of the tour. When we first land in New York, you will have some time with Cardinal Johns, who is anxious to be the first to welcome you to America. There will be some time for you to rest and recover from the jet lag, then an hour or two with the Archbishop. After your audience, he will host a private dinner for you and a few dignitaries.

"The next morning, the president of the United States will be flying into New York to meet you, along with the secretary of state and our ambassadors to the United Nations. This will consist of two parts: breakfast privately between you and the president, along with a working session with all parties. The president, being a Roman Catholic, wishes to have a private exchange to share his personal views before he adjourns to play the public role of the president in the larger setting. Essentially, the United States would like some assistance from the Holy See, acting as emissary in a certain region of Africa.

"Early that evening, you will celebrate mass in Madison Square Garden with over fifteen thousand in attendance."

"Sounds like a fruitful day. It will be a bit different from my last visit, as a seminarian on holiday."

"The next day will be a travel day. We will have a midday flight to Los Angeles, allowing you to have a restful afternoon, again adjusting to the time change. A private dinner with the Archbishop of Los Angeles will conclude the day.

"The following day, there will be a short parade to the Los Angeles Coliseum where, weather permitting, there will be an outdoor mass for over eighty thousand. After the mass, you will spend the afternoon in an informal gathering of a handful of Bishops invited to an audience by your host.

"There is then another day for travel, shortened by the time change heading East. You will arrive in Boston in time for a late meal with Cardinal Welty. This visit to Boston is solely a private visit with the Cardinal and a rest stop before continuing back here to the Vatican. How does that sound, Holiness?"

"It sounds as though I'll be spending most of my time with men holding shepherd's croziers, rather than with members of the flock. Francis, your last-minute task is to find an opportunity in each city for me to spend some time with regular Catholics. I want to have a small audience, for an hour or so, with a half-dozen people. No agenda, no pre-planning. Can you arrange that for me?"

"You will give the Guard fits, Your Holiness. But I suppose they can use the spontaneity to their advantage."

"How do you expect this to go, Francis? Do you expect a warm welcome in America?"

"Of course, Your Holiness. The believers in the United States are most excited to be the site of your first Papal Tour."

"And how about my brother Bishops; is there any indication of what they think of this little visit? Is there any indication about what my brother in Los Angeles is interested in discussing?"

Slightly less assured, Francis suggested, "I believe they just wish to get to know you, Holy Father. Most of them were not in the Conclave when you were elected. They don't really know you. I believe they only wish to hear your thoughts on the Church. They might do well with some reassuring that the Church is still relevant after all that has gone on over the last few years."

"Very well, Francis. I can certainly assure them that the Church can weather these scandals, just as Our Lord has led Her through the past scandals. But I will not let them off the hook for their part in the disrepute."

Silence gripped the room as Pope John's mind moved to what those conversations might look like…and Francis was afraid to think about them.

After a moment, Francis broke the silence. "Holy Father, we will be leaving for the airport immediately after your mass tomorrow morning. They can hold a takeoff slot for a little while, but the airlines don't have the latitude that they used to." With that, Francis bid the Pontiff farewell and left for his offices. He had some new plans to make, with only one day before their departure.

When she saw Monsignor Hellman leave the Pope's study, Abrielle entered and asked if there was anything that she could bring him. She was looking for an excuse to speak with him; she still felt somewhat awkward whenever she was in His Holiness's presence.

"Thank you, Abrielle, I would like some fresh tea when you have a moment to spare."

"Of course, Your Holiness."

She left so quietly that when she returned an instant later and Pope John looked up, his first thought was to wonder whether she had yet left. Instead, he said, "Abrielle, your stealth and speed will forever astound me."

As she prepared him a cup, she interrupted the newspaper he was reading, saying, "Your Holiness? May I wish you farewell?"

The Pontiff looked up, embarrassed that he was ignoring this lady who was only here to serve him. "I'm so sorry, dear lady. Please sit with me for a moment."

"No, Holiness. I was only concerned that in the activity that will surely build between now and tomorrow morning, I may not have the chance to say goodbye. While I realize that you will only be gone for a few days, you will be missed here."

"That's very sweet of you to say. You should enjoy the quiet. Perhaps go away for a few days."

"Yes, Holy Father. I also wanted to ask you to please be careful. Please allow your Guard to look out for you."

"I will. Rest assured. Please don't worry about me. I have wonderfully dedicated men looking out for my well-being."

"Is Inspector Guidice going along?"

"Do you know Giuseppe?"

"Only by reputation; and, of course, he has been kind enough to greet me when he visits. I know that he has known you his whole life and would give it for you."

"Well, you seem to know quite a bit about my old friend." The Pope said this with a little conspiracy in his eyes and his smile. "You should let me formally introduce you the next time he visits."

"That's certainly not necessary. What does he need, talking with an old housemaid? I am just grateful that there are men who care for your safety."

"Well, although Inspector Guidice doesn't have any official role on a trip like this, he insisted on accompanying me. And truth be told, I'll be very glad to have him along. He's a very special man; and he would do well to get to know a lovely lady such as you."

Abrielle blushed slightly, bowed deeply, and backed out of the study.

The balance of the day followed a similar course, with a steady stream of visitors who were either involved in planning the trip or wished to say their farewells. Although there was a typical pattern to his days, the activity and excitement built throughout the course of this particular day. When Pope John finally retired close to midnight, he felt prepared to walk out the door, without the distractions that might otherwise accompany him. He was ready to spend time meeting with his family of believers.

As dawn broke, the Papal Apartments were already in full motion. His Holiness was returning to his study after saying mass, with his sacristan in tow. The sacristan, responsible for the care of the vestments and vessels used in the mass, had been busily preparing the items the Pontiff would use on his trip; and he now bore an additional two suitcases that would be added to the luggage collection currently accumulating in the dining room.

In a blatant attempt to keep the morning's routine to a minimum, Monsignor Hellman had assured Pope John that there would be a lovely and light breakfast awaiting him on the airplane. Surprisingly, it took the Papal Retinue only fifteen minutes to load the small caravan of vehicles headed to the airport. It occurred to Pope John that he was not the first Pontiff to be so carefully managed by his professional staff. It also occurred to him that he was not the first Pontiff to be given a quick escort out of Rome.

Fiuminicio International Airport was thirty minutes away. The caravan headed west out of Rome to the beltway, then south briefly before heading west again. At this point, the Pontiff knew that his car was pointed directly at the northern Sardinian coast. His lack of homesickness over leaving the Vatican was now punctuated by thoughts of his true home. "Well," he thought, "perhaps someday this too will feel like home."

As the group arrived at the airport, they paused briefly at a special security checkpoint and then proceeded to a hangar on the edge of the airport grounds. Sitting with its nose just poking through the hangar doors was a late-model Boeing 757. The Alitalia aircraft had been reconfigured for papal flights, and the Pope was among the last to board. There was room toward the back half of the plane for a small contingent of press and staff from the Vatican, along with a few journalists from the visited country. At some point during the flight, Pope John would be expected to greet them all and answer a few polite questions, all of which would allow the American papers to run stories on the day of his arrival. The middle cabin was reserved for personal staff and any of the members of the senior clergy that might be accompanying the tour. Finally, the first class cabin gave His Holiness maximum privacy during his journey. All but one of the seats had been removed, and in their place were two rear-facing seats and a small conference table, allowing the Pontiff to conduct meetings or private audiences along the route.

Once Pope John arrived on board, it was only a few minutes before the door was closed and the plane began taxiing toward the runway. With wheels up, the waiting game began. Pope John was not an enthusiastic traveler; it was only the joy of arriving and seeing new faces that carried him along. The nine-hour flight was tightly scheduled to break up the monotony. He would have several meetings with top staffers. At least two hours would be spent with Monsignor Hellman, reviewing correspondence that they had saved just for the occasion. He had two major homilies to polish, along with personal notes to review for the audiences he would have in the United States. Finally, he would host a young journalist from *Time* magazine for the last hour or so of the flight. His Holiness had granted an interview to the prestigious and influential magazine in order to facilitate a day-in-the-life portrayal of the tour. Of course, with only a slight chance of controversy in the piece, they had assigned a journeyman reporter rather than a marquee journalist. Monsignor Hellman had intentionally scheduled the meeting for the end of the flight. This way if any unplanned topics were to come up, there would be very little time before the landing process, at which point the captain would banish the reporter to the third cabin, where she could be safely strapped in with a seatbelt.

When the plane finally touched down in New York, the sluggish entourage disembarked a little more slowly than they had emplaned. At this end of the trip, Pope John was the first to move and was in the awaiting car and on his way to the hotel before most of the group had even stretched their legs and pulled their bags out of the overhead bins. As his car approached the Plaza Hotel, New York City bustled with midday crowds. The NYPD had established a notable presence in front of the hotel on the Grand Army Plaza, complimenting the less-obvious contingent of Secret Service, which held primary responsibility for the Pontiff's protection.

Pope John exited his car in front of the grand awning, complete with its gold finials, and paused for a moment to enjoy the fresh air. He noticed at once that one of the flag poles overhead carried the banner of the Vatican. The front door staff briefly greeted the latest dignitary to visit their fine establishment, and they were, by training, aggressive in their welcome. This was something quite new for the Pope. He made his way through the cavernous white and gold Nouveau-Rococo lobby toward the elevators. Monsignor Hellman's assistant, having arrived the evening before, had checked the entire party in an hour earlier, allowing the group to move quickly through the public spaces and into an awaiting elevator. Pope John rode to the top floor, where he would occupy a small suite. Rather than facing out toward Central Park, his room was on the opposite side of the hallway and thus faced inward toward the courtyard and pool. The Secret Service had recommended this as an added security precaution, which the Pontiff found somewhat amusing, given that his bedroom window at home looked out on Saint Peter's Square. This was the Roman equivalent of Times Square, not Central Park.

Suddenly alone again, but now in an unfamiliar city, the Pope settled in quickly for a short rest. He recalled that his old friend Giuseppe had asked to meet with him about an hour before he was to leave for the Chancery Office, the seat of the New York Archdiocese. It seemed that no sooner had he closed his eyes than he received a phone call. Monsignor Hellman's assistant was providing a wake-up call service while they were on the road, to ensure that everything continued to run smoothly. He stepped into the marble bathroom, took a quick shower, and felt refreshed for his evening's activities. Pope John knew that these westbound trips made for very long first days, but he was feeling surprisingly ready for the balance of the day.

The Secret Service agent sitting outside the door was already familiar with the Inspector General of the Vatican Police and had greeted him warmly. Giuseppe knocked twice on the door, paused, and as he entered saw the Pontiff emerging from the back bedroom.

"Wonderful to see you, Your Holiness. I trust that your flight was uneventful."

"Yes, Giuseppe, it was very smooth, although I will never get used to being cooped up so long. No one likes me to wander around the airplane too much, so I end up confined like a bird to a cage. How has your visit been to New York, your 'advance work,' I believe you called it?"

"It has been very enjoyable to visit the United States again and practice my English a bit. And it has been very interesting working with the Secret Service on their plans. I must admit that I think it bothers the Guard a little bit that I am here, when your protection is rightfully their duty. You may hear a little bit about that from the colonel on your return."

"That's neither here nor there. I am not terribly worried, neither about my safety in America nor about the jealous complaints of my colonel."

"I can assure you that he has taken great precautions on your behalf. In addition, the Secret Service seems to value a flawless visit very highly indeed. I would never have imagined the resources that have been put at our disposal."

"Very reassuring," the Pope said, a little too sarcastically for Giuseppe's liking.

"Holiness, I am here because I'm also concerned about you and your safety. I wish you would take these precautions more seriously. I recognize that sane people wish you no harm; but that doesn't make you safe. I am grateful that you have allowed me to join you on this trip."

"Giuseppe, I don't mean to be disrespectful of the work you do; and if I give you that impression I am very sorry. I still don't understand the internecine battles within the Vatican. The fact is, I don't want to care about them. But I do need to learn to understand the landscape." Pope John wasn't talking about the Swiss Guard and their ego any longer, and Giuseppe knew it.

"Your Holiness, now that the tour is underway, I don't feel there is much more that I can do with regards to personal protection. It's probably best that I stay out of the way of the

Secret Service and the Guard anyway. With your permission, I want to fade into the background for the balance of the tour and just observe."

"Certainly Giuseppe, but you say this with a bit of a conspiratorial accent. What exactly will you be observing?"

"As you can imagine, with so many important figures converging at the same time and the same space, there are numerous meetings around the meetings. There will be a variety of old friendships to reacquaint and new relationships to build. It might prove useful at some point to understand those dynamics. As you said yourself, a bit of family feuding can spring up within this group."

The two men stood and walked toward the door. Intentionally trying not to sound too intrigued, Pope John shook Giuseppe's hand gently and said, "Whatever you think is best; I trust your judgment. Perhaps when we return to Rome, you can share your observations. I'll invite you to lunch; there's a lovely lady in my household that I should like to introduce you to." Pope John didn't realize it, but Giuseppe had already begun his dossier on Abrielle.

As he left the Pope's suite, Giuseppe headed down the hall to the elevator, descended to the lobby, and found the Rose Club off of the Fifth Avenue lobby. At the entrance to the restaurant, Giuseppe found his old friend Paul Regalo.

The two law enforcement veterans had met early in their careers at the FBI training grounds at Quantico. While officially called Marine Corps Base Quantico, the facility also plays host to various facilities for major law enforcement agencies, including the FBI Academy, the FBI Laboratory, DEA training, and the Marine Corps Embassy Security Group. Back when Giuseppe had been a rising star in his state police force, he was given the opportunity to participate in an exchange program at the FBI Academy. There he met a very young and very fit Paul Regalo. The two hit it off and always kept in touch. Paul kept his friend apprised of opportunities to visit, and over the years Giuseppe had done a prolonged stint at the FBI Laboratory as well as several shorter training courses. By the time Pope John had invited him to Rome to take over the Vatican Police, Paul had been stationed at FBI headquarters in Washington, D.C., for some time. Giuseppe asked Paul to wrangle him an invitation to meet with the Embassy Security Group, sensing that Vatican City was not unlike a very large embassy. He wanted to understand strategies for defending a highly porous site in the midst of a bustling city.

"Paul, I am so glad to see you." As his friend turned to greet him, he said, "I hope I haven't kept you waiting too long."

The two men embraced, as Paul took the chance to remind his old friend of his usual tardiness. "I expected nothing less. I showed up five minutes late, thinking I might give you a fighting chance, but you didn't take advantage of it."

"Fortunately, His Holiness granted me time before his schedule got completely away from him. I wanted to assure him of all the good work that has been done in preparation."

"Well, that's not fair," Paul laughed. "I will never have an excuse as good as, 'I was with the Pope.' By the way, I am grateful that you alerted me to the visit early enough that I could talk my way onto His Holiness's security detail. No offense, but while it's great that I can see you, a friend of His Holiness, it will be really special to be in his company."

"I am really grateful that you are so involved in this tour. He is very special to me, almost like an uncle; I've known him so long."

A lovely young hostess approached and offered to seat them.

On the way to the table, Paul started up again, "It never ceases to amaze me. Ever since Pope John was elected, it's been hard for me to imagine you as a personal friend. I know you too well. Does he know that I can't drag you to mass when you visit without the guilt of the bad example you're setting for my kids?

"Yes, unfortunately I get to have personal lectures from the Vicar of Christ on my poor religious habits." Giuseppe sat down and, focused on adjusting the napkin in his lap, shook his head at the sorry direction the conversation was headed. "Give me a break. You realize that you highly devout, daily mass attendees are pretty rare these days."

"I understand, but standing with the minority is frequently the right move. So, how is the Holy Father, if I can ask?"

"Of course you can. He looked quite happy to be here and ready for the activities to begin. If you only knew him as a parish priest, or even as our Bishop, he was such a gregarious man that it's hard to imagine the adjustment to living in a bubble. But enough about overly pampered, old Catholic men; how are your overly pampered wife and overly talented kids?"

"Everybody is doing really well. They are disappointed that they won't see you on this trip. Have you found anyone to spend your time with in Rome?"

"Not yet, although Pope John just said something to me that sounded like he's going to play matchmaker. How about that for an arrangement—introduced by the Pope? No pressure there, right?"

"Perhaps he's thinking, as I do, that the right influences could do your social and spiritual lives both some good."

"Paul, I'm not a fallen-away Catholic. I'm more of an *unmotivated* Catholic. I believe everything I'm supposed to believe, I'm just no longer sure that I need the Church as an intermediary."

"And I think, when you stop seeing the Church as an institution and an intermediary and more as a community that you participate in, that you will find the Church that I know. I wouldn't want to belong to a club either, if I thought its mission was to control my life."

Giuseppe listened thoughtfully, although not without skepticism.

Paul continued, "It just cracks me up that you are actually friends with the Pope, and you're the one who disdains the Church."

"Well, that may be a little stronger than I would put it; but my sentiment toward Father Franco is personal and born out of the knowledge of what a good man he is. Most people in his life, especially today, love him without really knowing him."

The conversation then turned to their more traditional topics of law enforcement, world politics, and sports. They renewed an endless debate about football versus football, as in the NFL versus Series A. Before they knew it, it was time for dinner, so they settled deeper into their booth and ordered. The familiar patter of their past conversations returned easily, and they nearly overstayed their welcome, as the waiter started to wonder if they would ever give up their table.

Finally, they sipped down the last of their espresso and parted company, assured that they'd be seeing quite a bit of each other over the next few days. And Paul extracted a promise that Giuseppe would visit Washington the following spring, when all the kids were home from school.

Chapter Seven

After Giuseppe left, Pope John sat down to review his notes for his meetings later in the day. Although it had been a very long day already, he still had his meeting with Cardinal Johns and what was billed as a "small, intimate" dinner. When he and Monsignor Hellman arrived at the Chancery Office, just ten or so blocks away near the East River, they were greeted warmly by His Eminence, Michael Cardinal Johns, Archbishop of New York. Cardinal Johns was standing just outside the front door in his finest starched cassock. The rich red sash around his waist, along with the pectoral cross that hung from his neck but seemed to point wherever he looked, only served to emphasize his girth. For some reason this struck Pope John, although even he didn't understand why; there are plenty of cherubic Bishops in Rome. As the Pontiff mounted the stairs and extended his hand to Cardinal Johns, the Cardinal bent to meet the Pope's hand and kiss the *Annulus Piscatoris*, the Ring of the

Fisherman. The ring symbolizes the office of the Pope, as successor to Saint Peter in leading the world's Catholics. By kissing it, the Cardinal paid respect and allegiance to Pope John for all those around to see.

After stepping inside, the Pontiff met a line of staff waiting to greet him. Pope John was overjoyed to be able to immerse himself in a crowd of "real" people, but he found himself being ushered through the crowd and into the Cardinal's office almost immediately.

Once inside the dignified, wood-paneled office, Cardinal Johns offered a chair and said, "Your Holiness, it is so gracious of you to make our city the first stop of your papacy."

"My dear brother, America has played such a wonderful role in our Church over the last century; and where else, other than New York, to begin a visit to your beautiful country. Did you know that I've been here once before?"

"I didn't. When was this?"

"Longer ago than I care to remember. It was during a holiday while I was studying in the seminary."

"I trust that you will be seeing our fair city from a slightly different vantage point this time around. I am quite sure that you didn't address thousands from the floor of Madison Square Garden on your initial visit."

Pope John chuckled, "Well that's certainly true enough. I am greatly looking forward to our mass tomorrow."

Just then the door opened and in walked a seminarian holding a tray of tea and cookies. The Pope noted two things: first, the Cardinal apparently had the same bumper crop of seminarians that he had at the Vatican; and second, the Cardinal happened to stock his favorite tea. This struck him simultaneously as both very kind and a little unnerving. To think, someone in Los Angeles at that moment was probably fussing about the kind of soap he preferred or how he liked his bed to be made.

Once the two priests were alone again, Pope John returned to the topic of tomorrow's mass. "Is there any theme that you might like me to touch on tomorrow, during the mass?"

"No, Your Holiness. I am sure that whatever you wish to share with us will be thoughtful and well inspired by the Spirit."

With that, he flashed back to the Conclave in which he was elected. When he was still Cardinal Calliendo, he had one brief conversation with Cardinal Johns, and it was the first time they had really ever spoken in person. The Cardinal struck him at the time as quite content and unenthusiastic, even at the thought of electing the next leader of the Church.

Cardinal Johns had remarked to him, "I believe that we need a mature and steady hand to wear the Fisherman's Ring." He recalled thinking that this was a subtle suggestion that the Conclave should look for a man other than the wildly popular—but perhaps too young—Cardinal Welty of Boston. He only later learned that his own name was being circulated and that Cardinal Johns was expressing his support. After the sweeping excitement of the following few weeks had settled down, it occurred to him that while Cardinal Welty was not significantly younger than he was, there was probably no shortage of history between the two reigning monarchs of American Catholicism.

Returning to the moment, Pope John asked, "Are there no current events in your diocese that you might wish me to comment on, in order to reinforce my appreciation for your community's needs?"

"New York is so large and diverse; there are few issues that matter to a majority of any crowd. As you undoubtedly know, New York is a melting pot and has been for centuries, ever since the first Europeans shared space with the indigenous population."

"Perhaps, then, we might discuss this theme, reinforcing the importance of ministry to immigrant populations. The

Church has certainly played an enormous leadership role historically in New York's immigrant history."

"Yes, Holy Father, historically we have seen waves of Catholic immigrants come to our shores, and the Church has successfully ministered to them. Today, however, most immigrant groups are non-Catholic. We likely will play a diminishing role in the immigrant story over the next decade."

The thought that ran through Pope John's mind was Christ's injunction to help the visitor and the foreigner. He thought, "Why doesn't my brother Bishop see this as an opportunity rather than simply a demographic shift?"

The two men continued to talk for nearly an hour, although the conversation turned increasingly away from weighty topics and more toward the mundane—the itinerary for the tour, the interview he granted to *Time* magazine on the flight, even his routine around the Vatican. Cardinal Johns had arranged for a private room for Pope John to rest and freshen up before dinner; but as he bid a temporary farewell to his host, the Pope couldn't shake his bewilderment. The Church had granted this leadership position to a man who seemed almost like a bystander. The conversation around routine matters animated the man more than the opportunity to minister to a staggering population shift. He seemed to have decided that achieving the Red Hat—the most potent symbol of a Cardinal—was the reward for a life of service, rather than an extreme call to greater service.

After a few hours reviewing correspondence with Monsignor Hellman, the two men made their way down to the main floor, where a small reception had gathered before the private dinner Cardinal Johns had arranged. In attendance, and all quite punctual, were the Auxiliary Bishops, who helped minister to the massive diocese, along with several notable dignitaries. In all, there were sixteen invitees; nearly all were Roman Catholic, with the exception of the Mayor of New York, although even his wife was Catholic. For absolutely all of the guests, this likely marked the most significant dinner party that they would ever attend and one they would talk about for years.

The Cardinal and host introduced Pope John to his guests. The Pope chatted with them amiably for about a half hour, until dinner was served. As was customary, the host offered grace before the meal. The guests dined on a splendid, if simple, meal intended to make their guests feel welcome. Given their travel schedule and the time changes, Monsignor Hellman had specifically requested a meal that wasn't too rich. There was spinach and goat cheese ravioli intended to remind the Pope of his childhood, a seafood soup that reflected the modern Sardinian diet, and a traditional wine, which because of the island's history resembled a Spanish wine more than an Italian one.

The dinner dragged on a little longer than Monsignor Hellman had hoped, but the conversation had been very enjoyable. Concerned about tomorrow's busy schedule and looking after His Holiness, he stood and asked Cardinal Johns for permission to retire for the evening. At this, all the guests rose in unison. Pope John made his way around the table, personally thanking everyone for welcoming him and somehow managing to reference a particular topic that he'd discussed with each of them personally. After the long farewell, Monsignor Hellman thanked their host again and led the Holy Father outside to their waiting car and security detail. The short ride back to the Plaza was even quicker this time, with the lighter evening traffic. The two of them moved quickly to their rooms without much conversation, both men quite exhausted from their extended day due to the time change.

* * * * *

The next morning, after a good night's sleep, Monsignor Hellman once again rapped on the Pontiff's door. They reviewed the day's schedule; it would be a perfect example of the odd combination of the secular and religious natures of the Holy See.

The Monsignor escorted His Holiness down to the lobby of the hotel, where they seemed to pick up additional security officers every few feet as the cordon collapsed around them. They skirted the edge of the famous Palm Court, and just beyond they entered a meeting space called the Terrace Room. At nearly five thousand square feet, the room evokes the feeling of an Italian church, its columns spread across a richly painted ceiling, creating the feeling of flying buttresses in a medieval church. In the center of the room, which was now surrounded by security, sat a conference table set for ten; however, on the room's mezzanine was an intimate setting for two next to a small buffet table. At the foot of the small staircase, Monsignor Hellman nodded to the president of the United States and left His Holiness in his capable hands.

"Holy Father," said the president, as he bent to kiss the Fisherman's Ring, "how nice of you to make time on your visit for this meeting." They had met briefly once before, at the coronation of Cardinal Calliendo as Pope John XXIV, although at that meeting there had been no time for discussion.

"Think nothing of it, Mr. President. When Monsignor Hellman and I heard of your interest in speaking, we immediately knew that we must make time."

"Well, Your Holiness, I took the step of ordering a small buffet for us to share. I hope that wasn't too presumptuous. We have only twenty or thirty minutes until the others arrive. I wanted to have a few minutes alone with you to share my thoughts, before I must put on the mask of one head of state speaking to another."

As they both rose to prepare plates for themselves, the Pope responded, "I appreciate the hospitality, especially since in some ways I am your host here at this lovely hotel. I also appreciate your candor during this meeting and will accord you all the respect due you in our next. What is it that Holy Mother Church can do for you?"

"I am very concerned about the issues of piracy in East Africa. I am also quite concerned about the poverty that is driving these desperate men to such measures of risk-taking and about the increasing number of children being recruited. This will be getting out of hand soon; I am concerned that some in the Middle East might wish to conquer and colonialize the nation of Somalia in order to keep the Gulf of Aden open for their merchants. This would set Somalia back, returning it to colonial rule. With the majority of the nation being Sunni Muslim, there are several nations that might invade and claim to be a stabilizing force, even over the objections of the East African Community."

"I have been hearing similar things from my diplomatic corps," replied the Pontiff. After some further consideration, he continued, "But what exactly do you think that we could do to assist? As you say, the nation is nearly entirely Muslim."

"Yes, Holy Father. However, according to my intelligence sources, your newly appointed Apostolic Delegate is very well respected in the region and with the members of the East African Community. I wish to beg your assistance in helping us negotiate for at least some temporary solutions. The USAID is willing to help funnel additional economic assistance to the area, and I would like to ask the Church to help us to place it in the most beneficial places. However, I cannot get my Congress to open the flow of money unless the violence diminishes greatly. We will need to negotiate some quid pro quo in advance. If the Church can broker this, it might further its stature in the region."

"*Quid pro quo,* hmm, the American's favorite Latin expression," the Pope said with a little smile as he put his tea cup to his lips and pushed his plate away. "Well, it sounds like a worthy topic of discussion and certainly the goals are laudable. Let us entertain the rest of the group in the discussion and I will certainly throw my support in early."

The two men sat for their remaining minutes together, discussing a little of the behind-the-scenes of the coronation that the president had witnessed. Pope John inquired after the First Lady, whom he had recalled being unusually striking; and the president said that they would be together in a secured box for the Papal Mass in Madison Square Garden later. As the door opened at the far end of the room, His Holiness told the president, "Please tell your wife that I will add Saint Margaret to the litany of saints during the Eucharistic Prayer in her honor. I believe that she is named for her. You can tell her that I will pray for her intentions during this mass."

The president was speechless for the first time since he had entered politics thirty years earlier. He could only smile and nod.

As the crowd formed around the conference table, they seemed somewhat surprised to see the two heads of state descending the small staircase together. The group included the Secretaries of State for both nations, the U.S. Ambassador to the Holy See, and the Papal Nuncio to the United States. Once all the greetings had been completed, the group sat together. The discussion was really just a longer version of what had just transpired between the two principals; and they both seemed anxious to get to a conclusion.

The president finally spoke up during a lull in the conversation, and the Pontiff took his clue. "Holy Father, the United States would like to formally request the Holy See's intervention into the piracy issue. We are willing to offer financial support and to potentially put that at the Catholic Church's disposal, if we can be sure that you are making progress on the matter."

The Pope responded with similar formality. "Mr. President, I will ask my diplomatic corps to investigate the matter further, with an eye toward how much we believe we might accomplish. At that point, we will provide you with a recommendation as well as a plan for carrying out that recommendation. Will that suffice?"

The others at the table were somewhat surprised by the clipped and professional tone of the exchange, but they were also pleased that the two men were driving to a tactical conclusion. After a bit more clarification by the professional diplomats on both sides—those who had to execute the instructions—the group concluded their business.

As the group disbanded, Pope John instructed Monsignor Hellman to pass to the president two documents, the Papal equivalent of backstage passes to a rock concert.

They would allow him and his wife to join a small gathering after the mass concluded later in the day. Then the Pontiff realized that Monsignor Hellman was leading him to an adjoining room.

"Holy Father, yesterday you asked me to assemble a small group of believers in each city for you to converse with. In the time we have remaining this morning, we have just such a small group. Unfortunately, because of the limited notice, I had to work with the hotel concierge to assemble a group of the faithful from within the hotel staff, and obviously they have had no real time to prepare for the meeting. They will undoubtedly feel awkward and uncertain—"

"Nonsense, Francis. This is perfect. I can't thank you enough for making this happen, and I am sure that I can put these folks at ease and have a very good conversation. The fact that they haven't been selected from some group of the Bishop's friends and haven't been able to 'prepare' should make it all the more effective."

The Pontiff entered the room, where a single empty chair sat facing seven others in a semicircle. There was shock on the faces staring back at him; undoubtedly, they thought they were part of some practical joke when they were told earlier what was to happen. The Pope asked Monsignor Hellman to excuse himself and then sat down in his appointed seat. The folks around him were too scared to move or say anything.

After a few seconds, he asked them to rearrange their chairs into a full circle. He wanted this to be a discussion, not an audience. He was afraid to bombard them with questions, for fear of putting them on the defensive. The first things he could think of to say were, "What do you think of the Catholic Church," "What would you change if you were in my job," and "Why are you in the Church?" But no, these wouldn't do. Everyone would get very quiet and insecure. He decided to try a different tack.

Pope John started, "Thank you for taking time from your day to spend with me. Until one year ago, I was Father Franco Calliendo, a simple priest from a poor village in Sardinia, Italy, and it would make me very happy if you could try to think of that while we are together. I'd like to start by giving you a chance to ask me questions...anything that you would like." The group remained quiet, with the most adventurous looking around at each other, hoping to nominate someone else to be the first to speak up.

Finally, a middle-aged man in a chef's uniform said, "Holy Father, can you tell us what it's like to be elected Pope?"

Pope John spent several minutes recounting the emotions he had felt when it became obvious that his name had been circulated among the Cardinals. He shared the progression from surprise, to false modesty, quickly followed by self-doubt, then concern, and finally resignation. Once the election had concluded and the results were announced, he shared that he had felt a surprising comfort with the decision—he knew that the Holy Spirit would help him through whatever was to come. He didn't stray too far from a simple answer, because this wasn't supposed to be about what he thought; but with that first exchange, the group opened up a little.

"Holy Father, were you involved in Vatican II?" Yes, he was; although the Council seemed to have as many meanings as interpreters…

Then the questions kept coming. "Why do we keep changing the liturgy?"

"Well, some of it is a search for a greater communion among the participants, but much of it can be traced to having too many theologians in the Vatican." This response elicited a collective chuckle from the group.

"What do you think of the current role of the laity in the Church?"

"It has been a wonderfully fresh breeze, the kind that you always want to feel more frequently…"

"Why do we have so many scandals in the Church?"

"We need to remember that the Church is really *you,* but the bureaucracy is human and very fallible…"

"How are you going to stop the abuse that's going on?"

"The best weapon against that abominable behavior is to shine a light on it and hold everyone accountable…"

"What are we going to do if these scandals chase off even more vocations?"

"Our primary role is to pray for those vocations and support them. Then we have to work to make service, both religious and lay, more a focus of our daily lives…"

By the end, the group had really gotten to the heart of the matter, and Pope John hoped that he had earned their trust with his candid answers. "Can I put you all on the spot now? I think you've uncovered some very key issues, and I want to hear your answers to your own questions." Starting with the first person who had spoken and working his way around the group, he remembered each person's question:

"What do you think it would be like to find yourself as Pope, and what would you like to do with the job?"

"What do you think about the post-Vatican II Church? Do we need a Vatican III?"

"What do you think about the liturgy, good and bad?"

"How can the laity play a more active role in the Church?"

"How do the Church's scandals reflect on Her and how should we handle them?"

"What should I do about the child abuse scandal around the world?"

"How should we increase vocations to religious life, and what if we can't?"

Each person took the Pontiff's questions, in turn. As he expected, their questions demonstrated a particular topic that they had given a good deal of thought to, and the conversation became quite lively. By the end, Pope John could hardly get a word in edgewise, but this was what he wanted. He needed to know what real Catholics thought about the most pressing issues of the Church. In the end, he was pleasantly surprised, not by what they said, but by how much it rang true with his own beliefs.

Sensing that Pope John would never willingly break away from a group such as this, Monsignor Hellman quietly entered the room after nearly two hours. He suggested that the Holy Father needed some lunch and time to rest before the mass later in the day at Madison Square Garden, which promised to be a marathon under hot lights.

Pope John acquiesced and thanked the group profusely for their candor and animation. At this, he could see by their expressions a sudden worry that they might have become a little too informal and gone a little too far as the conversation wore on. As he approached each of them individually to say goodbye, the first few people attempted to kiss his ring or bow. He pulled them up to embrace them. By the time he got to the last young lady, a member of the housekeeping staff, she threw her arms around his neck and kissed his cheek. He was very pleased that he had made her that comfortable. He thought, "Maybe there is a way to be in this role and still connect with real people."

Monsignor Hellman again led the way up to their rooms, where a lunch was waiting for Pope John. He invited the Monsignor to sit with him. He had so much spinning through his head, and he wanted to share it with someone. He also wanted to reinforce for Francis that this was exactly what he had hoped for when he gave him the assignment.

After lunch, the Pope rested for a few hours, wrapped in the optimism that he felt in the Church. Not that everything he had discussed with his small group had been positive— quite the opposite. However, he was heartened by the engagement and willingness of the laity, even after all the confusion and disappointment the Church had served up. This was a fantastic place to begin; he vowed to tap into more of this energy.

By four o'clock, he had freshened up and put on a fresh cassock for the ride to Madison Square Garden. Although he had been there before and had celebrated mass before larger crowds, he knew that tonight would be special.

The ride down Fifth Avenue was one that he looked forward to, although he had been advised that the ten-minute trip could end up taking up to three times as long. The caravan ventured in via the underground entrance, and after the Pope was escorted to the Green Room, which was serving as the Sacristy for this evening, Monsignor Hellman made his way to a pre-mass logistical briefing. When he returned, several other Bishops had arrived and were resting in leather armchairs that dotted the room. He shared the gist of the briefing with the assembled clerics.

"Apparently, there was quite a scene an hour or so ago. Security found that a large number of folks had scalped their tickets to the mass, and that these were fetching very high sums on the black market."

"Outrageous," said one rotund Bishop in the corner, "to think that someone would sell a ticket to a holy celebration. Those were supposed to have been dispensed to active members of each parish."

Monsignor Hellman continued, "This was complicated by the fact that apparently there are a large number of counterfeit tickets floating around. Once there was a market, the con men got involved. There are many people who arrived, only to be greatly disappointed."

The irritated Bishop chimed in again, "Serves them right if you ask me." At this, Monsignor Hellman grimaced at the cleric and turned to Pope John.

The Pontiff waded into the conversation with more conciliation in his voice. "Your Excellency, putting all modesty aside for a minute, I am concerned that our most active brothers and sisters find it *necessary* to sell the opportunity to celebrate the Lord's Supper with us—not because of the sale, but because they need the money so desperately. That is the shame. I am equally disappointed that some of our brothers and sisters, who were so anxious and able to pay scalpers to celebrate with us, were then duped out of their hard-earned money. Monsignor Hellman, please instruct the door staff to collect the names and addresses of anyone surrendering a counterfeit ticket and arrange for us to send them a memento with our regrets."

"Yes, Holy Father, at once."

Within the hour, Madison Square Garden was full and a half a dozen concelebrants were dressed for the mass. As

Pope John stepped into the arena, the processional hymn rose twenty decibels, as the already engaged throng of people felt moved by his presence. The celebration proceeded just like any other liturgy, but it was hard to mistake the specialness of this day for the attendees.

When the Pontiff rose to deliver his homily, he spoke extemporaneously to the adoring crowd. No one had ever heard of such a thing—a Pope addressing a gathering like any parish priest on Sunday. He shared three main thoughts with God's people. He reminded New York of its prominence on the world stage as a home for immigrants, and he cautioned that the Church must lead that continuing embrace, rejecting notions that those days are over. He encouraged evangelization of those in other communities, within the bounds of respect for other faiths. These two notions he tied back to the early Church and its willingness to take chances for the message of Jesus. And finally, he promised that the Church would see itself revived by that spirit of the early Church, but they must each be willing to work for it. This was a Church of the involved, not the spectators.

As the mass continued, there were moments of profound emotion for many, such as watching the Vicar of Christ celebrate the Last Supper, directly obeying the command of Jesus. These moments were contrasted with profound joy as the music carried the thousands through the communion lines and concluding with the recessional hymn.

By the end, Pope John was both exhausted and exhilarated. He spent almost an hour in a reception room that was set up for the city's Catholic elite to join him after the celebration. The president's wife leaned in as they were introduced and thanked him for his kind gesture; he could tell that she was genuinely moved.

* * * * *

The next day, the entourage had a late morning, with a comfortable breakfast together in a quiet, private dining room. Afterward, they made the slow trip in midday traffic back to the airport for the next leg of their journey. The flight to Los Angeles was longer than Pope John had expected, and he was grateful that they had nothing planned for the afternoon. In Los Angeles, the Pontiff's caravan pulled in to the Peninsula Beverly Hills Hotel in western Los Angeles, near the former movie back lots of Twentieth Century Fox in Century City. His suite provided a lovely terrace and rooms filled with overstuffed chairs. It turned out to be a restful time that allowed each of them to recharge for the big day that would follow. Monsignor Hellman was given the afternoon off, and the Pope begged him to find some restful activity rather than sifting through the never-ending supply of correspondence that was still being forwarded to him daily.

In the early evening, Monsignor Hellman collected Pope John, who noticed a bit of pink on his secretary's cheeks. He had apparently done as requested and found some time to enjoy himself in the beautiful weather. They departed for the Chancery Office for a private dinner with the Archbishop. Archbishop Juan Suarez had been recently installed as the Ordinary for the greater Los Angeles area and had not yet been created Cardinal Suarez. He had offered the private time to allow Pope John time to get to know him better as well as to prepare for a very busy day to come.

The two men became fast friends and, to Monsignor Hellman's eye, seemed to be almost able to complete each other's thoughts. Despite his relative youth, the Archbishop had intellectual credentials as well as pastoral; Francis could tell that the Pope was quickly developing a fondness for him. Pope John recounted his time in New York in some detail for his new comrade, and the younger cleric seemed genuinely interested in both the conversation with Cardinal Johns and the crowd of hotel workers. The Archbishop assured him that he would find the group assembling the following day to be equally engaging.

Regardless of the casual day and the enjoyable conversation, Pope John was clearly fatigued after another day of westward travel. At the Archbishop's suggestion, Monsignor Hellman called the car around and the brother Bishops embraced. Archbishop Suarez was clearly choked up when he shared with the Pontiff how touched he was that his invitation was accepted. "Your Holiness, I will forever be grateful for the kindness that you show me by engaging me as an equal. I will remember this week for the rest of my life."

"You are my equal and my brother, Juan. I thank you for your hospitality and thoughtfulness, and I look forward to the rest of our time together. *Vaya con dios.*"

The next morning began with the Archbishop and his Auxiliary Bishops venturing to the west end of town to join the papal entourage at the hotel. As they all gathered near the main lobby, outside the hotel sat an unusual sight for Beverly Hills—the Popemobile. Just a block north of the hotel, the customized Mercedes truck met Wilshire Boulevard for a six-mile, two-hour marathon of a papal parade. The parade traveled from Beverly Hills to the Chancery Office, which allowed tens of thousands of Catholic Angelinos to see His Holiness in person.

Along the route, Pope John felt warmed by the excitement and energy emanating from the throngs of people.

He knew that any papal parade drew nearly as many non-Catholic spectators as Catholics; and he loved knowing that the mixing of the two groups might win over one or two hearts today. To those along the path of the parade, the event seemed to have motion; however, to the Pontiff standing still at a railing inside the confines of the vehicle, such occasions sometimes felt static. For Pope John, however, these were intoxicating events. Just as when he stood looking over the crowds at Saint Peter's Square, this wasn't a mass of people but a collection of stories. As the truck moved along, he would pick out someone thirty feet ahead—perhaps a grandmother holding a baby—and focus on them as he passed. He would consider their story and what that grandmother was whispering in the baby's ear, and he would feel utterly grateful to be a part of their lives, if only for a few seconds. He knew, because he'd once done the math, that he would connect with about one hundred people per mile; and today, that meant "meeting" more than five hundred people on the way to say mass.

When they arrived at the Chancery, the celebrants gathered to rest, have a light lunch, and chat for a while before the mass was scheduled to begin. About thirty minutes before the mass, they rode in a small motorcade to the Los Angeles Coliseum. As they processed into the stadium, nearly one hundred thousand people were singing the processional hymn, and Pope John realized that he was grinning like a schoolboy. He didn't know these people, but he was overjoyed to be here, with them, right now.

At the conclusion of the celebration, as he was leaving the stadium, he paused and looked back over his shoulder. He missed these people already. They had shared something special together. He realized there was a tear in his eye, he loved them and wanted to do something special for them. The tasks of removing his vestments and riding back to the Chancery were completed largely in silence.

Once back at the Chancery, he was provided a room to rest for a short time while his next audience was assembling. The Coliseum Mass was an event organized by and for the Church in Los Angeles. The balance of the day would be spent talking with a broader group, Bishops representing most of the west coast of North America. These men were quietly invited by Archbishop Suarez for the purpose of sharing their personal thoughts on the state of the Church. As they all took their seats in the Archbishop's library, Pope John noticed that there were five guests as well as his host. Even with such an august group, Pope John found it necessary to break the ice.

"Brothers," he said as he looked at each of them in turn, "I am so grateful that you each traveled here today. I would love to have visited each of your homes; and the Lord willing, someday I might be able to. Nevertheless, I'm grateful that I don't have to wait for such an eventuality in order to speak with you privately." He then turned to Archbishop Suarez, "And a special thanks to you, dear brother, for helping me to connect with this group."

"Your Holiness, we are humbled by the invitation and grateful to meet you." This voice was from a man known to him only from Monsignor Hellman's briefings. "What is it that you wished to share with us?"

"I was actually hoping that each of you could share something with me…the state of the Church, as you see it."

The group shared for about the first thirty minutes without managing to say much that was challenging or inspiring. They each talked about their struggles to keep the Church relevant to believers, their struggles to encourage vocations, and their concerns about the encroachment of other denominations on their congregations. The Pontiff listened thoughtfully, sometimes interjecting a benign question to confirm his understanding…and that he was listening.

After each of the men had spoken, except for their host, Archbishop Suarez quietly entered the conversation. "Holy Father, please correct me if I misspeak; but, brothers, I don't believe that His Holiness traveled halfway around the world in order to hear us talk about our everyday struggles. After all, he was one of us only one year ago; I believe he understands those issues. If I were in his position, I would want to understand in what ways we have found to inspire participation." He looked to the Pontiff for confirmation before proceeding. "Holy Father, each of us has been focused on the realities of the disengagement of our people. The scandals in the Church, locally and abroad, have discouraged believers. But in some ways, the shortage of vocations requires us to look for an opportunity in all of this to remind the faithful that *they are the Church*. We are teaching the children of God to grow up, take ownership of their own vocations, and lead each other in ways that they used to rely on our brother priests."

Pope John responded quietly with a smile. "I too have been looking to understand the workings of the Holy Spirit in some of these issues."

One of the other visitors added, "Your Holiness, we have been focusing on the development of small faith communities, which return us to our early roots in the Church. Without diminishing the importance of the larger community or sacramental celebrations, we are nourishing the laity to find their vocations to each other."

Another joined in. "We are very excited about the ministries of outreach to the immigrants in our communities. This has been a great outlet to our lay ministers, who are rapidly learning that there is a real blessing in service that we priests have been secretly hoarding."

The Pope asked quizzically, "How so?"

"My lay ministers now understand that when they serve, they receive more than they give. One old friend called me just last week to say, 'How dare you keep this a secret. If I'd listened to your call years ago, I wouldn't have missed all these wonderful experiences.' He no longer looks at the immigrants as needing something from him, but rather as offering him an opportunity to give, to learn, and to grow."

"That's wonderful news. I never thought about our reluctance to encourage lay ministry as 'hoarding,' but I suppose we haven't explained the blessings as well as we should. Thank you for sharing that." Pope John looked around the room. "What is there that I can do to serve you in this work? What can Rome do to support you?"

Another of his brother Bishops joined in. "Holiness, I'm not sure that there is anything Rome can do. In fact, anything that you do may run the risk of sidetracking the effort. This is about empowering our brothers and sisters who have been led to believe that their contributions are less than those of the professed religious. We are trying to reverse that mindset and open their imagination to the possibilities of lay vocations. This movement, if I can call it that, goes back to the roots of our Christian Church. It is very much a believer-driven approach—out of necessity, if not also correctness." At this last statement, the Bishop feared that he might have stepped over a line.

The Pontiff responded thoughtfully, "Brothers, I can't tell you how gratifying it is to hear that the Church is alive and well and that *we* are staying out of the way of the Holy Spirit. I have been concerned for some time, as you clearly have, that the fruits of the Second Vatican Council have been allowed to grow stale. Please continue this work, with my sincerest support and blessings. Promise to write me and share your evolving thoughts on how this can be exported throughout the Church. Know that, even as I endeavor to stay out of your way, I will pray earnestly for your successful cooperation with the Spirit." After a moment he added, "If I can be so bold as to add a word of advice: stay close to the faithful, brothers. You need each other to sustain your respective vocations."

Archbishop Suarez, as the host, stepped in. "Holy Father, on behalf of us all, I want to thank you for your kindness, generosity, and support. We should like to impose upon you further, if you will allow us."

"Of course."

"Will you allow us to join you to celebrate mass together tomorrow morning, before you leave for the airport?"

"You must know that I am leaving at five o'clock for my flight. I was planning to say mass in my hotel room before heading off. I would never think to ask that of you."

"Holiness, we have discussed it with Monsignor Hellman, but of course he didn't wish to speak for you. I have offered to use my private chapel here if you so desire. That will save you some time in packing and unpacking your vestments and vessels; and at that hour of the morning, the detour will be only a few minutes."

"Are you sure? Have you all discussed this?"

"We have, Your Holiness. We can think of nothing more worthy than to send you with our blessings and allow you to feel our unity with the Vicar of Christ."

The meeting ended solemnly, and the men regrouped later in the day for dinner. This event was significantly less serious and centered more on Pope John getting a chance to get to know the stories of each of the Bishops. He was amazed at the diversity of their life experiences. The thing they held in common, which was clearly the intent of

Archbishop Suarez, was their commitment to the pastoral care of their people—hands-on pastoral care.

* * * * *

In the predawn hours, the Pontiff arrived at the Chancery in a simple white cassock and was shown to the chapel near the back of the building. It was beautiful in its simple design. The men vested and shared the celebration of the mass together, even singing a few short hymns *a cappella*. After the closing blessing, they removed their vestments and escorted Pope John and Monsignor Hellman to their car. The driver was snoozing behind the steering wheel when they arrived, but the security detail was watching the surrounding street intently. Pope John looked at each man in turn, reminded each of something he had said that had touched him, then embraced each like a brother who wouldn't return for a long while. As his car pulled away, the clerics stood on the driveway, none of them wanting to move.

Once in the plane, Monsignor Hellman briefed the Pontiff on the remaining stop on their way home. They had been over it numerous times, but he knew that his boss liked to be thoroughly prepared. The stop in Boston was one that His Holiness had requested, inviting himself to visit Cardinal Welty. He wanted to seek the advice of the man who was highly influential in the College and who had been his most serious rival in the balloting. This would be an unofficial visit, not covered by the media except as a private meeting between the Pope and the Dean of the American Catholic Church.

When they were done, Monsignor Hellman left Pope John to enjoy a light breakfast and a short nap. After breakfast, there was a scheduled interview with an Italian reporter who had been with the tour since they had left Italy. The two men had joked that they should wake the reporter and conduct the interview while her defenses were down. Instead, they stuck to the plan and the Pontiff enjoyed his breakfast after takeoff, while watching the rising sun out his window.

The interview he granted was not what he had really expected. Much like the interview on the way to the United States, this was timed to deliver fresh news to the European media immediately upon his arrival back home. He had expected to keep the discussion very businesslike and not get into personal feelings and details. Instead, the journalist began by observing that His Holiness didn't appear to be acting like a caretaker. She further observed that he clearly wasn't greeted as such in America, but rather, "The Americans seemed to really love you. In fact, even the non-

Catholics I interviewed seemed to hold you in very high regard."

All of this seemed to ignite a desire in the Pontiff to elaborate on what a moving trip it had been for him. He shared some of what he had learned from the laity and clerics alike. He shared that, from his first homily, he had felt the Spirit moving in the Church and that there were endless possibilities. Far from feeling like a caretaker, as some had imagined, he felt empowered to lift the Church on his shoulders, if need be, and carry Her where she needed to go.

Chapter Eight

Monsignor Hellman joined Pope John for lunch. They both felt compelled to discuss what they had experienced over the last few days and search for their logical next steps; for they both knew that upon arrival back at the Vatican, they would be besieged by questions. When these sorts of tours went well, Bishops around the world would be inquiring about the list of future papal visits; journalists would be asking for the Holy Father to clarify statements he made; and thousands of individual believers would be moved to write supporting letters, to reinforce ideas that the Pontiff had shared in his appearances. Many of these ideas would come from actual statements of his; others would be the product of rumor and extrapolation.

"Monsignor, I cannot thank you enough for the success of the tour, in particular our meeting with the hotel staff in New York. What did you think of our visits?"

"Holy Father, I am pleased that you are pleased. I too thought that the connection you made with the faithful was most profound. You have rallied people to the cause of the Church and created a great upwelling of support. I am quite confident that those individuals who have had a chance to see you in person will be more articulate about the importance of the papacy in their communities. It touches them to feel so close to you."

"Certainly, Francis, you don't mean to suggest that my mere presence is enough to incite the Church to take up the just causes of the world?"

"Perhaps I was thinking on a more superficial level, Your Holiness. I was speaking more of the faithful's sense of history and connection to the Throne of Saint Peter. For that matter, I was also going to say that I felt a palpable response from your brother Bishops during your visit as well. It was clear to me that they endorse your succession and look forward to your representation of the Church as its public face."

"Again, Francis, it sounds as though you are thinking of me more as a figurehead, and I know that you don't mean to give me that impression." Monsignor Hellman was quiet, as though he was considering the correct answer to this, but Pope John continued. "I was very pleasantly surprised by our reception, all the way around. I didn't suppose it was false modesty, but as we left the Vatican, I expected a polite reception that would be driven more by curiosity and formality than by genuine affection. Francis, I felt genuine affection from the people of America."

"Without a doubt, Holiness. I could see a genuine warmth from the people, especially in the parade through Los Angeles."

Changing directions rather suddenly, and looking directly at Francis as though to gauge his reaction, Pope John said, "I was disconcerted by my conversation with Cardinal Johns, however. His complacency was startling."

Monsignor Hellman didn't really react, which was disconcerting in its own way for the Pope. He had been wondering for some time if his peers were just taking up space, content to play the role and not taking up the important issues within the body of the faithful.

"Francis, do you understand why this concerns me? I'm afraid that my brother Bishops are creating a presence in the world that it just cannot tolerate. The world, including all of our faithful, is in constant search for leadership. I'm not sure that we all appreciate that challenge. If we are perceived as relics from the past, the world will move on without us; it won't waste its time waiting for us."

Francis nodded noncommittally. "As you know, I believe the Church plays a stabilizing role in the world. I believe humanity likes to experiment, whether with social structures, political systems, or, pardon me, even with sexuality; but the faithful look to Holy Mother Church as a thread of constancy throughout history."

"Yes, Francis, but you are more practical than me. Do you think we can play that role if we aren't, by and large, viewed as likable? We certainly cannot, if we are not inspirational. It concerns me that people are ready to think the worst of us, and our apparent indifference to that fact only makes it worse. Most important of all, the lack of inspiration means that we aren't encouraging souls to look to their Creator.

"I shouldn't be so hard on my brother Bishops, however. I was so amazed by the turnout and enthusiasm of our people, in New York as well as in Los Angeles. It's nonsense in many ways to bask in the enthusiasm of the faithful and then to chide their local Bishop for being less than inspiring."

"There is a lot of wisdom in that statement, Holy Father."

"The Madison Square Garden mass was an amazing experience. I know that I have regularly greeted larger numbers of people, but the energy of so many in such an enclosed space was electric. I felt truly blessed to be celebrating with them. And as I have already told you, I am grateful for the event that you organized for me with the workers at the hotel in New York. Those were such special people; I almost can't believe that they were so hastily assembled. Of course, it took a little coaxing on my part to encourage them to open up; but, oh, when they did, it was a wonderful exchange. I learned so much."

"I am glad that it went so well for you." Francis didn't continue, because Pope John seemed to be building up a head of steam.

"And then, the conversation that I was able to have with the Bishops in Los Angeles…" Pope John looked out the window of the aircraft into the heavens beyond. "As disconcerted as I was by my conversation with Cardinal Johns, I was delighted by the Bishops in Los Angeles. These are exceptional men, Francis. They are true servants, thinking only of how they can inspire hearts to God. Just spending a few hours in their embrace was like a mini-retreat for my own vocation."

"That's wonderful to hear, although I must say that it's still surprising to hear the Holy Father discussing needs in his own vocation."

"I know, Francis. It's important for you to remember, if you are to be a counselor to me as well as a secretary, that I struggle along with the rest of the Children of God."

"Yes, I know that I should."

"All of this enthusiasm puts me in mind of my first homily as Supreme Pontiff. It may be time for me to continue to teach on those themes and to worry less about offending the sensibilities of some of my brother Bishops."

"Do you sense that there is concern by some of the Bishops, Holy Father?"

"I know that there is. I did not share with you, Francis, but Cardinal Welty personally penned a note to me in the week after the Conclave to express his disappointment in the implications of my homily. He did it very politely, mind you, but the tone was…parental, almost."

"Well, Holy Father, I'm sure that was not the Cardinal's intent. When he told me of the great honor of serving you, he spoke in the most glowing terms about what you might mean to the Church." Francis knew that he was being a little expansive in his characterization of the conversation.

"Be that as it may, this is some of what I hope to discuss with Cardinal Welty during our visit this week."

"It has been a whole year since that day, and I am sure that the two of you will have a very interesting conversation.

If I am not out of line, I would suggest that it was wise of you not to press the themes of the first homily too quickly in your pontificate. You were able to make the points you wished to make—to plant the seeds, so to speak, for later harvest. Even the most anxious farmer must allow for time, quenching rain, and the rays of daylight to work their magic. After all, the history of the Church is measured in millennia, not individual pontificates."

Not wanting to over-exercise his arguments on the topic, Pope John said simply, "Perhaps you are right, Francis: patience is a virtue."

Francis didn't want to be perceived on the side of the inflexible, so he added, "When we return to Rome, may I help you to draft some correspondence? You could select a constituency of Cardinals whom you trust; open a dialogue regarding your first homily and potential improvements in the Church that could help it to realize its potential. This way we could move the questions forward without arousing fear in the College."

"That is a wonderful suggestion, Francis."

Chapter Nine

The next morning, Pope John woke in his suite at the
Ritz Carlton overlooking the Boston Public Garden and ate
breakfast in relative quiet. Nearly all of the Papal entourage
had continued on in the Al Italia charter back to Rome, as
there was only a single private meeting left to be held. Only
the Pontiff, his secretary, and a small detachment of security
disembarked the plane for this meeting. It was to be with
John Cardinal Welty, Archbishop of Boston and one of the
reigning princes of the American church. The secret of the
Conclave, known to only a handful of the billion Catholics of
the world, was that John Welty had come within a hair's
breadth of being elected Pope instead of Franco Calliendo. At
the outset of the last Conclave, the assumption among most of
the Catholics of the western world was that an American
would be elected and that it would be he who would ascend
the Throne of Saint Peter.

After breakfast, the two men made their way to the seat of the Boston Archdiocese and were escorted to Cardinal Welty's private study. Francis Hellman introduced the men officially in his capacity as Papal Secretary, and awkwardly in his capacity as the embodiment of Welty's offer of loyalty to the newly elected Pontiff. Monsignor Hellman expressed his thanks to them both for their trust in him and excused himself, wishing them an enjoyable conversation.

The two men had not been together since the final days of the Conclave that had created Cardinal Calliendo as Pope John XXIV and his first public mass. During that mass, he had delivered the first notable address of his papacy; what has since been referred to simply as The First Homily. This meeting was ostensibly being held to discuss that first address and some correspondence from the Cardinal that followed over the ensuing weeks. Deeper still, it was an opportunity for both men to discuss some philosophical issues that the Pontiff believed needed addressing but his host wished to be left for future generations.

"Holy Father, it is wonderful of you to make a detour in your plans simply to meet with me. You look very well. How have you enjoyed your visit to the United States?"

"What a wonderful country, full of very generous people. They were so welcoming. Did you know that I have been here once before, when I was young?"

"No, that's wonderful. I am sure that you know by now, we are very grateful that you chose to visit here on your Grand Tour." The choice of words was odd, implying that perhaps this was to be his *one* tour.

"I only wish that I had sufficient time to spend in some of the other great cities, such as Boston; it is clearly a city with a great Catholic heritage. But either way, I couldn't step foot on this continent without making my way here to visit with you and seek your counsel."

With a degree of false modesty, Cardinal Welty replied, "My counsel? What could there possibly be that I could impart to you, Holiness?"

"Please, dear brother, you have worn the red hat much longer than I and understand the ways of the Curia far better. I am most anxious for your thoughts on these early days of my pontificate. You are fairly known as a true prince of the Church."

The Cardinal managed to hide his surprise by the reference to "early days," knowing as he did that the College didn't expect this to be a long pontificate. In fact, the advice he was given as the votes began to turn away from him was that the Church wasn't yet ready for an American Pope but that perhaps a short reign by a benign caretaker could be just the bridge to the next Conclave.

"Holy Father, as I have already expressed to you in my correspondence, I was somewhat taken aback by the tone of your first public sermon. I thought it was a somewhat unusual tone to strike, given that these first addresses are often taken as the direction of an entire pontificate."

"I did intend to do precisely that. I took the letter you wrote me to heart, however, and have been more delicate in my sermons since then. Of course I read your letter with great interest and respect, but I thought it best to discuss when we had an occasion to be together, to be certain that I had taken the meaning correctly."

"Like you, Holy Father, I take the role of the laity in the life of the Church very seriously. I am concerned, however, if the direction of your pontificate is to call the role of the clergy into question and denigrate their vocations." Hurrying along, he continued without waiting for a response. "Now, I don't believe this is what you intended, but it could certainly be taken that way by both clergy and laity alike."

"In some respects, I did mean to send that message." Here, Pope John paused slightly for a response, which he received only in the form of a half-hearted gasp. "Of course, I don't mean to denigrate the vocation of myself or any of our brother priests; but I did want to make clear, to clergy and laity alike, that religious life does not confer special status. Those professed religious who fail to understand the importance of service are missing their calling, and there is a corresponding responsibility for the laity to take ownership for the health of the Lord's Church."

Sensing that he might be driving the Pontiff to renewed excitement about his opinions, the Cardinal chose a different tack. "Many of your brother Bishops are grateful, in my humble opinion, that you chose to downplay these sentiments in your later sermons and writings. We were initially concerned, as I told you in my letter, that this might further discourage vocations and enthusiasm for the priesthood. It would be my privilege to continue this dialogue with you behind the scenes if you should like to explore these issues."

"Your Eminence, I am most grateful that you should wish to do that for me." He said this in all sincerity, but he noted the risk that it could be interpreted as sarcasm. "I should like to engage your counsel on all great matters before the Church. One of the things that you will come to understand about my views, however, is that I believe the clergy can be the Church's worst enemy when it comes to a lack of enthusiasm, both among vowed religious and those discerning a vocation."

"To put this in a more practical context, Holy Father, I would refer you to your earlier statement regarding the amount of time that I have been in leadership roles in the Church. It's important for you to always keep in mind that the College is a self-perpetuating organization. I don't want this to come across as overly crass or cynical, but it is a political institution in the true sense of the word. It is an institution in which men's feelings and emotions naturally play a role. One must consider these things if one is to be successful over time. As you also said, this is early in your pontificate; and you want to make the most of its entire duration. You wouldn't want to find that bureaucratic obstruction was interfering with your goals. This is where I can help you; understanding the pace of change and the correct method to present your ideas, in a way that they will receive the greatest encouragement, rather than confrontation."

"You are right, of course, dear Cardinal. I appreciate your assistance."

"You understand that any change creates a fear-response among most men."

"But should we permit senseless fear to be the determining factor?"

"No, but let's discuss your first homily specifically. Do you still think that it's appropriate to say that the members of the laity are the primary ministers in the Church?"

"I do. History tells us that that was the condition of the Early Church. This was the point where the Church was at its most robust and people were growing in their faith because they owned it personally. Besides, I think that even if this weren't our roots, the lack of vocations necessitates opening our minds to the laity as ministers to each other."

"But doesn't this diminish the role and authority of the clergy?"

"I think it's a challenge to the clergy, yes; but in the way that an engaged student creates challenges for a teacher. Passive, complacent students never challenge their teachers."

"But aren't these also the students that attempt to disarm and overthrow their teachers? They attempt to develop their own following, formally or informally. Don't we risk the students ultimately coming to believe that they are a teaching authority, usurping the Church's magisterium?"

Pope John thought about this for a few moments. "The Church has regularly taken its teaching authority too far. Recall, Cardinal Welty, that at many times over our history, we have maintained a point of faith so dearly that we would cajole, imprison, excommunicate, and even kill those who would dare to disagree with us. Many of those teachings are no longer held as true by the Church herself. By what misguided sense of enlightenment should we continue to be so dogmatically certain? If history has taught us anything, it should be that the more stridently we fight for a position, the more likely we are to decide later that we were incorrect. Today, that sense of self-righteousness and self-protection has led to some of the most heinous scandals, unimaginable to the faithful. I have come to believe that if the clergy served better, focused on the simple messages of our Lord, we would inspire more vocations."

"Why do you keep implying that the clergy are not serving adequately?"

"I speak of myself primarily; which is what I aim to improve in myself from the Throne of Saint Peter." This unnerved the Cardinal because of the potential inference of the Pope's use of his authority to speak *ex cathedra*, that is, "from the Chair." When a Pope speaks in direct reference to that authority, it is deemed to be unchangeable and infallible. Popes have only done this on a handful of occasions in the history of the Church, contrary to popular belief. "I believe that Christ's message was simple, intended to direct our attention to his Father and to service to each other. If I can serve more simply, I can encourage others to do the same."

"So then, why would you begin your pontificate by pointing everyone's attention to our unfortunate scandals? Doesn't that defeat the purpose of your ministry and bring disrepute on the Church?"

"My discussion of the scandal isn't what brings the disrepute; the behavior of our brother priests and Bishops already did that. My role is to be forthright about our behavior and let the world know that we are willing and able to admit our own faults. When we try to avoid doing this, the truth isn't lost on the world; the world only sits in wonder at our arrogance and begins to question our authenticity. These are the moments when I believe the laity has every right to be discouraged and view our teachings as suspect."

The conversation continued down this Socratic path for some time, meandering into and out of various subjects.

Pope John finally said, "I am grateful, Your Eminence, for your willingness to engage me in this way. I desire your continued counsel and prayers. However, as you know, I haven't really spoken publicly of these thoughts since my initial address and your kind letter of clarity that followed."

Cardinal Welty was caught off guard, wondering if all of this was merely an academic exercise. "Holy Father, I must again commend you for the very touching sentiment and informality of your homily as well. With all respect to your beloved predecessors, I am so grateful to be able serve at times such as this and with you as our Supreme Pontiff."

"Cardinal Welty, you will be such a wonderful counselor with which to share these ideas and from which to learn. I was pleased to be able to plant some seeds during my first official address, but I am not so arrogant as to think that I will be the only farmer in this field, or that I will have to be the one to reap the harvest. That is only for the Lord and His Church. I am reminded by my secretary, for whom I owe you great thanks if I remember correctly, that the Church marks time in millennia, not in pontificates."

The two men enjoyed the balance of their time together, discussing the more banal aspects of the Papal Tour. At the conclusion of their scheduled time, Monsignor Hellman and Cardinal Welty's personal secretary arrived and knocked on the heavy door. After a brief pause, they entered and found the two clerics sitting with smiles on their faces as they turned to the door.

Monsignor Hellman spoke first. "Your Holiness, I believe that it is time for us to return to the hotel and catch up on some correspondence."

"Of course you are right, Monsignor. Please allow the Cardinal and me a few additional minutes and we will meet you shortly."

As the door closed quietly, Pope John turned to Cardinal Welty. "Your Eminence, I just wanted to thank you again in private, brother to brother, for your continuing counsel. I haven't said yet that I know how difficult it must have been to send the letter that you did after the Conclave and my first public mass. It is only in such boldness, however, that I will receive the esteemed wisdom of my brother Bishops. I look forward to more conversation with you over the coming years."

"Holy Father, you do me much more honor than I deserve. I am grateful for the way in which you received my letter and your willingness to entertain conversation with me on these topics. I hope that, at the least, you understand my love for Holy Mother Church."

The two shook hands briefly and the Cardinal bowed to kiss the Pontiff's ring. He then led him to the foyer of the building, where they met their lieutenants and said their final goodbyes.

Chapter Ten

After the brief drive through crisp, sunny Boston, Monsignor Hellman escorted Pope John to his hotel suite. He left momentarily to collect the papers that they needed to deal with during this layover. While in his room, Francis noticed that his room phone was signaling a message; he punched the button to retrieve it. The voice on the other end was that of Cardinal Welty's personal secretary, whom he had just met that morning. In a tone that was more instruction than invitation, the young priest let him know that he was being invited to a private dinner at the Union Club in downtown Boston. He should announce himself at the reception desk just inside the front door, where he would be escorted to a private dining room.

Monsignor Hellman took the message down on the hotel pad on the nightstand, equal parts intrigued and annoyed. He had been instructed that the invitation was for him alone and that "His Holiness need not know." This posed an interesting issue for Francis, who had planned to work the afternoon away with Pope John, have a quiet dinner in his room, and get his first good night sleep of the tour. This, however, would likely be a dinner worth attending.

When he returned to the Pope's suite down the hall, he unloaded the satchel of correspondence that had arrived ahead of them. There were letters from a variety of Papal Nuncio, or ambassadors, from around the world; administrative orders that required his signature; and a piece of follow-up correspondence from the president of the United States, detailing the next steps from their prior meeting. The cache had been carefully filtered because of the limited time available for office work during the tour; and nearly every item required him to dictate precise instructions, if not whole letters, in response.

They worked through a light lunch and for several hours afterward. Partially as flattery and partially because he needed to get to his secret dinner, Francis sought to bring the session to a close. "Holy Father, I am not sure that I can keep this up with you for much longer. Would it be possible to call it a day and complete this work during our flight home tomorrow? Given that we will be alone on the charter, we should have no interruptions as on our typical flights."

"Of course, Francis. I would be foolish to think that I can carry this on through the evening. And you are correct, some work will make the trip move much quicker…not that you aren't a splendid conversationalist. Would you care to join me for dinner before you retire for the evening?"

Francis laughed. "Thank you for the reprieve and the compliment. With your permission, I would like to defer the invitation. I am anxious to enjoy a restful evening and hopefully be back to full alertness for our time together tomorrow. I believe the pace is catching up with me."

He collected the work that had been completed, added it to the remaining materials, and bid Pope John a good night. As he walked away, knowing he was leaving the Pontiff alone in a strange hotel suite with only a contingent of Secret Service outside, he had a pang of guilt. Again, this was muted by the building curiosity over the invitation to dinner with the Cardinal. It had been roughly a year since they'd been alone: the day the Cardinal let him know of his appointment as the Papal Secretary. Since that time, he'd been through the awkward episode of receiving the letter from Cardinal Welty for the new Pontiff, scolding him on the occasion of his first mass. That had immediately created some tension between Francis and his new boss, tension that took some months to completely subside. He was anxious to have the first opportunity to discuss this with the Cardinal.

Francis took a cab, as instructed, to the far side of the Boston Common and arrived at the Union Club a few minutes early. It was clear that he was expected, but he was inexplicably held in the reception room for what felt like ten or fifteen minutes.

He was led to the end of a long hallway, past a well-staffed butler's station. When he was finally shown into the private dining room, Francis could tell that there had been a meeting going on while he had been waiting in the lobby. Cardinal Welty stood at the head of the table and walked over to greet his guest. Francis realized that he must have evidenced some surprise on his face, because the Cardinal immediately led him around the dining table and introduced him to the other diners. First, sitting to Cardinal Welty's right, was Luigi Cardinal Compeccio, whom Francis knew from internal Vatican correspondence as a player in the bureaucracy of the Curia; although in his shock at the moment, he couldn't remember exactly what his role was. Next to Compeccio sat Cardinal Johns of New York, whom Francis had always assumed was antagonistic to his mentor. As they had recently been together, their greeting was quite informal. Sitting across from these two men was Michael

Cardinal Somers, Archbishop of Westminster in England. Next to Cardinal Somers was an empty chair, presumably for Francis; although he took it rather reluctantly.

As he sat down, he noticed Cardinal Compeccio hastily sliding some papers into a leather portfolio. Before they disappeared, he noticed a header on the papers in red that appeared to be a kind of logo. The words were *Custodes Tempus*, which he knew to be Latin for "The Time Keepers." He'd never heard of such an organization. Was it a Committee of the Curia that had escaped his notice? That didn't ring a bell as the department that he associated with Compeccio.

Francis was conscious of who was hosting this dinner, or running this meeting, or whatever this was. He waited for Cardinal Welty to speak.

"Monsignor Hellman, Francis, welcome to our conversation. I'm sorry if my message didn't indicate that others would be here. I flattered myself in thinking that you'd be more likely to attend a private get-together with me than a stuffy Church meeting."

"Your Eminences, I apologize if my surprise in any way comes across as disappointment. I am honored and delighted that you would invite me to dine with you." Turning specifically to Cardinal Welty, he added, "Cardinal, I do always enjoy our conversations; but I also am in your service and trust that you would have only asked me here with the best purposes in mind."

Cardinal Welty pushed a button on a console in front of him and a waiter appeared seconds later. "Gentlemen, in front of you are menus. We can order now and begin our conversation while we wait for our food. Gerald will also ask the kitchen to prepare anything special, within reason, which you might desire." It was clear that this was his club and knew the staff well. He let each cleric order in turn, and when Gerald came back to the host, Cardinal Welty ordered an elaborate four-course meal, along with two bottles of very respectable wine.

"Francis," the Cardinal asked as Gerald left the room, "would you be so kind as to give us your thoughts on the Papal Tour?"

"Certainly, Your Eminences. His Holiness has shared with me that he has been very pleased at his ability to connect with 'real people.' He is pleasantly surprised by the keen outpouring of affection. I believe he genuinely misunderstood the drawing power of the office and believed that since people didn't know him before his election, they might somehow be apathetic toward him."

"What about his private meetings?" Cardinal Welty continued, testing how far his young protégé would go with this insider's report.

"Well, Your Eminence, he thoroughly enjoyed his visit to His Eminence Cardinal Johns." Here the young Monsignor thought it better not to share too specifically. "He greatly appreciated the hospitality of the Cardinal, and the whole City of New York for that matter. Before the Papal Mass, I arranged for him to meet with a group of workers at The Plaza Hotel. Apparently, His Holiness was really able to get them to open up after a while and share their heartfelt thoughts on the Church. I took from his comments afterward that they were very respectful but reinforced some of his preexisting beliefs."

"How about his trip to Los Angeles? Did he find that as edifying?"

"He met with a number of Bishops from around the western half of both North and South America. They were invited at the request of Archbishop Suarez to meet His Holiness and have a town hall meeting of sorts, although it was obviously something much more than it sounds. Again, my understanding is a bit sketchy, but it appears that he found some kindred souls among that group. I can only assume that the Archbishop chose them based upon what he believed to be Pope John's feelings on the evolution of the Church."

"Very good, Monsignor. I am grateful for your assistance; you see, we hope to continue to provide counsel to His Holiness on these matters, so it's helpful to understand where his influences are coming from." He looked around, assessing the group. "My brother Bishops, allow me to share my own conversation with His Holiness. As you would expect, we spent the majority of our meeting discussing the First Homily on the role of the laity and the deficiencies in the clergy."

Cardinal Johns interrupted, "He didn't say that, did he?" dispensing with the usual formalities of title.

Cardinal Welty continued without missing a step. "The message of that address was clear, and His Holiness wished to discuss my letter of reproach. I shared my concern that I believed his statements about the clergy could be demoralizing to our brother priests and counter to our efforts on vocations; and I shared my concerns about encouraging the laity to overextend itself in teaching ministries."

Cardinal Somers chimed in, "Did His Holiness seem to understand the gravity of where this could lead? The good Lord knows that I live on the vanguard of this debate. The missteps of the Reformation are finally coming home to roost in the Church of England. Why would we allow the same mistakes, when we are starting to win back some of these souls to the magisterium of Holy Mother Church?"

"Indeed," Cardinal Welty continued, "but it is not clear to me as yet that our Holy Father fully understands the situation. By the end of our discussion, he seemed to indicate that he understood at least that he should be taking more measured steps in his public comments, and perhaps that he should be even more willing to confer with the College before such addresses."

"Well, that's good," Cardinal Johns added superfluously.

"Monsignor, it pleases me to share one additional detail from my conversation with His Holiness, which I wish the rest of the group to hear as well. He credits you with some wise counsel toward moderation in his public addresses. I knew that my recommendation of you to your current position was a good one, and you have done me proud, so thank you."

Monsignor Hellman was clearly moved by the pride that he felt. "I apologize that I didn't ask very specific questions regarding the tour. I'm sure that it goes without saying that if I had thought that you would like to know, or that we would be having this meal together, I would have certainly dug deeper. I am glad you are pleased with what I have accomplished."

The Cardinals all nodded and smiled slightly at Cardinal Welty. He had done well in placing Monsignor Hellman in the Papal Household. At this, Cardinal Welty pushed the button on the console in front of him, signaling to Gerald that he could serve their meals. It was clear to Monsignor Hellman that Cardinal Welty was the leader of this group, whoever they were, and that he was proud of Francis and his potential.

With wait staff coming and going over the next twenty minutes, during which soup and salads were served and cleared, the conversation turned to administrative matters and gossip about which Bishops were likely to retire and when. As the entrée was served, Cardinal Welty dismissed Gerald and made the grand gesture of standing and serving wine to his guests personally, beginning with Monsignor Hellman.

"Monsignor, it occurs to me that when you joined us this evening, you may have felt yourself a bit out of place; and now you may feel yourself to be in a somewhat inferior position to be taking an active part in this conversation. Our hope is that when you leave tonight, you will feel yourself as a true part of this group."

Monsignor Hellman looked at each cleric at the table and, looking at his mentor, confirmed, "You know me very well, Your Eminence. I am humbled to be here with you all tonight, and I would be honored to be counted among your acquaintances."

"More than acquaintances, Francis, we are joint collaborators on the future of the Church. Let me ask you, why do you think His Holiness was open to your encouragement to moderate his rhetoric?"

"I have offered him an alternative outlet for his ideas. I persuaded him to begin a correspondence with a select group of Cardinals for advice on the practicality and the pace of changes within the Church. My goals were to provide that outlet, encourage him to include you and others in that dialogue, and to begin to look at this as a Century Plan of sorts, rather than feeling constrained by the limits of his own pontificate."

The Cardinals looked at each other, smiling and nodding, almost as if Francis were not in the room. They seemed to share the same, unspoken thought. Francis thought it wise to quit while he was ahead.

Cardinal Compeccio decided not to be sidelined in this conversation. "Cardinals, we are clearly blessed to have such a competent man in place in the Papal Household. I can assure you that I will keep very close tabs on the sentiment of the Curia and all other major players in the Vatican. There is really little chance that His Holiness will attempt to manifest any great changes without consulting the power base within the Vatican."

"Thank you, Cardinal Compeccio. I know that we are all well assured." In saying this, Cardinal Welty came across to the Americans as slightly sarcastic in a way that slipped by his intended victim. "My chief concern, as you know, however, is that our Holy Father would feel empowered to do something rash and not to consult with the Curia or the College." Turning to Francis, "We are all most grateful for the wisdom and patience that you have shown, Monsignor."

All conversation stopped for a few minutes as Cardinal Welty used his console again to move the evening's program along. Their dishes were cleared, and a cart was brought in containing a colorful and fragrant buffet of desserts. Each of the men took their time making their way over to the cart and assembling their own private collection of confections. When they had all made their way back to their places and Gerald had been given an opportunity to serve coffee, tea, and espresso to the various constituencies, it was time for the conversation to reengage.

Cardinal Somers was next up around the table, and it occurred to Monsignor Hellman that this group had probably met several times before and knew that this was the appointed time for a roundtable. His Eminence picked up where he had left off earlier. "Monsignor, it is wonderful to have you here with us and to know that we can count on you to continue your thoughtful counsel to His Holiness. I mean no disrespect in this, but because of his relative sheltered history of ministry, I am not sure that he understands the stakes in this regard. Luther's Reformation, which of course quickly spread to my own country, should not have been allowed to fester in the first place. We know precisely what comes of the laity getting it into their heads that they can challenge the Church's teaching authority at will. I trust that we won't find our own Pontiff leading the next Reformation."

It occurred to Francis that Cardinal Somers was playing very fast and loose with history. Martin Luther was a monk and not a lay revolutionary; the Church in his time did almost everything it could think of to quash the Reformation—from burning books to people; and since those days, the Roman Church had adopted many of the reforms suggested by Luther. All he could think to say was, "Thank you for your confidence, Your Eminence."

Cardinal Johns alone was nearly silent—and nearly asleep, it appeared. He seemed almost disinterested. All he said at his appointed turn was, "Thank you for taking the time to join us this evening, Monsignor." Cardinal Welty was apparently going to do nothing to draw him back into the conversation.

Now it was his mentor's turn to lead the conversation, and he addressed no one in particular, which by default granted Francis an equal footing. "My brothers, I feel that this has been a very productive evening, and I am grateful to each of you for accepting my invitation to join me here. While I am pleased to see the reception of His Holiness here in America, I fear that it might encourage him to some erratic behavior, and I think that among ourselves we need to begin to speak candidly."

Before he continued, he looked as his brother Bishops and eyed Francis cautiously out of the corner of his eye. "We must remember that his election was followed by some unexpected expressions of opinion. I worry that his, how did you describe it Monsignor, 'pleasant surprise' of a reception in America, might encourage a renewed freedom of expression. I am not wholly convinced that His Holiness has fully embraced the importance of the College's role as counselor. After all, he had precious little time in the red hat himself before being elected Pontiff. He may, in fact, confuse his role as one of absolute power and authority, rather than as a king among princes who must be brought into conversation. I think Monsignor Hellman has done us a great service in helping to shape His Holiness's thinking on our role.

"We mustn't, and I believe we won't, allow for the radical reversal of roles that our Pontiff has espoused. Holy Mother Church has evolved and works the way that it does for a reason. We must guard the majesty of the Church, the strength of Her teaching authority, and the respect of the clergy. We Bishops will continue to respond to challenges from the laity to our authority, even in matters of so-called transparency, with a firm hand on the wheel and protecting the Church.

Turning to Francis, he concluded, "Monsignor, can we count on you to help us guide His Holiness toward a more moderate course?" The question came across almost as the introduction to a vow; and Francis quickly learned why.

"Of course you can, Your Eminence."

"Very well." Cardinal Welty scanned the table one last time, looking for any sign of objection and then continued. "We, the leaders at this table, are part of an unrecorded society of the Church. You won't find the name of our society in any official papers; although it will surprise you to learn that there is an entire section of the Vatican Archives dedicated to our papers and a record of our work on behalf of the Church. When one of our members ascends to the Throne of Saint Peter, they reconfirm the Papal sanction on our mission; and only that Pontiff, or the reigning leader of our group, knows how to access that particular archive." He paused again, this time to see if Francis raised any concerns or expressed any apprehension.

"Monsignor, I tell you this only to assure you that our group has no sinister motives or purpose, only the perpetual success of Holy Mother Church, even through periods of internal dissent and turmoil. Our work began during the time of the trial of Galileo, when the Church appeared to be divided into two camps—those who wanted to rush headlong into the future without understanding its implications, and those who simply wanted to stick their heads in the sand and deny everything. In actuality, there was a third camp, which understood that denying reality would serve the Church poorly; but they wished to maintain Her sacred role in measuring out the changes of time. Our founder was His Holiness, Pope Urban VIII; and while he was a longtime friend of Galileo who understood the importance of his discoveries, he objected to Galileo's attempts to embarrass the Church. He did what needed to be done and ultimately supported the sentence of heresy. His Holiness understood the importance of the Church managing the pace of change and was mindful of the need to ensure this through the ages.

"Our society is known as Custodes Tempus, and our members are recruited in each generation by the preceding generation through a very careful and methodical process. Occasionally going forward, you will receive correspondence related to Custodes Tempus that will bear our name, the first will be from me and will include a roster of the entire membership. You are charged with memorizing it and then destroying it, because none of our documents are ever out in the public domain. We have only two kinds of correspondence: documents which are about to be destroyed and documents which our leadership has placed in our secret archive. Do you understand?"

"I do."

"Do you wish to be commissioned as a member of Custodes Tempus?

"May I ask a few questions?"

Trying not to show his surprise, Cardinal Welty agreed, "Of course you may."

"You implied that sometimes our Supreme Pontiff is not a member of the society. In those cases, how do you discern the correct path for the Church, when it might be in contravention of the will of the Pontiff?"

"That's a very astute question, Monsignor. I neglected to mention that the society is always composed of a majority of the College, usually a very large majority, which as you can imagine is a self-perpetuating reality. What may surprise the average Catholic is that Popes are often chosen as compromises between extremes—caretakers, if you will. That is the case with our current, though beloved, Pope John. He was viewed by most of the College as someone who would quietly lead the church as a grandfatherly figure. While my name was added to the ballot, a majority in the College was unwilling to elect another Pontiff who was likely to serve twenty or more years, especially one that would also be the first American. I actually agreed with them, because as you now know, I prize stability and evolutionary change in the Church above all else. In conference with my fellow society members, we decided to push for Cardinal Calliendo, and the decision was made to attempt to place you in his household."

Francis only nodded, uncertain of how to respond to such a revelation.

"Remember please, Monsignor, that we have never asked anything of you other than your service to the Holy Father. All of your counsel to him has been honest and natural for you, which is why we wished you to take that role. Remember also that I asked you to serve in that same capacity for me. There was no ulterior motive; we believed that we knew of your earnest love of the Church."

"I understand." Francis was willing himself back to the group.

In order to seal the bargain, Cardinal Welty continued, "There *was* one other reason, my dear Monsignor. It was quite clear to all of us that you would likely be created Bishop by the next Pontiff, whoever that should be. Our society is actually quite small, and over the course of history, we have had few members who weren't ultimately created Cardinal. Your admission is testament to our belief in your potential."

Francis nodded again, trying to conceal his smile.

"Then I shall ask you one final time, do you wish to be commissioned as a member of Custodes Tempus?"

"Yes," was the strong reply.

With that single word, the four other clerics rose from the table. Cardinal Welty escorted Francis to the window at the far end of the room, where he was circled by his elders. They placed their hands on his head and his shoulders and prayed over him, a mix of thanksgiving and commission for service.

As Francis left the dinner, his mind was racing. The thought of returning to the hotel and joining his normal routine in the morning was almost unbelievable. His mind was so preoccupied that he didn't notice the café across the street, lit from within and creating a dramatic contrast to the dimly lit side street. Had he glanced in the café, he would have noticed Giuseppe Guidice, sitting over a cup of coffee and surrounded by the remains of his own dinner. His self-appointed mission had been to understand what was going on *around* the official Papal Tour. The fact that he saw Monsignor Hellman leaving by a side entrance of the hotel was curious enough to draw his attention this afternoon, and his instincts had been repaid. Over the next few minutes, the payoff was even more dramatic, as he watched Cardinals Johns, Welty, and Compeccio leave the same posh club. In their company was a fourth man in a red sash who fit nicely into the screen of Giuseppe's smart phone as he snapped his picture.

All that was left was to try to figure out how to raise the topic with his friend, his boss, and his Supreme Pontiff.

Part III—Search for Impediments

Chapter Eleven

Back on his feet after his medical scare, Pope John reflected that his Papal Tour to America seemed so long ago, and the path he had followed over the past two years was difficult to discern at times. He looked forward, with a renewed strength of vision, to bringing about the best parts of the plan that he had been so afraid to execute before his supposed stroke.

The plan was set to begin in earnest with a meeting with a most influential person, Luigi Cardinal Compeccio, Prefect of the Congregation of Bishops. Cardinal Compeccio, the leader of the selection process for new Bishops, had been one of the few members of the Curia who embraced him early in his pontificate and provided both counsel and encouragement along the way. Today, Pope John would share the news of how he intended to move forward with his plans.

The Pontiff held a note from Cardinal Compeccio as he pulled the velvet rope on his desk:

Holy Father,

In enquiring after your health, Monsignor Hellman informs me that you have begun to return to your regular routine in the Apartments. I certainly don't want to be an imposition in any way, but it would do my heart glad to lay eyes on you in your renewed health as soon as it suits you.

Until then, I remain your most humble servant,
L. Compeccio +

Less than fifteen minutes later, Cardinal Compeccio made his way toward the Papal Apartments, hot on the heels of the young seminarian who had brought him the good news of his invitation. Normally, he engaged these messengers in conversation along the way and walked slowly, maximizing the opportunity for others around the Vatican to see that he was invited to visit the Holy Father. In this case, however, he was more anxious to arrive at his destination. Monsignor Hellman had made only vague references to change, and the Cardinal wished to dig for some details. He understood Hellman's reticence; they had learned over the last few years not to discuss too many specifics together for fear that Pope John would come to believe that they were discussing things behind his back.

As he approached the Pope's study, the seminarian went his own way and the Cardinal noticed Abrielle just a few steps down a side hallway. He turned to greet her, saying, "Good day, Signorina. How are you this fine day? Isn't it wonderful to have His Holiness up and around?"

"Yes, Your Eminence." She said this without emotion and without so much as turning in his direction.

"Signorina, are you well?"

"Well enough, I suppose."

Had she been looking toward the Cardinal, she would have noticed the perturbed look on his face. He took a step closer to her, saying, "Shouldn't you be a little more courteous to a visitor to the Papal Household? And I'm not just any visitor, I am a friend and guest of His Holiness, not to mention a prince of Holy Mother Church."

"Your Eminence," she said as she turned toward him, "I mean no disrespect to Holy Mother Church, nor to my Holy Father, but—"

"Well then, that's better. It's nice to hear you acknowledge my status."

"—please don't confuse my respect for the Church with personal respect for you. Don't mistakenly believe that I will ever treat you with the respect that is owing to your office. I have had too much experience to make that particular mistake."

As her voice was starting to rise, Cardinal Compeccio was concerned that someone might hear her and inquire. God forbid that person might be the Pope. He thought better about pressing the point and turned away, saying to no one in particular, "Thank you, Signorina, I wish you a good day as well."

The Cardinal was shown into the Papal Study by the seminarian on duty in the outer office. The room was brightly lit with the morning sun, and Pope John had the windows open so that he could listen to the crowds bustling in Saint Peter's Square below. There was also a wonderful coffee service set out, along with some miniature pastries.

"Your Eminence, how wonderful to see you today. I am so glad that you were available to get together on such short notice."

"Holy Father, I hope that my note was not too overt of a self-invitation." He crossed the room to where the Pontiff was sitting and bent to kiss his ring. "I was so delighted to hear that you were doing well that I couldn't wait to see you in person."

"No, no, I have been so encouraged by the prayers and support from my close friends and confidants. I feel a bit ashamed that I didn't use more of my recuperation time to spend with all my friends."

"Well, Holiness, as much as we wished to see you, we knew that you were under strict orders to rest and recover fully from your stroke. We are just glad that it was God's will that you recover so quickly and completely."

"I am sure that it is in no small part due to the petitions from you and all those who wish me so well. Please, pour yourself some coffee if you wish and help yourself to a treat. Abrielle is going to great lengths these days to keep my spirits buoyed by sweets."

The Cardinal settled into a chair opposite Pope John, and when he looked comfortable, the Pope continued, "You know, brother, that my recovery was so wonderful that it has confounded the physicians a bit. While I would not wish to downplay the workings of Our Lord in my life, I suspect it wasn't a stroke after all. I think that it was something much less dramatic, which was only confused with a stroke because of my advancing years. You never hear anyone cry 'stroke' when a child gets dizzy and falls down; people just assume they have overexerted themselves."

"That is an interesting perspective, and I suppose that it's true. I had assumed that the physicians used that term only because they saw other evidence, not just jumping to wild conclusions."

"I don't believe the conclusions were wild, but the symptoms of a stroke can be confused with so many other things. Unfortunately, their speculation became public before the brain scans were reviewed and my recovery proved so quick. They believe now that it may have been something as simple as food poisoning. Their problem is that food poisoning is usually more evident in stomach issues than in issues of the head, as I had."

"Well, certainly they can close the book now that you are doing so well and we can put the whole episode behind us. It's been two years since your grand tour of America and now over a year since your last trip abroad; perhaps we should make a big show of the blessings of your health and the stability within Holy Mother Church and announce a future trip."

"Actually, brother, it's timely that you bring up such a topic. I have wanted to confer with you about some decisions that I made during my recovery. I believe that the Holy Spirit used the forced downtime of my recovery to sow the seed of inspiration in me, to move forward with renewal of the Church. Given your tremendous experience, as well as your esteem within the College, I will need to rely on your counsel as I ponder some of the practical matters."

Cardinal Compeccio was aware that he needed to cultivate this reliance, but he equally hoped to stop these plans in their tracks, if at all possible. "Well, of course you know that you can always count on my support, Holy Father. May I enquire, however, about your certainty? I don't believe you wish to say that Our Lord struck you down so that you would listen to him better when you were stuck in bed."

"Oh my heavens no, dear brother. I only mean to say that I took advantage of the time in recuperation to discern the true motives behind my ideas. As you know, I've long struggled to be sure that I was free of selfish motivations. In calling upon the Holy Spirit, I was able to receive clarity and conviction that these are truly healthy ideas for the Church."

"And you speak of practical matters, Your Holiness. Perhaps I need to be clearer about your plans before I could help you with the practical matters. After your very successful trip to America, you were kind enough to invite me into a circle of correspondence with some of the western Bishops. We've discussed a variety of things within that group over the last couple of years; would you care to share your newfound thinking?"

"It may be most helpful to start from the practical conclusion and review the thinking behind them as necessary. I'm sure that we will be having many discussions on these topics over the coming years."

"Your Holiness, it is reassuring to hear that we are not rushing into anything. What is it that I can help you with first? In your first letter to our little group, you suggested rather dramatically that we should purge the ranks of the Church's leadership to set Her on a new trajectory."

"Yes, Your Eminence, I began with that possibility, although I fear that I didn't explain my reasoning too well. Now I believe that this is one of the things that we must proceed with immediately. At the time, it was only the pragmatic conclusion at the end of the chain of beliefs I was exploring. Today, I have a clearer grasp of the importance and necessity of these beliefs, specifically as a result of my recent discernment process."

Seeing this notion of certainty reenter his vocabulary, Cardinal Compeccio was disturbed. He was struggling with dueling perceptions: was the Holy Father springing into action, or was he taking a thoughtful approach? "Holy Father, I was heartened by your next letter to us, in which you seemed content to allow the Bishops to continue to experiment on their own. I agreed with you that it is important to allow sufficient time for the Bishops to continue their discernment process as well—to not leave them behind in this process."

"This is a very reasonable view, brother. Leading up to that letter, I had procrastinated so significantly in the appointment of a Synod that I felt I owed it to all of you to explain my self-doubt. I had also spoken to Cardinal Suarez about the changes in his diocese and his request for reinforcements; it was my hope to further encourage him by publicly acknowledging the experiments that he was attempting. Unfortunately, my insecurities were still present at that point."

"Your final letter to us included a suggestion that we could widen the circle of conversation, which I was also grateful for. Your patience in these important matters serves the Church well. Do you now wish to accelerate the process of change, without the opportunity for a broader consensus to form?" The Cardinal was most interested in the opportunity to reinsert doubt into the mix. With the Pontiff in relative solitude and reflection during his recuperation, he seemed to gain greater conviction about his dramatic plans. These were changes that no Pope should spring on his brother Bishops.

"While I haven't told you the breadth of what I'm proposing exactly, you have sensed correctly where my heart is. My intent is to move with all due speed to set these plans in motion. My request of you is to assist me with the practicalities of what I propose; I would like to leave the Holy Spirit in charge of the inspiration, however."

"As you wish, Holy Father. It would seem that no matter how well-fashioned the plan already is in your mind, your first step would be to call a Synod of Bishops for discussion. This will not only assure those in our inner circle of your desire to remain true to the plan you discussed with us, but also allow you to widen the circle to include others who will help to drive the changes."

"I don't disagree, dear Cardinal, but in fairness, I should be clear with you about a few things. First, invitations to the Synod will be limited to those who are likely to cooperate in its mission. I am not looking for a consensus or a traditional quorum of the influential. Second, I'm not looking to put a generalized question to the Synod; I will present them with my intent and ask them to help us shape the plan of action."

Cardinal Compeccio rose from his chair, clearly disturbed. It was very unusual for him to visibly disengage in the middle of a conversation like this, and it was evident that his thinking was being pushed faster than he could handle. The Cardinal took a few moments to collect his thoughts. He completed a lap of the study and was standing behind his chair, seemingly unable to express what he was thinking or even to retake his seat.

The Pontiff continued, trying to soften the impact and looking genuinely for guidance, "Dear Cardinal Compeccio, I'm sorry if I've distressed you. There must be something in what I've said that causes you to struggle more than I expected and to think beyond the practicalities. Please let me know what you're thinking. This is precisely why your counsel is so important to me at this juncture."

Hoping to recover both his composure and the confidence of the Pope, the Cardinal answered, "Holy Father, I hope that I've not given you the impression that I disapprove of anything you are suggesting. That would be far beyond my role or competencies. Perhaps I just need to understand better what will be put before the Synod for Consultation in order to provide you with useful counsel." In one phrase, the Cardinal had named the process and at the same time attempted to broaden the role of the Synod. "I do believe that we should ensure that some of the more influential Bishops are in attendance. Structural changes will require a great deal of support from the Curia in order to go smoothly. Can you share a general outline of the plans with me?" Cardinal Compeccio sat back in his chair and poured himself a cup of tea, a gesture tantamount to waving his hand across the floor and challenging the Pontiff to lay out his case.

The entire conversation was starting to feel a great deal like the exchange he had had with Antonio just the day before. Pope John seemed to be continually reminded that Popes are not monarchs with unlimited power; and try as he might, there was a chance to be tangled up in the vast bureaucracy of the Church. For the first time, he asked himself, "I wonder if other Pontiffs have started down this path, only to be hamstrung by the Church itself. Perhaps the Holy Spirit has tried to impose change before, and failed."

"I thank you for your candor. I recognize that I should have discussed this with you all in more detail along the way; however, it was only during my recuperation that I found the clarity of mind to see the whole picture. In short, I'll propose a three-point plan for the Bishops to implement." He was now allowing a bit of semantics to work its way into the conversation. "The first point of the plan is fundamental; the other two are imperatives that follow from it. I believe that we must refocus everything on supporting the laity in their work as the Church. We have slowly, but not so subtly, elevated the clergy to the point where the laity has forgotten that it is the Church, not the institutional hierarchy. Out of both spiritual and practical necessity, we need to augment the clergy with the vocations that have been suppressed for centuries in the laity. This will be a cultural shift, I know. It will involve expanding and elevating the ministries available to the laity, putting the administrative roles of the clergy in their proper perspective, and in doing these two things, eliminating these silly power struggles between some clergy and the laity."

"Holy Father, this sounds a great deal like your famous first homily. I believe the fallout from that should speak for itself. As you say, these are cultural changes; and even if they are the correct course to follow, it will take a generation or two to realize them."

"I understand that. The fallout, as you call it, is what planted the seeds of doubt in my mind. I now see the concern that was expressed as self-interest and not in the best interest of the Church as a whole. They are a product of the insularity and clergy-centric history of the Church, rather than recognition of some legitimate incapacity of the laity."

"You said, Holiness, that this goal leads naturally to some imperatives?"

"Indeed, the first we've already discussed: the need to restructure the leadership of the Church. I believe that this self-elevation of the role of the clergy has created a side-effect that administrative roles and hierarchy are admired. I believe that service must be the driving principal of a missionary church, and in order to drive that notion into the culture, we must start at the top with those who must lead by serving. My notion isn't just to bring in fresh faces, but to put the Bishops in closer ministry with the laity. Step one will be to clean our house of those who are incapable or unwilling to serve closely alongside God's People. Then we will encourage them to live and work in parish ministry, just as our apostolic predecessors did. This will require locating and placing a large number of new Bishops into smaller territories. Cardinal Compeccio, this is where your role as Prefect of the Congregation of Bishops is so critical to making this plan work."

"Again, Holy Father, I will serve you in whatever capacity you wish. However, you asked me to discuss all this with you because of my experience. My experience tells me that this is a massive undertaking, fraught with risks and potential complications. I'm concerned that it might end up turning out like the First Italian War of Independence."

Pope John heard this as a veiled reference to Charles Albert and the folly of the Sardinian. Charles was routed in the First War and then unilaterally renounced a successful armistice with Austria. That move ultimately led to a resounding defeat at the hands of an incited Austrian Army, one so bad that Charles was forced to abdicate in favor of his son. To all Sardinians, this was the metaphor for hasty and ill-planned action. Pope John was the one to rise this time from his chair. He took a couple of audible deep breaths, letting his companion know that he understood the insult and was deciding his fate. As the Pontiff circled the study, it was clear that he was also deciding whether this conversation would continue and if there was a continuing role for Cardinal Compeccio in their little circle. To make that point, he walked behind his desk and shuffled some papers around, implying that there may be a better use of his time than continuing this conversation. In the end, he decided that he needed an insider at this stage of the process, if for no other reason than to understand what the certain wave of opposition was going to produce. He decided to engage with flattery; as he sat down, he looked the younger Cardinal in his face as if to say, "we're in this together."

"Absolutely correct, my dear brother. I will need your counsel. Everyone knows that you have a noble pedigree; almost certainly better suited for this task than I am. With six princes of the Church in your family history, and more degrees and honors than I knew existed, you have been seemingly raised to be a leader of Holy Mother Church. Yet it has fallen to me to complete this task, and I would be foolish to disregard the tools that Our Lord puts at my disposal, including you." Then he continued, with a resolution that hadn't been present in his voice a moment earlier. "What I need you to accept, however, is that this will be a discussion of how to accomplish these goals, not whether we should attempt to accomplish them. The Church must move back to Her roots."

"As you wish. Let's then discuss the practicalities of this process. Not only will the Congregation of Bishops be an important ally in this process, but so too will be the balance of the Curia. I would also assume that many of the changes you propose would affect members of the College. There will certainly be some potential obstructions there. Do you consider these to be significant issues?"

"Obviously, I consider all issues to be significant. Ideally, the Holy Spirit will have moved the entire College and Curia together. Unfortunately, that is rarely the case. However, I understand the only legal stumbling block to be the potential resistance of the College; and at the end of the day, the College is composed of those that the Vicar of Christ believes should be included."

"Certainly, you're not suggesting that you would demote the very men who elected you?"

Pope John ignored the sharp rise in the Cardinal's voice and the aggressive position he took in his seat. "My good Cardinal, I said no such thing. But the College is a deliberative body which moves by plurality. The size and composition of the College is, however, my decision. This is another exercise where I would like your assistance."

Cardinal Compeccio visibly relaxed in his chair. "I believe you suggested another imperative from the elevation of the ministry of the laity. Can you share any more insight there?"

"Certainly, I can. In my mind, the focus of the Church should be on service, and the only practical way to live out that mission is to unshackle the laity. By extension, I believe that all things that are of value should be put into service to our mission. I think that the accumulated wealth by the Church has become nothing more than a reflection of our self-importance. Over the centuries, what were initially good works—namely, patronizing the struggling artists of history to tell the story of our Creator—have come to symbolize grandeur. As with our roles, I believe that we should lead by example with our possessions. We should publicly express the goal of putting our treasure to work in the service of our mission. This is a goal that could take decades, if not centuries, to realize. However, I believe that by putting a plan in place and beginning to exercise it immediately, we will start to lead by example."

"Don't you believe that the Church puts enough resources to work in missionary service already? Won't this risk looking like a hollow gesture?"

"Actually, no. My missionary projects are accomplished, as you know, through a special collection from the faithful each year. It's merely a pass-through. At the same time that we ask for that collection and preach to the faithful about tithing, we collect their money rather than liquidating any of our boundless assets. On top of this, we continue to allow our bank to be shrouded in mystery and spot lit with scandal. The world has little faith that we behave as we preach; and rather, we should be challenging the world everyday by our example."

The two men sat for a while longer, discussing the next steps and the likely pace of assembling a Synod for Consultation. There was another somewhat heated exchange when the discussion turned to potential invitees; but ultimately, Cardinal Compeccio conceded to work with Monsignor Hellman on a draft list. Pope John knew that, so long as he structured the agenda correctly, there would be little chance of the attendees redirecting his plans. In fact, it might be good to have the obstructionists present, so that they could dispense with any nonsense right up front.

When it was time for his visitor to leave, Pope John made a big show of bringing the discussion to an amiable ending. He escorted the Cardinal to the door of his study, where he embraced him in front of the assembled onlookers. "Your Eminence, I am always so grateful for your counsel and assistance. Let's continue to toil together for the good of Holy Mother Church."

For his part, the Cardinal bent again to kiss the Pontiff's ring, being careful to show due reverence to the role that he hoped to hold himself one day.

Chapter Twelve

After Cardinal Compeccio left his study, Pope John reflected on the conversation they'd had. He couldn't be sure what had just happened; but one thing was certain, he shouldn't have shared so much of his plans at this first meeting. It was one thing to share the full breadth of the plans with Antonio. It was another thing entirely to lay them out for a scion of the old guard. He had been grateful for the counsel and friendliness shown to him by the Cardinal, especially during the early days of his pontificate; but he had always sensed that he should be somewhat cautious. "I haven't even shared the most ambitious elements with Cardinal Suarez," he thought, someone with whom he felt a unique bond.

Now he found himself wondering which Cardinal Compeccio was the genuine article. Was his true nature that of the conscientious, but loyal, counselor? Was he really the obstructionist who always seemed to be lurking somewhere in all of his advice? Always one to be plagued by doubts, he even began to wonder if he should have invited the Cardinal into the open correspondence that he had begun after his visit to America.

He snapped out of it when he remembered that he still had his lunch with Giuseppe to look forward to. It would be the first time they could really spend time together since he had gone back to his regular schedule. Whenever he had meetings like this morning's, he was especially grateful to have some long and loyal friends close by, like Giuseppe and Antonio.

As if she sensed that he was thinking about her boyfriend, Abrielle appeared in his doorway. She rapped lightly on the jamb before he had the chance to acknowledge her. He couldn't help himself when it came to her, but when he looked up he smiled, "Yes, dear Abrielle? What can I do for you?"

"Holy Father, I am sorry to bother you, but I would like to find some time to discuss a few mundane tasks, if you are up to it. I've been trying to wait until you appear to be back in full swing before bothering you."

"It's no bother. In fact, it would be a welcome relief from the usual schedule." He stood and offered her a chair. "Oh, listen to me, going on about such a privilege that I have. How are you doing, child?"

"I'm doing much better, as we all are, now that you are doing so well."

"Well, you certainly saw me at my worst. Like some poor young lady who's been selected by the family to care for the doddering old uncle."

"Holy Father, I certainly hope that you know how grateful I feel, each and every day, to serve you and your household. My only thought during that first dreadful week was that I might lose you. That was too much to bear."

"You will be pleased to know that my physician can find nothing permanent in my brain scans. In fact, he's starting to come around to my thinking that this might have been only a strange episode of food poisoning or some such. Although it's beyond me how my symptoms could be what they were. But as with many unfortunate things in our lives, Our Lord has seen fit to bless me during this problem. I won't bore you with the details, but for much of my pontificate I have been vexed by an idea that I couldn't appropriately value. As I was recuperating, I was able to take myself through a methodical discernment process, which I dare say most Pontiffs don't have the luxury of doing."

"And you reached the conclusions you were looking for?"

"I would say they were slightly different. I was looking to prove my idea's worth…or not. Either way, I wanted to feel some certainty that I was on the Lord's path. In that regard, it was successful."

"That's wonderful news, Holy Father. I am happy for you. I have been concerned for you and your well-being. I suppose that I am just absorbing some of Giuseppe's anxieties."

"What is my old friend anxious about?"

At this, Abrielle realized that perhaps Giuseppe hadn't shared any of his recent concerns directly with Pope John yet. This caused her to become flustered. "I don't know…I mean, I must have misunderstood something he said. I hope that I haven't said something to cause you unnecessary concern." Trying to change the subject, she said, "I saw Cardinal Compeccio when he arrived. He seemed to be in good spirits. I trust that your conversation was productive."

"Well, I suppose it was, in its own way. He provides a good view for me into the inner workings of the Vatican. Not having spent much time here before my election, I'm still a relative newcomer."

"I'm sure that the Cardinals are quite helpful to you." The way she said this, it was almost in the form of a question. It certainly carried no confidence in the delivery.

"Don't worry about me, dear. I often think that you and our dear Giuseppe are overprotective of me."

The two of them chatted for another ten or fifteen minutes, mostly about Giuseppe. They shared a good laugh about his tendency to be overprotective of everyone. They supposed that it was this same nature that led him to his vocation. When they finished, Abrielle stood to leave, grateful to excuse herself from a conversation in which she had arguably overstepped her bounds on several occasions. She made a mental note to reintroduce a little of the old formality to her dealings with Pope John, and as soon as she crossed the threshold, she remembered that she hadn't brought up a single one of the household items she had meant to discuss.

A short while later, Monsignor Hellman was leaving the study, having just concluded their daily meeting to review correspondence; Giuseppe arrived for a private lunch. The two men passed in the outer office. They were somewhat acquainted, having both served the Pontiff during his entire tenure. It struck the veteran policeman that the Monsignor appeared quite curious as to what he was doing there, but Giuseppe thought it might be useful to keep him guessing. He delighted in the feeling that Hellman was off guard; then he turned his attention to his purpose for being there.

He closed the door behind himself and approached the Pontiff. "Holy Father, thank you for inviting me to lunch. I had only wished to talk to you for a short while." In spite of their personal history, whenever he was in the Papal Apartments the prestige overcame all else and he bent to kiss the Pope's ring. Pope John responded by grabbing his hands and pulling him into an embrace.

"Giuseppe, I can hardly believe that you and I have not spent any real time together since I fell ill. I am so glad to see you."

"Your Holiness, it's certainly understandable that you have needed the quiet and now have an enormous load backed up, I'm sure."

Pope John led his friend back through the door and the outer office. He had already asked Abrielle to set up a lunch for them on the terrace, much as she'd done when he and Antonio had met. He had determined to make the terrace his private space and to share it freely with his personal friends. As the two made their way up the stairs, Pope John described the space and how important it had become to him, wanting Giuseppe to appreciate the honor he was paying him. When they arrived at the top of the stairs, they found Abrielle waiting to descend past them. She had hoped to be gone before they arrived. As she stood there, backlit by the midday sun, she looked radiant, and Giuseppe forgot where he was. He walked straight up to her and planted a kiss on her lips. She startled and took a step back, blushing. This was the reminder that he needed of where he was and who he was with.

He turned back toward Pope John and somewhat bashfully said, "I'm sorry, Holiness, I forgot myself for a moment."

For his part, Pope John was beaming like a proud uncle. "Nonsense. True affection should never be contained artificially. Your expression is beautiful." Winking at Abrielle, he said, "Now shouldn't you be getting back to work?"

She left silently, as if walking on a cloud, and the two men took their place at the table she had prepared lovingly for them. The discussion began about Abrielle. Pope John was glad to now be fully included in their little secret, and he would encourage Giuseppe to talk about her as much as he liked. But Giuseppe wanted to talk about the Pope's schedule and how he was approaching this new chapter in his papacy. Neither of them seemed to remember that the lunch was originally supposed to be a meeting, with a purpose.

When Pope John casually mentioned that Cardinal Compeccio had just been by to check on him, he didn't realize that the conversation was just about to take a more somber turn. In fact, it hadn't occurred to him that Giuseppe would necessarily even know who he was referring to. To his surprise, the mere mention of his name caused Giuseppe to put down the bread he was holding and sit upright.

"Father, do you truly feel that you can trust the Cardinal?" Giuseppe had been the one person he could count on to call him by his more humble title, at least when they were truly alone.

Now it was Pope John's turn to be surprised. "Why on earth would you ask me that?"

"I'm sorry, but there's something I never told you about your tour of America. You'll recall that I wanted to come along in part to understand what was going on *around* the official events of the visit. What I never found a way to tell you was that I followed Monsignor Hellman to a most unusual dinner party on our final evening of the trip. While it was a suspicious group of individuals, I made the decision to keep the news to myself, determining that it was unfair to fill your head with needless political intrigue."

"Well, Giuseppe, you certainly have my curiosity piqued now. Please go on."

"Present at the dinner, which was held at a very elegant social club, were four Cardinals of the Church, along with your personal secretary, Monsignor Hellman. Three I recognized: Cardinals Welty and Johns from the United States; Cardinal Compeccio, who you just mentioned; and a man I later learned was Cardinal Somers of England. I later did some research and discovered that Cardinal Compeccio arrived on a flight booked outside of the normal Vatican travel agency. Based upon his itinerary, I determined that he flew to America solely for that dinner. All five men arrived at the dinner separately and left separately."

"Isn't that interesting?" It was clearly rhetorical...and highly noncommittal. "I didn't know that Cardinals Compeccio or Somers were in town." What went unsaid was the Pontiff's assessment that perhaps he now knew which Luigi was the true Luigi.

Giuseppe chose to continue. "As I say, at the time I convinced myself that this was superfluous political intrigue and not worth bothering you over. After all, most Popes don't have their own foreign intelligence services, and it might be unfair to burden you with things that only appear interesting to someone in my profession."

"I also would have told you that you and Abrielle worry about me too much. It's very touching, but I understand that there will always be a swirl of politics around the Throne of Saint Peter. It does something, even to the best of men."

"That was my original thought as well. However, I'm much more concerned about your safety than I am about Papal politics. After the events of the last month or so, I am very interested in what Cardinal Compeccio might wish to discuss with you."

Pope John looked at his friend somewhat quizzically. He had a great deal of respect for Giuseppe's professional instincts and realized that his own questions might reveal as much to the policeman as his answers would. He went ahead nonetheless. "What do you mean when you say, 'the events of the last month'?"

Giuseppe suddenly felt some trepidation at what he had to say next. He had called this meeting, but he was still not completely prepared; and now that he was sitting across from his childhood pastor, Father Calliendo, he was unsure how to broach the topic.

"Father, I am now convinced that your illness was not a stroke and, in fact, not an illness at all." He watched the Pontiff sink back into his chair, letting the sun shine brightly in his eyes almost without noticing. He seemed to sense what was coming next. "I need to share with you what happened while you were unconscious."

With an unfamiliar weakness in his voice, the Pope said, "My friend, you have done a good job of keeping idle speculation out of my field of view so far. Are you sure that this is something that I need to hear?"

"Holy Father, my sworn duty, not to mention my love for you, compels me to share this with you. Your awareness of the risks you face may be the single best tool we have to protect you."

Giuseppe went on to tell Pope John about the scene that had transpired after a private lunch nearly a month ago. The Pope had later told him that this lunch was the last thing he remembered before his illness. After the lunch, he had taken a walk in the gardens behind the Papal Apartments. During the walk, he had collapsed. Friends who had accompanied him would describe that he appeared disoriented, then weakened and sat down. He quickly lost consciousness, and the Swiss Guard kicked into action. They rushed the Pontiff to the Papal Apartments, where a fully stocked medical clinic is in place; there they were met by the Pope's primary physician. During the next few hours, the staff managed to stabilize his condition and ran a battery of tests, including a CKMB blood test. Creatine Kinase MB is an enzyme that is found in the bloodstream mainly when heart tissue is damaged. Because of the sudden onset of weakness and dizziness, the physicians wished to identify a heart attack if one had occurred, so they could take the appropriate next steps.

Giuseppe described the somewhat odd conversation that he had with the physician later that day, in which the doctor made an offhand comment about how quickly the test results came back. While the test itself only takes about fifteen minutes for results, he had years of experience with the medical laboratory nearby in Rome, and he was surprised by its sudden burst of efficiency. He also commented that the first tests are often inconclusive, due to the fact that CKMB rises over eighteen to twenty-four hours, and it might take much of that time to get a solid result.

Giuseppe, now playing every bit the investigator, went on to coolly describe that he came back the next morning for the complete written test results. As he went through them with the physician, they both noticed how narrowly the sample had been tested. Other typical tests for food poisoning and miscellaneous conditions were absent. As a result, he exercised the full weight of his office and ordered that the sample be tested again for a broader array of possible conditions. When he returned later in the day, the doctor confirmed that the laboratory could not locate the original samples that were drawn. In anticipation of the police interrogation they knew was coming, the laboratory staff attempted to locate the medic who drew the samples, but no one recognized the signature. More confusion ensued because while the laboratory was able to locate the report in their files, the staff could not remember processing the samples at all.

Giuseppe now proceeded with caution, because he was trusting in the Pope's discretion. He described that, in his frustration, he sent a member of the Vatican Police—a former military medic—into the Papal Apartments to draw a fresh sample. That sample showed only some minor abnormalities; in reviewing the results with a doctor he knew personally, they concluded that the sample may have been too delayed to be truly conclusive.

During the next couple of days, the physicians followed the traditional diagnostic sequence and begin performing head scans, looking for signs of a stroke. He paused in the retelling, seeing that his friend was trying to piece all of the news together.

"Giuseppe, what does this all suggest to you?"

"First of all, we should stick to what we know. We know from the brain scans that you did not suffer a stroke. We know from the blood draw that I ordered—which would have coincided with a spike of CKMB if you suffered a heart attack—that you did not suffer a cardiac event either."

"So then, doesn't this mean that the most likely cause is the correct one? I probably simply had a bad case of food poisoning."

"I think that is possible; however, the amount of intrigue surrounding your diagnosis leads me to be concerned that the poisoning was not accidental. Continuing with what we know, we also know that your blood was drawn and delivered by a medic that no one knows or can locate; a copy of the results are in the lab's files, but no one remembers running those tests; the results came back almost immediately; and finally, they were much more narrow that your physician ordered." He paused a moment to let his friend catch up. "My experience tells me that a gap or coincidence can be expected, but several in a related chain of events are nearly impossible."

"So how do you propose to answer your concerns? I need to be careful to avoid needlessly stirring up more drama within these walls just now."

"I understand, Father. In fact, awareness of my concerns would only hamper my investigation." He picked up a slice of cheese, trying to look casual. "Do you remember my friend Paul Regalo?"

"Of course."

"I believe that I need to employ a trusted friend from the outside with top-tier skills in this type of work. I want to call him in to assist me in tracking down any possible evidence and determining if you were intentionally poisoned. If that proves to be true, we will be on the hunt for a potential killer."

"But can't we keep this quieter by simply keeping it between us and your department?"

"I thought about that already. Remember that I have been in Rome for only a little more time than you have. I'm not completely sure how intertwined my department is with some of the long-standing constituencies within the Vatican. I would feel more comfortable if the investigation were truly between you and me; but I will need some support, and I trust Paul with my life…and, I suppose, with yours as well. He is a very well regarded investigator with the Federal Bureau of Investigation in the United States—their equivalent of the federal police. They also, coincidentally, run some of the most well-respected laboratories in the world and are relied upon by major law enforcement agencies inside and outside of America.

"Father, I suspect that the best way to determine what was happening in your system at the time of your illness is to locate what remains of the original blood that was taken, if it still exists. We also need to document what really went on— who had possession of the sample and what, if any, tests were actually run on it. The medic who originally drew the blood is the key to both of these issues. Failing those two things, I want to ask the FBI lab to take a second look at the sample that I had drawn and determine if there is any more information to be gleaned from it.

"Finally, Father, Paul can operate under the radar within the Vatican, which is something that I can no longer do. There is always a benefit to dividing and conquering when it comes to investigations. In this case, I may need to play the role of the official investigator, while Paul is running down the more obscure leads."

Pope John relented. "Okay, you've convinced me. Invite him over and give him the run of the Vatican."

"Actually, I would like for us to call him together first. I would like him to hear from you personally that this is something that has your support."

"Well, let's get on with it then," Pope John said, rising from his chair. Then he looked at his friend with his best conspiratorial grin. "Does your friend not trust you, if you call to ask for assistance? What type of relationship of trust am I putting my reliance on?"

The two made their way quietly back to the Pontiff's study. They took up positions around the desk, and Giuseppe dialed his friend's number. He had warned Paul the evening before that he might need to call him very early in the morning and needed him to be available.

"Hello, this better be good, Giuseppe. I've been at the Bureau too long to be arriving at this hour. People are going to start rumors about me."

"Hello, Paul. Thanks for agreeing to be available. I wouldn't have asked you if it weren't so important."

"Oh, I understand, I'm just busting your balls."

At this, Giuseppe saw the perfect opening to reintroduce his two friends. "Paul, I have you on a speakerphone because I am standing in the Papal Study in the Vatican, with Pope John. We have a favor to ask of you."

Special Agent Paul Regalo swallowed hard, trying to forget what he'd just said. "Holy Father, it's very nice to speak with you. Of course I will do anything I can to help you and my old friend Giuseppe."

Pope John decided to let him off the hook, sensing his discomfort. "It's nice to speak with you, Inspector Regalo. Thank you for offering your assistance."

Giuseppe took control of the conversation. He reminded Paul about the news stories of Pope John's recent illness, suspected of being a stroke. He shared his suspicions that the Pope had been poisoned instead; and without letting Paul tear into his theory, he recounted the details of the blood tests, the missing medic, and the lack of an explanation for the illness. He concluded by saying, "Paul, I need a partner on this, preferably one that I trust completely and that no one in the Vatican knows."

"Well, my mother always wanted me to be a priest instead of a cop, so perhaps this will be my way of repaying her patience with my decision. I'll be on the first plane out and I'll be there by morning, if that's what you'd like."

"That's exactly what I need," confirmed Giuseppe.

At this, Pope John chimed in, trying to lighten the mood. "That will allow you to meet Abrielle also."

"I'm sorry, but who is Abrielle?"

Pope John looked at Giuseppe disapprovingly as he leaned into the phone. "I suppose I should let Giuseppe tell you about his special friend."

"Yes, Holy Father. But before I hang up and make my travel arrangements, I would like to pose a question to you. If there were no irregularities in the custody of the blood tests, has anything unusual been going on that would make either of you particularly suspicious?"

Giuseppe fielded this question. "I just shared with Pope John that when he visited America two years ago, I uncovered a clandestine meeting between a number of Cardinals and his Papal Secretary. I set the information aside at the time, believing that it was just politics. However, since I've come to believe that His Holiness may have been poisoned, this group's meeting has taken on new meaning."

Paul pressed both of them, albeit delicately. "What could these men possibly have to conspire about? With the Papal Secretary as a participant, it sounds more like a gossip session than a high-level meeting with political consequences. Beyond that, to involve attempted murder, it would have to have grave consequences. What possible motive could any of them have for wanting to see you hurt, Your Holiness?"

Giuseppe was a little put off by the note of skepticism in Paul's voice, but Pope John stepped in. "Gentlemen, there is another piece of information that I will review with you in detail tomorrow, when we are all together. Suffice it to say that I have shared some plans with Cardinal Calliendo and Monsignor Hellman, two of the men of whom Giuseppe speaks. These plans will likely upset the old, entrenched interests of the Church."

Paul pressed further. "Are these plans that will cause them heartburn or cause them to want a new Pope?"

"In short, I am setting some changes in motion within the Church. They will likely result in my replacing some of the Bishops with new blood. They will also, hopefully, change the imbalance of leadership by the clergy by refocusing it more on its core role of service."

"The group you describe doesn't sound exactly like a homogeneous representation of the old guard. What would connect these men in a way that they would trust Monsignor Hellman with information he might share with His Holiness? They would assume, wouldn't they, that his loyalties lie with Pope John?" Paul was struggling with how this all fits together.

"Gentlemen, I need to caution you that what I am going to share with you is of monumental secrecy. I am going to share something that is never discussed outside of the College of Cardinals. Monsignor Hellman is a member of a different generation, to be sure. But what even you don't know, Giuseppe, is that he came to the Papal Household at the express recommendation of Cardinal Welty, after I was selected over him in the Conclave. Further, I invited my secretary and Cardinal Compeccio into the planning of these changes, as thought-partners of mine." After this had a few moments to hang in the air, he delivered the final piece of the puzzle. "I have also just made them aware that I am moving forward with these plans as quickly as possible."

Somewhat annoyed, Giuseppe looked his friend squarely in the eyes. "I wasn't aware of this, Your Holiness; and if it's true, we are not just looking for a killer, we are truly in a race against time."

Chapter Thirteen

Special Agent Paul Regalo arrived at the Vatican the
next morning, somewhat bleary-eyed by the redeye flight to
Rome, but energized by the monumental questions circling
his mind. Less than twenty hours earlier, he'd had a phone
conversation with the Supreme Pontiff of the Roman Catholic
Church. During that call he had learned some information of
a type that few people, other than Cardinals, had heard over
the last two thousand years. He'd also been asked to help find
the Pope's murderer, before that person had a chance to make
a second attempt.

After that call, he phoned the home of the Deputy
Director in charge of the Washington Field Office of the FBI
to ask for permission to give assistance to the Vatican Police
Department in an investigation. He knew that these types of
requests were normally highly bureaucratic and even then
wouldn't fall to an agent in Paul's current role, but his mind
was made up that he would be on a flight later that day, even

if it meant the end of his career. He was putting on hold an investigation of significant consequence within the Bureau, the background of the next appointee to be Director of the FBI. He had just recently been granted this plum assignment, and he knew that this new request would not be taken well. During the brief conversation that followed, he was cryptic enough to keep the Pontiff's confidence and to send the message to his boss that this was serious business. The DDIC set the phone down for a few moments to double-check Paul's personnel file online. It confirmed two things from his memory—that Paul Regalo was a devout Roman Catholic and that he was personal friends with the Inspector General of the Vatican Police. He could be assured that this was an important matter also, but he still vowed to get the full debrief directly from Paul on his return.

It was a warm but slightly overcast day in Rome, and it occurred to Paul that this was probably how Rafael would paint the Vatican on a day that the Pope was under threat. He decided to leave the taxi at the edge of Vatican City and walk the last distance through the grounds to his friend's office. They had passed the Audience Hall along the south boundary; Paul could see the iconic Saint Peter's Basilica to his right just before they pulled to a stop along Via della Stazione Vaticana. As he checked in for directions to Giuseppe's

219

office, the checkpoint guard showed great deference to both his credentials and the name of his friend. As he started walking, he quickly realized why the taxi driver had given him a bewildered look, as this edge of the medieval city had clearly adapted well to the arrival of the automobile. He skirted narrow streets and parking places located on every available piece of tarmac. As he worked his way to the back side of the Basilica, he crossed the street and then the park in front of him. In the few minutes that it took Paul to arrive at the Civil Administration building, he had crossed nearly one-quarter of the breadth of the tiny city-state. In spite of the unusual approach he chose, he was now standing before a lovely architectural façade amid a tranquil park-like setting.

Paul snapped out of the moment as he found Giuseppe standing on the front landing waiting for him. The seriousness of the visit was written all over Giuseppe's face, and the two men exchanged their least familiar greeting since that first meeting all those years ago at Quantico. He followed his friend up one flight of stairs and back to his office in the far corner of the building. When the door had been closed, they sat opposite each other without knowing how to begin.

Finally, the Inspector General looked up at his friend and all the relief spilled out. "Paul, I can't thank you enough for dropping everything and making the trip on such short notice.

I trust that you didn't put yourself in an awkward position by doing so…but I also recognize that I didn't really give you any room to say no."

Paul smiled. "You did kind of pull out the big guns when you called me from His Holiness's office. You know me too well to think that I could refuse. Fortunately, my circumstances didn't pose a problem and the timing was pretty good, if one could ever say so about this situation." He chose to keep the true details of his docket to himself, although something deep inside encouraged him to share just how committed he was to helping his friend and the Pontiff.

The two discussed the prior day's phone call and the facts that were known, including the new revelations of some clear motives and suspects. Giuseppe reflected aloud on his disappointment that he hadn't followed up on the revelations from the tour. He also expressed some concerns about just how delicate their task would be: finding the missing medic and not arousing too much suspicion within this tight-knit community. For his part, Paul just couldn't wrap his mind around the fact that Pope John had almost been murdered and the most likely suspects were the Papal Secretary and a cabal of Cardinals.

"Paul, we have a meeting with His Holiness in about an hour. We should plan how we would like this conversation to

221

go. I'm sorry to say that he may not be the most cooperative interviewee."

"What is your biggest concern, that he knows more than he'll share or that he is really in denial about what happened?"

"I think the conversation yesterday shocked most of the remaining denial out of him. But he is a very wise—some might say cagey—old man. Remember, I say that with all the love in the world because I've known him for nearly my entire life. He will generally be one step ahead of us and will at all times be much more concerned about how the Church will come through this than whether *he* will come through this."

"Based on what he told us yesterday about his plans, do you still think that he has the same respect for the Church that he did when he arrived in Rome? I've been wondering all the way over here if he's become discouraged by what he found here and that's why he is working to dismantle it. At the very least, the thought that he might be the victim of a murder conspiracy should cast a pall over his admiration for the Church."

"I understand why you might think that, Paul. But to those who have known him back home, the irony of him being elected Pope is thick. He doesn't believe that the clergy is synonymous with the Church. He has long held beliefs that the clergy is too flashy, but even with all that has gone on, he will always defend the Church, and we must remember that it is his life."

"Okay then, I would really like to leave the first meeting with a clear understanding of the events on the day he became ill. I want to go through that in front of him, because some of the details that he doesn't remember may still jog some associations with people or other events."

"Agreed. In particular, I would like to dig deep into some of these characters who are connected to the meeting in Boston and the plans that he has been hatching. We need to understand the implications of what he is proposing and who would be impacted by it."

The friends were now back in their professional mindset and clearly excited at the opportunity to really work a case together for the first time in their careers. When they wrapped up the preparatory conversation, they set out for the Papal Apartments. Once again, Paul was struck by the on-again, off-again ambiance that he experienced—out of the hustle and bustle of the police office; out the front of the building to the idyllic park, whose walkways embraced the more private side of Saint Peter's Basilica like a pair of arms; and then continuing Paul's original path around the church toward the

Sistine Chapel. Then the two ducked into what Giuseppe called, "a quicker and quieter approach," which turned out to be cutting through the parking lot in the Belvedere Courtyard.

When Giuseppe led his friend through the complex known as the Papal Apartments, the contradictory impressions didn't stop. The first was the rich tradition contained in the artwork, and even the history that these very floors had ushered in over hundreds of years of visitors to the Holy See. The second was at how simple it all was—offices, accommodations, reception areas. Maybe, he thought, it wasn't possible to capture in mere architecture the theoretical majesty of an institution that traces its origins to God on Earth.

When they finally arrived at the door to the study, Giuseppe knocked and was called in. He introduced His Holiness to Paul with all the proper formality the occasion required. Paul's greeting of Pope John could only be described as fawning. He didn't just bend to kiss the Pope's ring, he genuflected and lingered as he kissed it, as if importing a greater loyalty than the typical visitor. At this, Giuseppe did the honors for a somewhat surprised Pontiff and formally thanked Paul for making the trip over to help protect His Holiness.

Paul spoke with the emotion and formality of the occasion: "Your Holiness, Inspector General, I am truly grateful for the opportunity to serve Holy Mother Church and the Vicar of Christ, during what may be one of the darkest moments in her history. I can't help feeling that I was born for this task, and I am quite certain that my saintly mother, Juliette Anna Maria Boccelli Regalo, would absolutely agree." He turned toward Giuseppe to continue. "When the day began yesterday morning, my official assignment was to vet the next Director of the FBI. When I called the Deputy Director to let him know I was leaving for Rome, I expected he might issue an ultimatum or fire me on the spot. It is a huge honor, and a feather in my cap, to be offered that assignment." Now as he turned back toward Pope John, "But there is nothing that I would not sacrifice to ensure your safety and the continuity of Peter's successors. I was going to be here this morning, regardless of what my boss said to me."

Pope John led Paul over to one of the upright chairs opposite his desk, inviting him to sit down, as he turned to his Inspector General, "Before we begin, can you and I speak privately for a few moments?"

Giuseppe understood that this was not an invitation and quickly followed after the Pontiff, who was already halfway through the door next to his desk. When the door was closed behind him, he realized that he was standing in the Pope's private room. This was a room that Abrielle had described to him but he'd never stepped inside before. He looked around for a few moments, granted him by Pope John, who understood the impression that such experiences had on people.

When the Pope had settled in next to the far window, he called Giuseppe closer to be sure they wouldn't be overheard. "Giuseppe, I know that you have a long history with Inspector Regalo, but is he for real? I'm only used to ancient nuns treating me with that sort of reverence and formality."

"I'm sorry, Your Holiness, I am sure that he is a little overwhelmed by his surroundings and a little jet-lagged after his sudden travel. But, you know what I think about his talent as an investigator."

"Is he clear-headed enough to be of assistance to you in the investigation?"

"He is, Holiness. I wouldn't want to go into this without his assistance. And as we've discussed, his ability to attract less attention will be a great asset. As you heard, he was selected to help vet the next leader of America's federal police force. He has fantastic skills and will be able to draw on great resources if we need them. By the way, they prefer to be called Special Agents, not Inspectors."

As Pope John led Giuseppe back into the study, the Pontiff took up his place behind his desk and Giuseppe took the remaining chair opposite. "My apologies, Special Agent Regalo, for keeping you waiting. My Inspector General and I had something that needed our attention before we could focus on this investigation."

"Of course, that's not a problem, Your Holiness."

"Also, before we jump in, I should tell you that after we have concluded our business today, I will ring the president and ensure that he knows how grateful I am for your assistance in these matters. I am quite certain that should buy you all the flexibility you will require in your other duties."

"I am most grateful, Holy Father."

Trying to get things back on track, Giuseppe jumped in. "Paul and I have decided that the best way to get our investigation moving would be to review the events of the day you fell ill. I believe that an hour or two before, you were having lunch with a group of people. Is it acceptable if we start there?

Pope John nodded and settled deeper into his chair, shifting it slightly to keep the glare from the window out of his eyes. He sensed that this was going to be no quick conversation.

Paul jumped in. "Can you tell me who was present and add a little background that might be relevant? Sometimes, small things can be important in a recounting like this, so don't worry about trying to be overly concise."

"Very well. Monsignor Hellman was present, as he often is during larger meals, just in case work topics come up in the course of the conversation. I believe we covered all the intrigue related to the good Monsignor yesterday in our call—he was recommended to me by my most likely rival, Cardinal Welty, upon my election."

"Yes, thank you for clarifying."

"Cardinal Compeccio was also in attendance. He is the Prefect for the Congregation of Bishops, responsible for selection and review of appointments. While Cardinal Compeccio was in that role before my election, he has been one of my closest friends in the Curia since my arrival. I believe we also covered the intrigue with the good Cardinal yesterday—he was present at the Boston dinner that Giuseppe spoke of, along with Monsignor Hellman."

"What can you tell us about his background?"

"He is one of the most ambitious of the Curia. One of those who seem to feel they are born to occupy the Throne of Saint Peter. In fact, perhaps he was. There are countless priests, Bishops and even Cardinals, in his family going back centuries. He has a wonderful pedigree of degrees from the very best universities and is a reasonably well-regarded theologian."

"Did anyone else attend the lunch?"

"Yes, it was a casual lunch, but one other friend of mine was there. Jacques Fournier is the Director of the Vatican Museum. We struck up a friendship one evening as I stumbled across him leading a team of restorers working in a corner of my private chapel. They believed that I was out of town and were horrified at the thought that they may have interrupted me on the way to prayer. I tried to assure him of no ill will by striking up a conversation about his work. It turned out that he had worked his way up through the museum organization as one of the foremost authorities on the Vatican collection. Over the last few years, he has given me the most protracted tour of our holdings that any nonemployee has ever experienced. Over the course of those walks, we have become close, and he has taken to playing the role of conversationalist at many of my smaller gatherings."

"Was anyone else at the lunch?"

"No."

Giuseppe took control again. "So two of the three attendees at the lunch were attendees at the dinner I stumbled across in Boston. Any idea what that group was doing together? Did you know that they were even acquainted before I told you yesterday?"

Pope John thought for a minute as he squirmed in his chair. "I did not really think they would be acquainted, but I would have no reason to believe either way. I have been thinking quite a bit about what they might have in common, concerning the politics of the Church, but I really cannot."

The two veteran police officers were unconvinced by the way the Pope avoided making eye contact, and they stayed silent, hoping he would continue to consider the question.

The Pope finally relented, "Of course, Monsignor Hellman and Cardinal Compeccio have both been a part of my deliberations on the changes to the Church. But the meeting in Boston would have predated most of the conversations on that topic. The only thing controversial up to that point was my initial homily, but the College challenged me into submission on that right away."

Paul couldn't help himself, "So you've been under challenge by the Cardinals since you were first elected?"

"It sounds more dramatic when you say it, but in some ways, yes. Not all Cardinals, mind you, but some have been very vocal about remaining within the bounds of what they consider to be acceptable statements about the evolution of the Church."

Giuseppe didn't want to push this too far, too fast. "Holy Father, can we turn to what happened after you fell ill in the garden? Who came around in the first few days afterward?"

"Between Monsignor Hellman and my physician, there were very few people allowed in to see me. For most of that time, I was unconscious and undergoing medical tests to determine the source of my illness. I suppose that Monsignor Hellman has records of who was coming and going."

"He will most certainly be our next interview; but of course, we need to be cautious about double-checking anything he tells us because of his potential involvement. Can you give us a quick review again about these plans for change, who knows about them, and who would likely be angered by them?"

"My plans are complex and not easy to explain, but I do think that the opposition will be clear from the description. Essentially, there are two primary thrusts: to encourage the laity to lead the Church, and to encourage the clergy to serve, rather than lead. It is my belief that the first is the rightful order of things, based on the historical Church, and that the way to set things right is to bring the second step to reality through the Bishops. I want to increase the numbers of Bishops and have them serve in parish life, closer to their people. Obviously, taken together these two things are going to rankle those who grew up believing that becoming a priest is an ennobling occurrence."

"Yes, but how many of those priests know what you're thinking of doing?"

"Fewer than a dozen…that I have told myself. Obviously, others could have heard through the Church's well-honed rumor mill. There is one additional step to the plan, which I should mention, although it's hardly as personal as the first two. In order to refocus the Church on our primary calling of service, and by Her example the laity, I am proposing to sell some of our vast art collection to fund service projects around the world."

"I agree," Giuseppe chimed in, "that this is not going to inspire the kind of angst that a Cardinal would feel at hearing he is in place to serve the laity."

Questioning his partner, Paul asked, "Who do we think are the most critical to interview?"

"Clearly Monsignor Hellman and Cardinal Compeccio should be interviewed, because of their ever-presence around these events. I will interview Monsignor Hellman, because we have a bit of an unspoken rivalry for Pope John's affection and my interviewing him will disturb him a bit. You should interview the good Cardinal, because being interviewed by an outsider will disturb him."

Pope John raised his concerns, "Are you just out to irritate everyone in the Vatican?"

"No, I'm sorry. What is understood between Paul and me is that interviewees are often the most candid when caught off-guard. Emotion tends to illicit secrets. We certainly need to interview Mr. Fournier, since he was present at the lunch and on the walk in the garden afterward." At this point, Giuseppe was up and pacing around the room, thinking. "Paul, I imagine we should wait on the others from the Boston dinner; they may have little to do with the immediate events that occurred around the illness. They just didn't have much opportunity. Do you agree?"

"I do. We should also interview the Papal Physician and those in the laboratory. Giuseppe, you should handle the Swiss Guard in attendance, as you will know the proper courtesy to show them. They should have a solid timeline documented."

"I think we need to keep our focus, however, on finding the missing medic and the original blood sample. If anything will tell us what really happened that day, it will be a detailed assay of Pope John's blood. Paul, can we rely on the FBI Lab to help us there, if we are successful in locating it?"

"Giuseppe, after His Holiness calls the president, my guess is that we will have all the resources we need at our disposal. Also, I have spent quite a bit of time working in and around the Quantico lab; I don't think that it's bragging to say that I should be able to sniff out any procedural irregularities in the Roman lab used for these tests."

The three continued to review the list of potential suspects and interviewees for another hour or more. When they were finished, the two policemen took advantage of an aging and tired Pontiff and took him back through the draft timeline one more time. They found no particularly good, new lines of inquiry; but by an exchange of glances, they agreed they would take one more crack at their victim in a day or so.

Sensing they were about to be shown the door, the two finally stood and indicated that the interview was complete. They had plans to meet with Abrielle for lunch; Pope John had insisted that she take the afternoon off when she heard of the plans.

"Holy Father, with your permission, we would like to break off this conversation. As you know all too well, I have been remiss in introducing my *special friend*—as you call her—to my friend Paul."

Turning to Paul, Pope John confirmed this. "Now that this morning's ordeal is over, I can tell you how especially close I have felt to Giuseppe since he was a young boy. When

I came to Rome, for what became my election, Abrielle was one of the first—and clearly the most special—person that I met. After my election, I came to regard her as a niece, and when she and Giuseppe found each other, my heart was really grateful. Perhaps something *truly* special and eternal can come of this strange role I find myself in."

"I was very excited to hear that Giuseppe has found someone. My wife and I have been praying for this for many years. He has become like a member of our family, although an infrequent visitor. I cannot wait to meet this special lady."

Pope John escorted the men to the door of the study. As Giuseppe started down the hall, the Pontiff tugged on Paul Regalo's elbow to hold him back for a private word. "Paul, I am sincerely grateful for your presence and for what you are about to do for me and for the Church. Please know that, whatever happens, we are connected by a bond of friendship and mutual service."

Paul was unable to speak, only to bow and kiss the Pope's ring. He turned and hurried after Giuseppe, who was clearly anxious to see his Abrielle.

Chapter Fourteen

The two men rushed back to Giuseppe's car on the far side of the administration building. When they followed the same route out of Vatican City that Paul had used to enter, he didn't feel quite so silly. Apparently, there are very few ways in and out. They followed the road to Via Aurelia, following the southern edge of the protectorate until they reached Viale Vaticano. The road turned north, wrapping the ancient arrowhead walls that protected the Vatican's flank in ancient times, but now only held the pontifical heliport. On their left, only a few hundred meters down the road, was a lovely white apartment building. The expensive units on the front edge faced the ancient city walls. Abrielle kept a small apartment at the northern corner of the building, facing a shaded and quiet court.

Abrielle greeted Paul like a long-lost brother. It was clear to him that Giuseppe must have given her a detailed account of the friendship that had developed between them over the years, and she was anxious to embrace another corner of her boyfriend's life. She had prepared a traditional, if somewhat heavy, Italian lunch: deep fried cod as an appetizer, or *filetti di baccala*, along with *pasta alla carbonara*, a mixture of bacon, black pepper, and pecorino cheese. The men ate heartily and the conversation was delightful.

Abrielle and Paul each wanted to know the other's history with their dear Giuseppe. The debriefing began with Paul regaling her with tales from Quantico, which sounded professional enough; although the stories finally shifted to their social encounters as they visited each other over the years, and those were decidedly less professional. As their friendship matured and Paul's family expanded, Giuseppe settled into a role as a long-distance brother and uncle.

As Paul told the tales, Giuseppe would occasionally jump in to share his memories; but when the floor was turned over to his better half, he was smart enough to sit back and yield history to her care. As one might expect, Abrielle's story of how she met and fell for Giuseppe was very touching. Because of the circumstances and the audience, there were even perspectives and insights that her boyfriend hadn't heard before. She described how she came to work in Rome and later came to work in the Papal Household. She explained how impressed she was by this relatively humble outsider, who managed to be elected Pontiff and looked at her with respect for her simple work. Later, that appreciation was transferred to the handsome policeman that, it turned out, was a very longtime acquaintance of Pope John. Initially she thought, "Any friend of his is a friend of mine." Just as her familial affection for the Pope grew, she started to feel a palpable, but altogether un-familial, affection for Giuseppe.

As their meal came to an end, Paul started to remember where he was, and why. He extended his regrets to his hostess but assured her that, when his work was complete, there would be more stories to tell. Now it was imperative to get to the medical laboratory and conduct his first interviews. Giuseppe would explain the details, so far as he felt comfortable.

"If you don't mind, dear lady," Paul said, "I will leave you two and get back to work. Giuseppe, if I could take your car, I can stop by later and pick you up."

"Don't worry; I'm sure Abrielle can give me a lift.

When they were alone again, Giuseppe turned to Abrielle, realizing that he had some explaining to do. He had let her know that his friend was visiting, but he had neglected to get into the details of the work to which Paul was referring.

"Bella, we need to talk about why Paul is here in Rome and what we are working on."

"I assume that it's a police matter and not any of my business. I understand that your work requires a measure of secrecy; and I realize after our lunch that you are quite good at what you do…not that I didn't already believe that."

"Well, I appreciate that very much. It is not often that there is much worth discussing about my job. After all, I am the chief of a police force in a city populated mainly by priests and tourists. Aside from the odd parking ticket and pickpocket, not much interesting happens on my watch. And thankfully, the pickpockets know to stay away because every inch of the place is under camera surveillance."

"Why on earth would Paul be here then, professionally I mean?"

"What I am going to tell you will shock you, but I want you to remain focused, because it concerns you in a professional capacity as well." Giuseppe paused for a moment to ensure that he had her undivided attention. "I have come to believe that His Holiness was poisoned and that this was the cause of his illness."

She gasped and started looking around the room. She also started to get out of her chair and immediately retook it, clearly uncertain of what her next move should be. "Are you sure? That cannot possibly be. I'm sorry, did you ask Paul here to help you put this fear to rest?"

"I don't want to get into too much detail right now, for personal as well as professional reasons. But as a member of the household who is not likely to be a suspect, I need you to be on guard. You are correct, I have asked Paul here to help me; but it's because I believe that the Holy Father is still in danger. Whoever tried to kill him a few short weeks ago likely has a greater urgency now to complete what he started. Unless we can locate some proof that will point us in the direction of the killer, I have every reason to suspect that he will make another attempt on Pope John's life."

"Giuseppe, I'm scared. What can I possibly do to help secure His Holiness? I would never have suspected that he was in danger before."

"As I have additional clues later, I will share them. But as it stands, we are at the beginning of this investigation. All I can suggest is that it's likely someone close to His Holiness, and therefore someone highly unsuspicious. Please be careful and be on guard." He looked at her with a mixture of concern and affection. "*Ti amo, il mio tesoro.*"

"I am your treasure, permanent and all yours." As she said this, she leaned in to kiss him tenderly. "I know that you are concerned about me, but don't be. From what you are saying, this is a crime of political intrigue, but of a most subtle nature. The killer is unlikely to pay any notice to me."

While she was refocused on the practicalities at hand, Giuseppe was still mesmerized by her kiss. He scooted in close to her on the couch, slipping his hand behind her waist. With his right hand, he reached up and caressed her cheek and leaned in to return her affection. He pulled her closer to himself, letting her hair fall across his face and sealing them off against the outside world.

They kissed softly, but it was clear from her response that she was pleased with his choice. She knew that he enjoyed the softness of her lips. It seemed to him that the slower they kissed, the more he felt the sensation of her. Yet he also felt an irresistible draw to her, and each shift in their lips stirred more passion in him. The kisses would ebb and flow, and he was exploring her mouth with increasing, then decreasing pressure. He hadn't even realized that his hand had left her face and was now caressing her. While his fingers had innocently found her left side, the base of his hand was beginning to explore his favorite part of her lovely figure.

Now he was fully conscious. As she let her body fall fully into his, he lay against the back cushion, willing it to lie flat and trying his best to absorb her into himself. His hand now reached back to her face as he tried to regain some control over himself and savor the taste of her mouth. "Dear God, how I love this girl," he thought to himself. Finally, he gave in. The arm around her waist slid to her firm, round backside; while his right hand found her hip, then her thigh, as he tried to wrap her around himself. He wanted to be enveloped by her. He wanted to be part of her.

As if somehow sensing his impending loss of control, Abrielle reached for his face, returning to a more tender and slower kiss. She needed to be strong for the both of them. Men, after all, couldn't be expected to maintain control. She loved being in his arms. She loved his touch and his kiss. She wanted to be fully his; but she really wasn't yet, not according to the way she was raised. Abrielle remembered the one time she had let things go too far with Giuseppe. It had been a wonderful moment of ecstasy, but the guilt and shame she had felt afterward was hard to overcome. The message that had been written on her face for the next few weeks created confusion in his mind and in their relationship. She couldn't bear that again. She thought to herself, "But why is this so much harder for us than for most people?"

Her mind drifted off to that time twenty years earlier, when she had lost her innocence. Not her virginity, but her innocence. This is the story that she had shared with Pope John just a few days earlier; and it seemed to keep popping into her consciousness more frequently now. She had been working in Rome for a short while, serving in the household of her former pastor. Abrielle was young and still somewhat innocent. She had caught the eye of her young pastor, who was moving to Rome for a plum new assignment and invited her along to keep his new residence. As it turned out, he also invited her along to keep him company.

When she recounted the story for Pope John, she took certain liberties in abbreviating the story. Her would-be consort groomed her for his advances. He found things in which she was interested and cultivated his own interest in them. They began to share more and more meals, until the day when he began alluding to the glory days of the Church, when the senior clergy thought themselves above the rules for commoners. When she attempted to rebuff him, he took no notice. His manners became more and more intimate, and it seemed as though he was "playing house." She came to believe in later years that he was craving a certain normalcy that his chosen profession didn't permit. Eventually he began touching her, not necessarily in a sexual way, but as a loving husband would. His instincts told him that it was perfectly natural, but the discomfort only grew in Abrielle's mind. Eventually, he approached her from behind while she was making dinner one afternoon, wrapped his arms around her waist, and bent to kiss her cheek. She shook him off, perhaps more violently than was warranted, and walked out of his house. She never spoke to him again, until their paths crossed again in the Papal Apartments. She shuddered at the thought.

Giuseppe, realizing that she was no longer in the room, asked carefully, "What's wrong, *il mio tesoro?*"

Seeing the connection for the first time, Abrielle started to wonder if her *no* to Giuseppe's advances might be a reflection of the disappointment she felt over the blurred lines with her former employer. "I'm sorry, Giuseppe. This isn't about you. I have a history that I am having a hard time shaking."

"I understand. But your husband has been passed for over ten years, right? He would certainly want you to move on and find love again."

"Oh, no. It's not my Marco. I know that he understands. In fact, he rescued me from these same concerns twenty years ago. But whenever I feel that I'm stepping over the line…you know, sexually…I freeze up and these old memories come back."

Giuseppe stood and strained to be thoughtful. "Abrielle, is this about the nuns back in school? I heard the same things growing up; and while I recognize that you are a better Catholic than I am, these things concern me as well. You know that those ladies didn't know the first thing about what they were saying. I'm not even sure that the Church knows what it's talking about. Teachings on sexuality are all derivatives from some philosopher's mind; Christ didn't teach on this subject."

Abrielle didn't want to get trapped in these same philosophical conversations. It was time to explain to Giuseppe just where she was coming from. She recounted the story again, striking a balance somewhere between reality and the version she told Pope John. Still she was careful to use no names. She really just wanted Giuseppe to empathize; her issues weren't just blind adherence to the Church's teachings, although that was there as well; they were complicated by the very real experiences that she'd had.

By the time she finished, Giuseppe had sat down opposite her. At various times, he reached out to touch her hand and give her courage to finish the story. "I'm so sorry that you had to go through that," he whispered. "It never occurred to me, in this day and age, that while the Church is holding us to an unnatural standard, some of its senior clergy are behaving with such hypocrisy. I mean, what two lovers do together is at least natural and honest." Giuseppe paused, not wanting to sound too self-serving in his diatribe against the Church.

245

"I know that you're angry, Giuseppe; and in some ways I suppose that I'm grateful for that. My only objective is that you get to know *all* of me. I do believe what the Church teaches; it's just that my issues go beyond that."

Giuseppe was incredulous. "Even though you know that Synods of Bishops quarrel about these topics, which then come to us as inviolable doctrine; and now you tell me that, even so, they don't behave to the same standards we should? If our eyes are open, they are teaching us by their behavior, every day, what they *really* believe."

"My treasure, I know that you don't share my beliefs. I know that, in your eyes, I'm either willfully ignorant of the way the world works, or I've been damaged by errant teachings. Unfortunately, I am who I am; I believe what I believe. I'm sorry that you have to share in that side of me as well."

His heart softened. "Theology aside, there is no side of you that I regret sharing in. You are the perfect partner for me, and I am very blessed to have you in my life." He looked deep into her eyes. "Thank you for sharing this with me; I know it was difficult."

She got up and started clearing some of the lunch dishes. "Back to the topic at hand, please. Is there nothing more that you can tell me about the danger to His Holiness? What should I be looking for?"

"We are focusing on those in attendance at his private lunch, just before he fell ill. In most cases, poison is relatively fast-acting, otherwise it would be a toxin that had built up in his system over time and we would have seen a gradual decline."

"I understand. I don't recall who was there."

"You shouldn't necessarily, because it was a small affair managed by the kitchen staff. Monsignor Hellman was there, as usual, along with Cardinal Compeccio and Jacques Fournier, the Director of the Vatican Museum. With the exception of Monsignor Hellman, the others were invited just because of their warm relationship with His Holiness. There was no business planned to be discussed."

"Wow, to think that one of them is even a suspect in such a heinous endeavor is breathtaking."

"Given your experience with the clergy, Abrielle, I'm surprised that you are so surprised. You, of all people, should understand how rules of moral conduct are very relative for some people. They can easily explain transgressions as necessary; no sins are absolute."

Abrielle continued cleaning, moving to the kitchen where Giuseppe couldn't easily see from her face that she was wrestling with something. While they'd only been together for a couple of years, he'd grown quite good at reading her expressions. Certainly it was a part of his police training that she would never grow comfortable with.

When she reentered the living area, he saw it immediately, but she beat him to the question. "Giuseppe, I need to share one additional detail with you, making you the only person who knows my whole story. My family, of course, knows for whom I worked when I first came to Rome; but they are not aware of why I left his employ. You and a few others know some of the story of why I left, but I've never shared his name. However, I may need to help you avoid some accidental entanglements."

"Okay, you certainly have piqued my curiosity."

"My former pastor, the man I left without warning because of his inappropriate behavior, is Luigi Compeccio." She paused to let the news sink in, but Giuseppe showed no overt reaction. "I'm concerned that if he becomes a real suspect, there will be claims of bias leveled unfairly against you; and I don't want him to try to get back at me by hurting you."

"First, you shouldn't worry about who is or who isn't the prime suspect. Second, I am always careful about how I conduct my investigations and will be doubly so with Paul to assist me. But most of all, I won't let him hurt you again; I promise you that. But it is helpful to know something more about the character, or lack thereof, of the person I am investigating."

Chapter Fifteen

Paul had learned that the medical laboratory used by the clinic in the Papal Household was part of the oldest hospital on earth, Do Good Brothers Hospital, four kilometers southeast of Vatican City on Tiber Island. *Ospedale Fatebene Fratelli* was a certified regional trauma center and, as such, was a bustling place with deep expertise in a variety of testing processes; but it was also a place that could be deeply disorganized during busy times. Paul had called the Chief of the world-famous FBI Laboratory, asking him to call ahead to ensure cooperation from his Roman counterpart. When he arrived, he was greeted warmly by the shift leader, who seemed to expect his presence.

Paul explained that he would like to start with the blood test results on His Holiness and work his way back through the chain of custody, all in order to better understand how reliable the report was and where its strengths and weaknesses might be. They agreed on a course of action, and

Paul was introduced to a lovely young lady, Maria, the manager of the laboratory's records room. They started by discussing her role and the procedures used in her area to check reports in and out of the files. He did not immediately share the fact that his own lab had already ruled the records a forgery based upon a number of minor discrepancies between it and the typical report from this lab. Paul was able to work with Maria in real time to confirm this theory. Maria first pulled the official copy of the blood test report that remained in the lab's files, along with a prior report for His Holiness created during his last physical. The comparison startled Maria, who quickly confirmed that the latest report did not follow their standard protocol for labeling the patient, nor the order in which the tests are reported. She dove back into the file, mumbling to Paul that the original order was not attached as it should be. She went on to explain that the details of what work was requested were usually attached to the results, allowing her audit team to confirm that they were fulfilling orders accurately and completely. She mused that it was almost as if the report had simply appeared in the files without the work being done at all. It turned out they were both thinking the same thing.

Paul suggested that they review the process beginning at the other end. Maria escorted Paul through the lab, past the beeping machinery, whirring centrifuges, and the quiet bank of microscopes. There she introduced him to Bernardo, a young clerk who had only been in his job for a short while and was working the intake desk in the laboratory. Paul pulled up a chair next to the bored young man and tried his best to start out with a lighthearted tone. Bernardo explained the range of sources that relied on their laboratory: smaller hospitals needing specialized tests, doctor's offices, specialty clinics, and insurance companies. He failed to mention the Vatican, but Paul later discovered that there had been no requests from the Vatican during Bernardo's short tenure. The two men walked through the process for logging in the various types of sample materials—blood, tissue, whole organs. Each request would be assigned a standardized code and put into the appropriate container. The patient, requesting medical facility, type of sample, and condition of the sample would all be represented in the code. There were also carefully coded descriptions for the tests to be run, which would also be attached to the container. All of these things would be printed automatically from the testing record that the clerk would log into the lab's tracking system.

With that useful background, Paul and Bernardo put the tracking system to the test. Bernardo got into the spirit of the investigation as Paul rattled off the various data filters that he wanted to check. Patient name: Franco Calliendo—a report was returned concerning a blood test six years earlier, when Pope John contracted the flu while attending a consistory as Cardinal Calliendo. Patient name: Pope John—none. Patient name: Pope John XXIV—none. They tried as many permutations as they could think of, but with the singular exception of the physical done a year earlier—and filed simply under John XXIV—this lab had never been asked to perform a test on this Pope. Then they attempted to filter for the tests that the Papal Physician was known to have requested, specifically CKMB, but each of the results came back with legitimate hospitals, patients, and codes in place on the record. All of these positive results would be double-checked by Maria before the day was out. Finally, they checked under the name of the doctor who had treated Pope John. Again, a small collection of results were returned, but each had a seemingly legitimate patient attached, and none were for the day in question.

Paul thanked Bernardo and excused himself. On his way back to Maria with the list of reports to search, he thought through the chain of custody and what this all meant. Apparently, a blood sample for His Holiness was never checked into the laboratory's tracking system. The report that supposedly represented the results of tests run in this lab was, by all accounts, a hasty forgery. Add this to the medic who disappeared, and it was hard not to wonder if in fact the entire blood testing process had been a hoax. Once back in the records room, Paul asked Maria for two favors. The first was to check the list of test records to determine if there was a legitimate report associated with the tracking system. The second was for an escort and introduction to the lab director.

Dr. Pietro di Alberto was quite polite and seemed to have expected Paul in the lab today. Paul explained that he needed to confirm a few details. When did he hear of Pope John's illness? *Immediately.* Would he be aware if a request were made for blood tests for Pope John? *Absolutely.* Was any such request made? *Absolutely not.* Would he be surprised to learn that a forged set of test results had been circulated and a copy was in his files? At this question, Dr. di Alberto nearly leapt out of his seat.

Now that he had the good doctor's attention, Paul found a receptive interviewee. The men reviewed the facility's certifications, which Paul had already checked with Quantico, as well as the basic standards set for its employees. With a quick burst of Italian into an intercom by the good doctor, Paul had a list of all employees who worked in the facility, along with their tenure. This would be sent to Giuseppe's boys and used to search against criminal databases. They also reviewed the security procedures, hours of operation, and which employees had access to which areas of the facility.

Just has Paul was about to leave, Maria poked her head into the office to let him know that she had found each record he had requested. Her files contained a legitimate copy of test results for each of the samples on his list. She had made a copy of each and clipped them to the original list he had presented to her, highlighting all of the points of comparison and organizing them according to test date. This too was part of Paul's audit, and Maria had passed with flying colors. This was not a lady for whom clerical errors or omissions were going to be commonplace.

Meanwhile, back within the Vatican, Giuseppe waited in the outer office of the Papal Secretary. Monsignor Hellman's assistant, a kindly older lady, offered Giuseppe a cup of tea while he waited; but after his conversation with Abrielle about clergy, along with the Monsignor's rudeness at keeping him waiting so long, Giuseppe was in no mood to enjoy his surroundings. When he was finally allowed into the inner sanctum, he was surprised to find the cleric hovering over papers on his desk and not rising to greet him. Rather than make a scene, he decided to sit patiently and thereby exaggerate Monsignor Hellman's attitude.

Finally, the priest looked up. "Inspector Guidice, my apologies to you for keeping you waiting. Our Pontiff's work is never done."

"I'm glad that you agree, Monsignor. That's why I'm here."

Monsignor Hellman looked perplexed at having the tables turned on him so quickly in the conversation. "I don't understand."

"Yes, but unfortunately I am here to ask questions, not to answer them. I need to go through the events of the day when His Holiness became ill. You and I haven't been able to speak about it so far, but I need to complete the file on what transpired so that we may close it."

"Certainly, I will help in any way that I can."

"Very well, Monsignor. Please share with me whatever details you know; and if you don't mind, I will take notes."

Monsignor Hellman began his account as the lunch was breaking up and Pope John invited everyone to join him for a walk through the gardens to walk off their meal. He provided little in the way of useful details, sticking to the most basic sketch of what had transpired. Toward the end of the story, he described how he ran ahead to the Papal Apartments to alert the physician to prepare the clinic. At the same time, the paramedics of the Swiss Guard were putting Pope John on a stretcher and attempting to stabilize his condition. Monsignor Hellman told how he had described the symptoms he witnessed to the physician in order to prepare him for the impending arrival.

"Did you see the medic who took His Holiness's blood sample?"

"I don't remember that there was a sample of Pope John's blood taken."

Noting a little uneasiness creep into Monsignor Hellman's expression, Giuseppe decided to press the point. "The Papal Physician confirms that he ordered a panel of blood tests. In the hustle of the clinic, he ordered a medic to take the sample, believing him to be from the laboratory's staff."

"As I said, I just don't remember seeing that. But you'll have to remember that I was also not able to stay in the clinic the entire time because of all the activity of the medical staff coming and going. The first thing we did was call in for back-up staff from a nearby hospital, which is kept on standby. But if you know a medic drew blood, why does it matter whether or not I saw him?"

"Because no one knows who that young man was or where the sample disappeared to." He paused for a further reaction and was rewarded with a nearly imperceptible glance.

"What do you mean? I remember hearing the doctors discuss the results."

At this, Giuseppe was a little disappointed. Perhaps the Monsignor was just surprised and not concealing anything. There was rationality to the answers, so he decided to switch tacks. "Monsignor, can we go back earlier in the day? Was there anything unusual about the lunch that you had with Pope John that day?"

"Not really. It was very informal; you know, not a working lunch. We discussed a wide variety of topics, as we often do when together."

"After His Holiness was stabilized in the clinic, and over the next few days, can you tell me who came by to visit or called to check on him?"

"Certainly I can. There were not too many. One of my official duties was to immediately call each member of the College and senior members of the Curia to inform them of His Holiness's condition. As part of that call, I asked each of them—those who live in Rome—to please avoid the Papal Apartments until they heard from me again. For the same reason, we limited the number of people who were notified to only those who required notification." After a pause of a few moments, he continued. "Of course, Cardinal Compeccio visited the clinic the next day. He had been present when His Holiness fell ill and needed to comfort himself after that sight. He spoke to the doctor at some length, about both diagnosis and prognosis."

"No one else visited?"

"Not that I recall."

"Monsignor, do you know Cardinal Compeccio quite well?"

"Not particularly. I made his acquaintance through his friendship with His Holiness, at meals just like the one we've been discussing."

"That's interesting." Giuseppe decided to drop the bombshell. "How is it, then, that His Holiness was unaware of your dinner meeting with him in Boston? You recall, during the Papal Tour."

Monsignor Hellman performed better than the policeman would have expected. He barely reacted. "I recall the dinner, of course. I don't recall if I ever mentioned it to His Holiness."

"To refresh your memory, you didn't. Do you care to tell me what the meeting was regarding?"

Thoughtfully, he replied, "I don't believe that I'd call it a meeting. It was more of a friendly gathering. I'm sure that we discussed Church gossip, but there was no official agenda. Cardinal Welty invited me to meet some of the other members of the College that I really didn't know well."

"There was no other purpose?" Again, he paused for a reaction, but found none. "I find it odd that Cardinal Compeccio would fly across an ocean for a single dinner, only for casual purposes."

"As I said, Inspector, I didn't know the Cardinal very well at all in those days. I would hardly feel comfortable characterizing his travel priorities."

Trying to shift gears quickly, Giuseppe said, "And you have no knowledge of our mystery medic…nor the missing blood sample…nor the falsified lab results that were furnished to the Papal Physician?"

Concerned that Inspector Guidice was better informed than he believed, the cleric decided to hedge his bets. "Inspector, I should be more comfortable taking you into my confidence, since you are also a friend of His Holiness." Monsignor Hellman got up from behind his desk and started to pace around the room. "I had never seen the medic, to the best of my knowledge, before that fateful day. I was being truthful about not noticing him in the clinic as well. Finally, I don't know his identity, to this day." At the far side of the room, he turned toward the policeman, who was glaring at him, waiting for the important details. "However, that young man approached me on my way home the following day. He presented me with the blood sample, told me that he was the one who had drawn it, and suggested that he was under instructions to deliver it to Cardinal Compeccio through me."

Incredulous, Giuseppe nearly yelled, "And you took it?" When he regained some composure, he continued in rapid-fire. "Did you ask any questions? Did it occur to you that the Pope's doctor didn't have a blood sample to go on? What did you do with it?"

Monsignor Hellman, Papal Secretary, took his time walking back behind his desk. Once seated, he looked Giuseppe in the eyes. "You must first believe that I would never do anything malicious to derail His Holiness's recovery. Once the young man, the 'mystery medic' as you called him, told me to deliver the sample to the Cardinal, it didn't occur to me to question him, nor to turn him down. What nefarious motive could there be for putting it in the hands of someone at the heart of the Curia? Earlier that day, I had also heard the Papal Physician discussing the test results; and I made the assumption that the sample in my possession must be some remainder. I jumped to the conclusion that this must be some protocol associated with papal tradition, of which I was yet unaware."

"And did you pass the sample on to Cardinal Compeccio?"

"Yes."

With that answer Giuseppe stood and excused himself, instructed Monsignor Hellman to discuss this conversation with no one, and hastily left.

Paul was sitting outside of a beautiful office building waiting for his call. They had constructed the sequence of interviews to maximize the surprise of the interviewees and to use all available information at each subsequent meeting. Giuseppe filled him in on what he had just learned, and they reviewed the best approach to their next confrontation.

Paul strode purposefully into the office building, up the grand staircase to the second floor lobby. There he introduced himself to the very proper gentleman on duty. "I am Special Agent Paul Regalo, here to see Cardinal Compeccio. No, I do not have an appointment. No, I do not wish to make one." These responses had the intended effect and the gentleman moved, more quickly than Paul would have expected, into the office suite.

He emerged a few moments later. "Cardinal Compeccio is finishing up a meeting and will be with you in only ten or fifteen minutes."

Paul decided this was prompt enough to not warrant making a scene and took a seat under the massive window opposite the staircase. After only a few minutes, a small cadre of clerics left the suite and a buzzer on the reception desk sent out its call. The gentleman stood and motioned for Paul to follow him. As they approached an opulent door, his guide stopped and Paul instinctively knew he was on his own.

Cardinal Luigi Compeccio was younger than he expected and more gregarious. He greeted Paul near the open door and invited him to sit in a comfortable chair where they could sit side-by-side. "Inspector Regalo, the Gendarmerie coincidentally just called me to let me know that you would be stopping by. May I offer you some coffee or tea?"

"No thank you, Your Eminence, I am fine." Paul noted that the Cardinal relaxed a bit at the proper use of the salutation. "Good," he thought, "I need to keep him guessing."

"What can I do for you today, Inspector?"

"First, I should be clear that I am not an Inspector with the Gendarmerie. I am a Special Agent with the United States Federal Bureau of Investigation. I am here in Rome to assist with the Vatican authorities."

"Very well."

"My initial line of questioning relates to your visit to Boston two years ago. Do you recall that visit?"

"Perhaps you could help with my recollection." The Cardinal was quickly becoming cagey. Paul had already researched his official travel records and confirmed that this would have been his only visit to the United States for at least a decade.

"As the Papal Tour was coming to a close, you flew to the United States on a private aircraft registered to a wealthy Italian businessman, whom you apparently know quite well. You met for dinner on the night of June twenty-fourth at the Union Club in Boston. Your dining companions included Cardinals Welty, Somers, and Johns, along with the Papal Secretary, Monsignor Hellman. Your sole purpose for the flight appears to have been this dinner meeting. Does that improve your recollection?"

Cardinal Compeccio was clearly uncomfortable at the detail of the policeman's notes. To make matters worse, he was unaware that anyone outside of the attendees had been aware of the meeting; now it occurred to him that the Pontiff was likely also aware of it. In spite of all these thoughts running through his head, he decided to bluster a bit. "I'm not sure why a private dinner between senior clergy of the Catholic Church would be of any interest to the FBI. Or perhaps you are simply doing the bidding of the Vatican Police."

"I am working at the request of the local police, not the FBI in this matter."

"And is the Vatican Police acting as an internal intelligence agency now, spying on members of the clergy? On whose authority would that be done?"

As he and Giuseppe had discussed, Paul decided this was the time to bluff a bit. "Monsignor Hellman discussed the gathering with us. Would you care to confirm his account of the agenda and purpose of the meeting?"

"I don't know what the young Monsignor might have told you, but it was a private meeting between senior clergy of the Catholic Church and not open to prying eyes. I will tell you that there was no formal agenda. As you can imagine, we have all known each other for many years, and we had spent a good deal of time together at the Conclave a year earlier, in which we elected Pope John. It was time to renew our friendship."

"Very well. I am sure that I will have a chance to confirm Monsignor Hellman's version of events when I meet with the American Cardinals on my return." That caused a slight squirm, and Paul could see the Cardinal making a mental note to alert his friends. "I'd like to turn our conversation now to the events immediately after His Holiness fell ill. What did you do with the blood sample taken from His Holiness?"

Now, true shock was written all over the Cardinal's face. All of a sudden, this whole scenario was becoming all too real. An outside police officer was connecting him to some secret meeting and now to destruction of evidence, in what he could only suppose was a serious police investigation. He struggled to answer the question with a question, one that didn't sound too evasive. "Agent Regalo, you are clearly a serious man concerned with serious business. What is it, exactly, that you believe I have done?"

"We know that you received a sample of Pope John's blood from Monsignor Hellman, the sample that was taken after he fell ill. I want to understand why that happened and, specifically, what you did with it after it came into your possession."

"I was not sure why it was being passed to me. Monsignor Hellman was not clear. I am a member of the Curia, the Prefect for the Congregation of Bishops, to be exact. Often around the Vatican, people assume that my office acts as sort of a Human Resources department for all things clerical. While this isn't true, I get many unusual requests. I assumed that the physicians had completed their tests and wished me to dispose of the remains, which is precisely what I did."

For some reason that he couldn't identify, Paul had the impression the Cardinal was telling the truth…at least partially. He believed that he was surprised to see the evidence fall into his lap; but he doubted somehow that it was really destroyed. He needed to probe a little further. "Weren't you concerned that the sample would be required later if tests needed to be rerun? Did it occur to you to save it for at least a little while?"

"Like I said, Inspector—sorry, Agent—I assumed that it was sent because there was a medical opinion that it was no longer needed. By the time I received it, I assumed it was spoiled. Doesn't blood have to be refrigerated or something?"

"And how did you say you disposed of it?"

"I didn't. I thought that an appropriate method would be to use the Sacrarium in the Sistine Chapel. It is essentially the sink in the Sacristy, which is used only to wash out sacred vessels that contained the Eucharist. It deposits its contents directly into the soil below the Chapel." Cardinal Compeccio was proud of how well he was thinking on his feet right now. He was equally proud of having actually *disposed* of the sample in a way that would make it nearly as difficult for Agent Regalo to retrieve as the one he was now describing.

Paul stayed just long enough to ask a few additional, unnecessary questions, to keep the Cardinal from realizing how important the blood sample was to him. Although he was disappointed at what he had heard, he retained a glimmer of hope that Cardinal Compeccio was lying. There were plenty of leads to follow up on, and Giuseppe needed his help on those.

He managed to find his way back to Giuseppe's office on his own and, once there, was directed by a junior officer to the surveillance room. Paul was surprised to find his friend sitting in the center of a very impressive amphitheater, surrounded by a video wall and technicians observing monitors at their personal stations. Giuseppe gave him the grand tour and introduced him to each of the technicians on duty. It turned out that every square inch of the public spaces in Vatican City was under video surveillance, as were many of the non-public spaces. Giuseppe let Paul in on the little secret of the Pope Tracker—as those in this room called it— the device that Pope John allowed the Swiss Guard to use to know his whereabouts. The Vatican Police were permitted to piggyback on the Guard's coordinate feed, and the team was using that to assemble a video cordon around the Pontiff's movements on the day of his illness.

One large monitor on the side of the room had been dedicated to a map overlay of Vatican City. On the map was a tracing of the movements of the Pope, with dots marking every fifteen minutes. All the cameras that covered that spot, along with coverage for one hundred meters in any direction, were cued up in the video recorders. The grueling task of watching those simultaneous feeds carefully on the master video wall was underway. Because the regular duties of the crew continued, the task fell to Giuseppe alone, who was using the mother of all remote controls to follow the Pope's movements and simultaneously look in all directions around him.

He paused the feeds when Paul returned, and the two now retired to his office to debrief each other further on their interviews. Paul's conclusion, perhaps stated more strongly than he believed, was that the blood sample still existed but Cardinal Compeccio was hiding it for some reason. They were in agreement that the meeting in Boston had some purpose that no one was willing to disclose, which made it highly suspect. Finally, no one was laying claim to knowledge of the mystery medic, leaving the two policemen now to place a lot of their hopes on figuring out who he was. Getting through the surveillance video quickly became their top priority.

At the thought of returning to the amphitheater, Giuseppe was obviously disappointed. Paul inquired, and his friend expressed frustration that they were just rehashing the same details they'd been through in the interviews. He also made some vague references to a conversation he'd had with Abrielle after their lunch ended. Paul could tell he was distracted and decided to make him a deal.

"Giuseppe, why don't you let me take a shift here? If you promise to drop me some on your way, you can take a nice buffet from your favorite trattoria to lovely Abrielle's apartment and enjoy a quiet dinner, just the two of you. I'll keep looking through the surveillance tape, and if we get a clear facial or license plate on the mystery medic, I'll have your men begin to process it through the appropriate databases."

"Are you sure, Paul?" This was the requisite response, but he didn't pause. "I can't thank you enough for being here and helping me like this. I will bring you back the best pasta in town and perhaps a little vino as well."

Giuseppe walked his partner back to the surveillance room and updated the arriving shift on the plan for the evening. They were clear that they were to give their full support to Paul. About an hour later, the Inspector General returned with a veritable feast, and his men forgave him for saddling them with endless questions from the FBI guy.

After eating, Paul really settled in—massive remote control in one hand and a Styrofoam cup of Chianti in the other. After another forty-five minutes, he had gotten the hang of the system. He decided to mark his place and focus on a targeted search rather than following the time-sequence. Advancing to the place and time at which Pope John arrived at the clinic, he isolated the nearest video feeds. Fifteen minutes later, he saw the medic approach with his messenger bag over his shoulder. He followed the feeds concentrically outward, retracing the medic's steps as far as he could, and dropped another video marker. He emailed this marker through the system to one of Giuseppe's team members, who then began to search additional footage, hoping to determine the arrival of the medic. Paul went back to the clinic video, this time looking to track the medic's departure. When his available feed was exhausted, he applied the same procedure and forwarded a marker to the technician.

He needed to stretch his legs. Paul was growing more comfortable with his surroundings and decided to take a short walk. If he happened across a small grocery store outside of the Sistine Chapel, which was admittedly unlikely, he hoped to refill his Chianti supply. His little walk turned into a twenty-minute stroll around the civil administration building in the cool evening air, and Paul was grateful for a clear head when he returned.

As he walked into the surveillance facility, the room was abuzz. The technician had been unable to locate any car or other means of arrival of the mystery medic. At first, it had also been very difficult to pick up his departure route. Then they noticed that they had been looking for a white lab coat as their cue. Sure enough, there was a white lab coat seen leaving the Papal Apartments; but oddly enough, the medic seemed to disappear behind the Post Office to the north of the Papal Apartments. This was odd for two reasons. First, he had arrived from a different route, north of Saint Peter's Square but south of the Swiss Guard barracks. Second, he had disappeared into one of the few blind spots in the surveillance system, almost as though he had some knowledge of it. This frustrated the technicians, who predictably dug in to unravel the mystery.

What the technicians described next was shocking. The medic had disappeared into the blind spot wearing a white lab coat and re-emerged from the far side of a nearby church wearing a Roman collar and windbreaker. His messenger bag was intentionally hidden beneath. They could only follow the medic, now priest, until he left the Vatican's grounds another block to the East.

Paul was suitably impressed by the work this team had done. He was not surprised when his follow-up questions were easily handled. They had run the video back until they found the clearest angle of the mystery man's face. It was being digitally enhanced as they spoke, and five different police agencies had been put on alert to run the photo through their databases as soon as it was ready. Before Giuseppe had a chance to share dessert with Abrielle, they should have a name to attach to their number one lead.

Chapter Sixteen

"Monsignor Hellman, I have asked you to meet this evening in order to dismiss you from your current position." His Holiness was direct and to the point. There was no sense in beating around the bush on this topic.

"Excuse me, Your Holiness. I can't begin to understand where this would be coming from. Is there some way in which I've let you down?"

"Certainly, Francis, you can understand that you occupy a position of extreme sensitivity. I must be able to trust you completely and never have cause to question where your loyalty—dare I say, interests—lie."

"Again, Holy Father, where is this coming from? What cause have I given you to confuse something that I've done with disloyalty?"

"Francis, I knew of course when I was introduced to you by Cardinal Welty that you were close to him. Because of my respect for him, I assumed that this was a positive endorsement that I should count in your favor. Now, that closeness raises concerns for me."

"With all respect to Cardinal Welty, in what way would an American Cardinal have an impact on the role of the Papal Secretary?"

"The strange thing is that I don't know exactly. And no, I know of no specific act of disloyalty; but your behavior has caused me to wonder exactly what I should know about that is clearly being kept from me." At this, Pope John realized that Monsignor Hellman was still standing just inside the door to the study and the duration of this conversation would make that awkward. He motioned for him to come closer and to take one of the chairs opposite his desk.

"Thank you, Your Holiness." After a pause, he rejoined. "I don't mean to be argumentative, Your Holiness, but the only thing clear about this conversation is that you wish to dismiss me. What exactly compels you to this decision?"

"I have come to understand that you are keeping company behind my back. Cardinal Welty is one, but there are others that you seem to be intentionally disguising. Do you care to elaborate and bring yourself back in to my confidence?" The Pontiff was not about to reverse his decision, but he felt the need to get to the bottom of what was going on behind his back.

Monsignor Hellman could assume the Pontiff knew at least one detail. "Are you speaking of the dinner that I was invited to in Boston?"

Pope John nodded.

"I was invited to a private dinner which Cardinal Welty was hosting for some of his friends in the College. Since I was there with you, as you would expect, the Cardinal wished to continue to expand my circle of acquaintances." Francis decided to try a little misdirection. "It's beyond me why he thought that someone like me would require more opportunity for introduction than you provide me in this role. Sometimes I think that these types of things are a bit of vanity on his part, wanting to be known as well-connected."

"Interesting. Go on."

"He had apparently invited Cardinal Somers and Cardinal Compeccio to join him for dinner. I think that Cardinal Johns heard about the dinner and our host felt obliged to invite him." Francis decided to improvise. "Cardinal Welty mentioned to the group that he had hoped to invite them all to meet with you while you were in town, but that the plans didn't work out."

Pope John saw an opening. "This all just doesn't make a great deal of sense to me, Francis. Cardinal Compeccio sees me regularly here at the Vatican. Were you aware that he boarded a private jet, solely for the purpose of your dinner? Why would he do that, if only to have the 'opportunity' to meet with me? More to the point, why would neither of you, whom I see regularly, ever mention the meeting? Finally, I'm not so old as to forget that you made an excuse of being too fatigued to dine together that night. In actuality, you were going out for a long evening elsewhere."

"Your Holiness, I can't speak to others' reasons for being there. I can only speak to what I was told and overheard."

Pope John was aware of the risk of sounding paranoid, but he felt the need to cut ties immediately. "Well, your lack of a rational explanation only leaves open the possibility that your role here is to keep abreast of my plans and let Cardinal Welty and his friends in on the details before I wish them to be. I have important work to do, and I need people close to me who are interested only in my well-being and my intentions. Do you care to share with me what commentary you provided to that group, that night or at other times?"

Monsignor Hellman realized that Pope John needed to believe that this was a thorough debriefing, so he decided to give a little. "Holy Father, you know very well that I have long been mentored by Cardinal Welty and that he is a conservative member of the College. When we all met in

277

Boston, you'll recall that it was less than a year after your election and…what you will probably agree became an infamous first homily. The Cardinals at that dinner simply seemed to want to be reassured that you had no other such pronouncements planned. By the time we arrived in Boston, you'd completed the American tour, and they were already somewhat comfortable that there would be no additional surprises."

"So this is the Conservative wing of the College, trying to keep tabs on me?"

"Holy Father, they simply understand that it's important for the Church to move at a measured pace. You have always accepted that point of view in the past."

"Francis, slow for slow's sake is not a choice they get to make. I don't care how much they feel they have a right to make it."

"Holy Father, this is not about their choice, this has been the way of the Church through the centuries. There is a reason that the College of Cardinals exists. They must guide the Pontiff, whoever that is, to see the Church in its rightful context—broadly and throughout the arc of history. This is not personal; they see it as their role."

Pope John stood as if he was about to dismiss his secretary for good. "Monsignor, I need someone in your role who is capable of reimagining the Church. I'm not talking about some fantasy Church that is a construct only of the imagination of some old fool in a white robe. I'm thinking as the Vicar of Christ on Earth and, with the guidance of the Holy Spirit, pointing Holy Mother Church toward a future most like her origins—a future of simple service, devoted to teaching others, through our example, about their Creator. You don't get to decide that you work more for a cabal of Cardinals than for me and chose to pick sides in the destiny of the Church."

Francis took his cue, stood, and moved toward the door. Before turning the handle, he turned to face the Pope. "Rest assured, Holy Father, I don't believe that The Time Keepers are some cabal. We all want the best for Holy Mother Church."

As the door opened, Pope John stopped him. "The Time Keepers? Why would you call them that?"

Francis silently cursed himself. "Oh, it's just a nickname that I've given to those in the College who have a conservative view on the pace of evolution in the Church."

"Monsignor, do you understand that I'm not discussing an evolution of the Church in any way? In fact, what I'm suggesting is a de-evolution, away from the modernity of the

Middle Ages and back to a time when the People of God were the Church and everything was to support them."

"But you don't have any right to redirect the Church in such a radical way, without even consulting the Curia and the College. They are leaders of the Church as much as you. What you have planned today will make your original homily on the lay uprising look like a comic strip."

"Lay uprising?" The Pontiff chuckled. "Is that what your friends are calling it?"

"No, Holy Father, that's all me. But what would you call it?"

"I think it's the right thing at the right time. We've spent centuries protecting our power. In the process, we're wrapping ourselves up in knots of rules and philosophies that are so complex they can't possibly keep up with the pace of change in the world."

"But why should we be concerned about the pace of change outside of the Church?"

"Because, dear Francis, we don't have all the answers. Until we admit that, we will continue to make pronouncements that make little sense at the time…or soon will make none. We are making ourselves irrelevant."

"And giving the world over to its own ideals is the answer?"

"Not at all. But rather than force the world to bend to our will, we should instruct by example. Strip everything away to its bare essentials. Teach the simple message that Christ taught, no embellishments, no philosophical liberties."

"And then what?"

"And then we trust. We trust God, our Creator, to fulfill our destiny through nothing more than His simple message."

"I'm still not getting it, I guess."

"Francis, isn't this what Christ did? He spoke a very simple message. The more the high-minded tried to wrap Him up in His own words, the more He cut through with simple ideas. If He were alive on Earth today, he would be confounding to all bureaucracy and entrenched interests, even in the Church we love."

"But the Church does that today. It stands up to powerful forces."

"Just not to the powerful forces within, huh? Within the Church, vast amounts of energy are wasted when people play politics and the ultimate goal is personal power, not service. Give this some thought, Francis. If you are correct, and the Church is still living this mission, there should be no objections to my plans. My plans are all about Christ-like service. They are about bringing people into a deeper connection with what their Creator wants them to be. Can you really imagine Christ sitting among the hierarchy of the Church today and allowing them to live so smug an existence?"

Francis walked back to the side of the desk where Pope John was seated, reached down for his hand, and bent to kiss the Fisherman's Ring. With that, and with no other words, he turned and walked out the door.

Pope John watched him walk down the short hallway. He wondered if, perhaps, he was a little too hard on the young Monsignor.

Chapter Seventeen

In the middle of the night, Monsignor Francis Hellman awoke, startled. His first thought was one of surprise that he'd ever fallen asleep; the preceding evening had been emotionally exhausting. He had run through such a gauntlet of emotions in his conversation with Pope John: surprise, anger, disappointment, and finally uncertainty.

For the balance of the night, he didn't sleep a wink and felt as though he'd replayed his entire life over in his head several times—although in no particular order. What haunted him most was his one and only parish assignment. He had always comforted himself that he was plucked from obscurity for the greater glory of God. But he always knew in the back of his mind that his mentors were saving him from a dismal start to a pastoral life. And now Pope John was proclaiming that the only thing that mattered in religious life was pastoral service and to inspire the laity to their own pastoral missions.

He tried. He would wake up early for the daily six o'clock masses at Saint Mary Church. He would read the homiletics—the shortcuts to a successful sermon—as he'd been counseled, to be fully prepared for each day. It took him a while to realize that, at dawn, the regulars weren't necessarily looking for a detailed exegesis on scripture. In fact, he began to feel that his thoughts were more interesting to himself than to anyone else. He began to see the congregants as unappreciative of his theological training. More than anything, he began to resent the fact that parishioners at other churches were fawning over some of his classmates. He would hear them referred to as "a breath of fresh air," continually invited into people's homes for informal conversation. But wait, he knew these guys; they didn't possess the intellectual gravitas that he could bring. Why was he so underappreciated?

Then there were the indignities, like being asked to spend time in discussion with the Women's Bible Study. He had nothing in common with these long-retired ladies, and he would often amuse himself by repeating the question over in his mind: is there a woman's Bible that we'll be studying? They were trying to relate to female figures in the Bible, to whom Francis had never really given any thought. Inevitably, one of them would want to talk about the role of women in the Church. He would have to reassure them, "Holy Mother Church elevates the role of women, evident no less than in the role of Mary in the life of Christ....Any trepidation about clerical roles is rooted in tradition; it was not intended as a slight against femininity....Women serve critical roles in religious life, and making them priests wouldn't enhance that in the least." He knew that these were tired consolations, but it was what he had to work with.

On most weekdays during the school year, he was expected to visit the parish school. Unfortunately for Father Francis, those days were almost harder than his evenings with the Women's Bible Study. He tended to gravitate toward the younger grades. The kindergarteners saw him almost as a mythical cartoon figure. That was a comfortable role. He didn't have to answer difficult questions, and everyone seemed excited to see him, including the teachers, who would get a short break. But any time he had to venture upstairs to the middle school grades, his self-consciousness grew. Somehow the tough kids still managed to stir his memories of his own awkwardness at that age. Without a doubt, however, the worst part of visiting the school was the diminutive nun that ran the place like a military ship. He could swear that she was his fifth grade teacher, come back to haunt him. She could see right through him and would not stand for his learning curve. He should come prepared to class and deliver a message that was age-appropriate for whomever he was visiting. As a result, he tried to sneak into and out of the school without being noticed. He knew the teachers would confirm his presence at their staff meetings.

Usually, he tried to find some quiet time after lunch to work on his Sunday homily. He understood that this was the major leagues. Morning mass was for the converted, who'd almost put up with anything he said. Sunday was when the discriminating Catholics would show up. These were folks who were capable of walking out of the church after mass and debating the quality of the message…right there for anyone to hear. If he could win them over, he would make his mark.

But inevitably, right when he was about to put his finger on just the right message, the phone would ring. The hospital? Oh, not again. This made walking the middle-school hallways seem like a walk in the park. How could he possibly be expected to become such an intimate part of someone's life on such short notice? These were, by and large, people he'd never really met. They were at their most vulnerable, and many were facing the prospect of dying. Father Hellman was expected to comfort them and know what they needed to hear. His therapist called this a conflict of the highest order. In reality, this was service at the most basic level.

Francis often ate dinner alone in the Rectory, because his Pastor was invited to some parishioner or another's home five or six nights a week. It was a regular movable feast, with the Pastor as the only moving portion. But that left Francis alone with his thoughts; and the late evenings were the hardest. He would take his time cleaning up after dinner, because by the time he retired for the evening, his overwhelming feeling was that he'd wasted another day.

Then he was fished from a sad obscurity by his mentor, who knew that his talents were better spent elsewhere. At least that's what he'd always told himself. Now he was conflicted. He saw the merits of what Pope John was telling him, that those menial tasks were not so menial after all.

Now, Monsignor Hellman could tell that dawn was about to break. He had turned his life over so many times in his mind, now it was time to turn it over to God. He dressed without showering and made his way to the Papal Apartments. He had decided to sneak in to the Papal Chapel and quietly attend His Holiness's morning mass. As he hovered around the corner from the entrance, he felt like an outsider for the first time; he noticed that the Swiss Guard was unusually visible.

It had been a fitful night for the Holy Father also. He had done his best to rest, but he had found himself getting up earlier than usual and heading to his chapel to pray before saying his morning mass. He was deep in his own thoughts as he went through the rituals. As he genuflected at the end of mass and turned to leave, he could have sworn he saw Monsignor Hellman sneaking out the door.

Back in his study, he decided to call Abrielle for some tea. He knew that she was busily trying to catch up after her day off with Giuseppe. Within fifteen minutes, Abrielle was setting up a pot of tea across the room. He could see that she was distracted and a little tense. Unfortunately, he would have to find time later to inquire about her. There were so many things going on right now.

Just then, the phone on his desk rang. It rarely did, and this particular ring signaled that it was a caller who had been given his private number. He lifted the receiver and Abrielle made a hasty exit, as she had learned to do in such cases. On the phone were Giuseppe Guidice and Paul Regalo. They wanted to update the Pontiff on the progress that had been made overnight in the search for the mystery medic.

Pope John listened intently. He was more concerned than ever when the men told him that the medic might actually be a priest. After his conversation with Monsignor

Hellman, Pope John was concerned about any hint of clerical disloyalty, and now somewhat more likely to believe it.

He filled them in on that conversation with his now–former Papal Secretary. As he recounted the story, he adopted Monsignor Hellman's moniker of The Time Keepers to generally describe conservative clergy and those who might wish to derail his plans. He made the connection that perhaps the medic was part of this movement, formal or informal as it might be. As he spoke, he realized for the first time the fear that he had placed in the minds of many clergy over the *lay uprising* they imagined him leading. Not that they were against the laity—he didn't believe that for a minute. But any challenge to the status quo could be so upsetting for anyone.

"Monsignor Hellman just told me that the dinner in Boston was an informal gathering. But he also avoided the simple, factual observations that I made. I'm not convinced that this group is without purpose, as he would like us to believe. It may be necessary for you gentlemen to expand your investigation and see if there are things that you can learn about their associations with one another, and perhaps an even wider circle."

Paul jumped in. "I can call in some resources from the FBI in order to check travel visas and see if there were any other gatherings we can confirm. We'll try to shake something lose quickly, but I really think the investigation is here in Rome."

"I agree. We need to stick to our game plan, Holy Father. We are trying to locate the medic or priest, who we assume is local. We are also not giving up on finding the remaining sample, although that is temporarily a dead end."

"Very well. I know better than to drive your investigation from the back seat."

Not ten minutes after they hung up the phone, Giuseppe had a note handed to him by one of his officers. It simply said, "Please come see me in my office when you have some time." It was signed Francis Hellman. As expected, Giuseppe immediately handed the note to Paul, and they were out the door of his office almost before they had a chance to think.

They arrived at the anteroom of the Papal Secretary's office and found Monsignor Hellman waiting there for them. He didn't really feel entitled to sit behind his old desk any longer, but he invited them inside nonetheless.

"Gentlemen, thank you for coming so quickly. You may not know it yet, but last night His Holiness dismissed me from my office." They knew, of course, but didn't say. "I have not felt it was appropriate to be here until you could be here as well. Frankly, I'm so confused that I'm not sure if my intentional disloyalty today is greater or lesser than my subtle disloyalties of the past." The two policemen looked at each other, not quite sure if or how to break the awkwardness.

Paul decided to be the instigator. "Monsignor, you obviously have something on your mind that you wish to share with us; just go ahead, please."

"When we spoke earlier, Inspector, I told you about the dinner I attended in Boston. In the course of telling you that story, I left out certain details."

"Go ahead."

"I was telling the truth when I told you that there was no formal agenda; however, the gathering was not purely social. The Cardinals who were present, Welty, Johns, Somers, and Compeccio, are part of an affiliation of senior clergy."

"Yes, The Time Keepers." Giuseppe was playing a hunch.

The Monsignor was shocked. "You know about them?"

"Please continue."

"I don't actually know much about them myself, but yes, they called themselves *Custodes Tempus*, The Time Keepers. They initiated me at that dinner and told me that the society is always composed of a majority of the College of Cardinals and often the Holy Father himself. Whenever the reigning Pontiff is a member, he reissues a secret charter to establish the society's rights to exist. They, in turn, act as a check on any future Pontiff who might stray too far from the will of the majority. In effect, they have found a democratic way to exercise influence over the Throne of Saint Peter."

"We should leave the self-serving editorials about 'democracy' out of it, Monsignor. We need to know the facts of what they asked you to do."

"Other than some basic questions about how the Papal Tour was going, to whom Pope John was speaking, etcetera, they only asked that I continue to exert whatever influence I could in the future. They asked nothing specific."

"So they inducted you to keep tabs on Pope John. Why?"

"You might recall that shortly after his election, Pope John gave a homily that some clerics viewed as offensive. They thought the new Pontiff was seeking to diminish the stature and role of the clergy. With his visit to America, they feared that the excitement might renew his energy. In fact, it did somewhat; after his tour the Holy Father began a correspondence with a handful of Bishops regarding plans for the Church."

"And you relayed that information to this group?"

"Oddly enough, that wasn't necessary. I shared my personal beliefs with His Holiness, just as I always had. But Cardinal Compeccio had become friends with him and was part of the correspondence circle. Custodes Tempus would have known everything it wished from him." Monsignor Hellman paused and looked at each man in turn. "Come to think of it, why does any of this matter? You don't really think that this group had anything to do with the Holy Father's illness, do you?"

Now the policemen looked at each other. Giuseppe spoke first. "Monsignor, the Holy Father fell suddenly ill after having lunch with you and Cardinal Compeccio. His blood test was falsified and the sample stolen…and then ultimately passed to you, and from you, to Cardinal Compeccio. You now tell us that you and the Cardinal are part of a secret society that disagreed with the direction of this Pope and considers itself as a check on Papal authority. What should we think?"

Monsignor Hellman slumped in his chair and looked at the wall, beyond the policemen. He whispered, "Dear God." When he had collected himself, he looked at his inquisitors and asked, "What can we do now?"

Paul handled this one. "We need to look at anything you have regarding this group. We need to hear anything that you can remember, which might prove helpful in either identifying the young man who gave you the blood sample or locating that sample."

"Certainly. The first thing I was taught was that all official business would be conducted under a letterhead containing the name of the society. I received a roster containing the names of all the current members, which I was instructed to destroy as soon as I had memorized it. The second thing I was taught was that only the current leader of the society knew the location of the official archives and that everything that wasn't bound for the archives was to be destroyed upon reading."

"And who is the current leader, if not His Holiness?"

"Cardinal Welty," came the somber reply.

"So you have no documentation from Custodes Tempus?"

"I have no official documents on the society's letterhead. The closest thing I have that might be of interest to you would be the correspondence that followed the Papal Tour. The originals are in the Papal Archives, but I kept copies here in the office for His Holiness's reference."

"Tell us about that correspondence."

"If you suspect that Pope John's plans are at the heart of all this intrigue, these letters will give you some insight. While he doesn't detail his plans, you will see two sides of his correspondence with a number of Bishops. The letters—"

Just then, Monsignor Hellman's cell phone rang. When he checked the screen, the reaction on his face showed that he clearly recognized the caller ID.

"Buongiorno. Yes, I understand." Then there were a few moments when the Monsignor was just listening. "No, of course I have not told them anything about us. What good would it do anyway; their investigation has nothing to do with us, correct?" He looked at the policemen, as if they could guide his conversation. "I thought you were going to destroy it. No, Cardinal Welty hasn't told me the location, but if you are afraid to retrieve it, I could do that for you." After a few more moments of silence, Monsignor Hellman clicked off.

Paul couldn't contain himself. "Who was that and what did they want?"

"That was Cardinal Compeccio. He was concerned that I might lead you to him."

"Was he referring to the laboratory sample?"

"Yes. He confirmed that it has been taken to the Archives of Custodes Tempus, which, as you can assume, are somewhere on the Vatican grounds. The good news for your investigation is that the sample still exists. The unfortunate news is that none of us seems to know why we're hiding it."

Paul turned to Giuseppe with a puzzled look on his face. Giuseppe read his mind. "Why would the Cardinal save the sample if it indicated foul play? Why would he hide it if he didn't know the reason?" He turned back to the Monsignor. "What else did he say?"

"At one point when he was referring to the archive for the society, he mentioned a number, fifteen twenty-one, almost synonymously."

Giuseppe wanted to get back to suspects and motives. "Yes, but if the Cardinal doesn't know why he's hiding the sample, perhaps it's a dead end. Certainly, *he* would seem to be a dead end. Let's get back to the letters."

Monsignor Hellman obliged. "The correspondence was primarily among a group of Bishops that His Holiness befriended on his tour of America. They had apparently been left with high hopes that change was imminent."

"And why wasn't it?"

"The Holy Father had second thoughts. In no small measure, I'm sorry to say, because of Cardinal Compeccio and myself. He was part of the correspondence circle, as a close friend and advisor to His Holiness. We continued to argue the practical side of things—the need to consult the Curia and the College, among other things."

"I will need to review those letters. Paul, I might be able to come up with a hint of who we should actually be considering a suspect, if not Compeccio."

"Gentlemen, I will turn everything over to you, but I doubt that they will be much help. The reason that the originals are part of the Papal Archive already is that they are highly philosophical; there is nothing personal or conspiratorial in them."

"How about the roster of members of Custodes Tempus? You said that you were expected to memorize it so that you could safely destroy it."

"Certainly I will write down all the names that I can remember. You will have to forgive me however; we didn't exactly have club meetings. I have never met many of the members."

Giuseppe settled in behind the Papal Secretary's former desk as he started to bring him papers to review. There were surprisingly few letters between His Holiness and the group of Bishops who were encouraging his plans. Paul headed back to the Gendarmerie to see if the FBI or any of the law enforcement agencies had come up with a match on the mystery medic.

Chapter Eighteen

By the time Paul arrived back at Giuseppe's office, the men looked exhausted. They had been meticulously scanning employment records for Vatican employees, hoping to turn up a match. Some of the records were catalogued in a database, but they quickly exhausted those and were now going through the more backward departments. One thing they had going for them was that all employees had been photographed going back almost twenty years; so if the mystery medic was working at the Vatican, they would have a picture. Another thing they had going for them was that they understood the urgency around finding this individual. While Giuseppe hadn't given them a thorough briefing, they had realized the connection to the Papal medical clinic and that this must have serious implications.

Paul settled in behind Giuseppe's desk and phoned Washington DC. A trusted friend, Special Agent Deana Cutler, had been tasked to assist him and was leading the electronic efforts. The FBI laboratory had enhanced the electronic photo file and was matching it against an Interpol database. This was a bit of a long shot, because there was no real reason to believe that this person was an international criminal. He was just as likely to be another cleric caught up in something he didn't understand.

Special Agent Cutler had taken it upon herself to also conduct some searches of airport security databases, specifically searching footage of people traveling through the main airports around Rome. She reasoned that if this person was involved in a crime of such staggering proportions, he might be professional and therefore not local. She told Paul that her hunch had paid off, though not nearly in the way she'd expected. She found a match in a scanned image on a passport for an American national who had been living in Italy for some time. The prior fall, Sam Walters had traveled home to Philadelphia for a vacation. His return trip had been captured by an experimental passport scanner at the Customs desk in Rome. Upon further research, she discovered that Mr. Walters had a Masters in Art History and had moved to Rome four years earlier. She found a reference to his thesis online, something about the art collection of the Vatican. She also found that he had been arrested for petty theft not long after arriving in Italy. The records she could access indicated that he had not been in any further trouble.

Paul thought to himself, "I'll be the judge of that." What he said was, "Deana, I can't thank you enough. I'm sure the Vatican Police can pick up his trail from there, now that you've provided us with a name. Can you e-mail me all that you've collected so far? I'll call you tomorrow with an update on where we are."

Paul pulled his cell phone out of his pocket and called his partner with the good news. "We've got a name on the mystery medic: Sam Walters, of Philadelphia. He doesn't seem to be a hardened criminal, but we need to talk to him as soon as possible."

"Ask Paulo to work up a dossier from our records to supplement what your team found and send a car to pick up *Father* Walters." Giuseppe thought he was being funny. "Right now, Paul, I need you to get over to the Vatican Library. I have run across some things in Monsignor Hellman's papers that might be interesting leads for us."

A short while earlier, the Monsignor had created a list of those persons he could remember from the roster of Custodes Tempus. Next, he was asked to turn over any correspondence he had had with each of these individuals, whether related to the society or not. It was only then that the cleric sheepishly remembered saving the cover letter that had accompanied the roster. At the time, it seemed innocent enough because it wasn't on the letterhead and oddly didn't seem to reference anything secretive.

As Giuseppe reviewed the letter, written by an obscure Argentinean Cardinal, his host was narrating. "I have never actually met the Cardinal, Inspector. I remember thinking at the time that it was odd that the letter wasn't on society letterhead and that it didn't even mention the society, or the roster that was enclosed. As a result, I assumed it was permissible to save it."

The policeman shushed him. "Let me read this please, Monsignor." Then he noticed it; the letter mentioned 1521 as well. He read it aloud. "...the work you do will help to assure that there will never be another 1521." He looked at the young cleric. "You said that Compeccio mentioned something about fifteen twenty-one on the phone just now?"

"Yes, he did. It didn't seem to make sense."

"Why does that date seem familiar?" He pulled out his smart phone and typed *1521* into the search engine. The results returned all sorts of real estate listings where the house number was *1521 Main Street*, and along with many other seemingly random results. Then he retyped it specifically as AD 1521 and repeated the search. The first result was an article on the Reformation. He scrolled quickly through the article. "That's it. That was the year Martin Luther was excommunicated. Why would members of Custodes Tempus be so obsessed with that year, Monsignor?"

"I'm not exactly sure. The society was founded by Pope Urban VIII almost a hundred years later. He was famous for excommunicating his friend Galileo for his heliocentric views. Some believe that his treatment of Galileo was harsh but was intended to keep from repeating the mistakes of the past. When Luther's popularity began to spread during the early Reformation, some believe that it was allowed to fester too long. Perhaps Pope Urban was hoping to avoid repeating the mistakes of the past; and perhaps Custodes Tempus is looking to remind itself of the same thing."

As the two men continued to review documents and discuss the implications of Pope John's plans, Special Agent Paul Regalo was racing across Vatican City toward the Vatican Library, *Bibliotheca Apostolica Vaticana*. As he raced around the *Casina Pio IV*, the Villa of Pius IV, ironically now home to the Pontifical Academy of Sciences, he took a shortcut through a small grove of palm trees on the south lawn. When the library building was in sight, he called Giuseppe for further instructions.

"Great, Paul, I think we've got some ideas. I'm not sure exactly what you're looking for, but I want to focus on anything having to do with the Protestant Reformation or the year 1521."

"Okay, give me a little bit of time to get my bearings and I'll call you back."

As Paul rang off, he bounded up the stone steps and through the arched doorway. He was shocked at how quiet it was, though he didn't know exactly why that surprised him. There was an attendant's desk just inside the front door, but no one was manning it. He found himself in what appeared to be a main reading room, but the room looked more like the Sistine Chapel than a library. Every vertical surface and the ceiling were covered with intricate frescos. It quickly became apparent that this was more reception area than library stacks. He searched around until he found a more utilitarian space, with traditional bookshelves and even a gallery encircling the space that contained more manuscripts. Paul scanned the perimeter wall for about thirty minutes, hoping to find anything that looked interesting, but he began to lose hope, realizing that he really didn't know what they were looking for. Just then, he thought he discerned a system of organization that he could decode. With a few minutes of more focused investigation, he located what he might be looking for—a collection of manuscripts related to Martin Luther and the early years of the Reformation. His Latin was not as good as it had been during his school days, but he located a book that appeared to contain the excommunication proceedings of Luther: *Decet Romanum.*

As Paul reached for the volume, a curator approached him suspiciously. "This must be the attendant I skirted on the way in," he thought.

She politely, but firmly, asked, "La lettura di passaggio, por favore?" When he seemed lost, she tried again. "Do you have a reading pass?"

"I'm sorry, I don't know what that is. But I am here at the request of the Vatican Police."

She was not impressed. "Well, why don't you step outside and call them. Actually, please step outside either way. No one is allowed in here without explicit permission and a piece of identification on file at the Vatican Police station. If you choose to call them, that's your business, but if you stay here I will be calling them."

Out of necessity, Paul sought better cell phone reception outside and phoned the Inspector General of the Vatican Police. "I have run into a little bit of a roadblock. Apparently, your little town has some pretty strict library procedures. I

304

will need you, or at least one of your men, here to help me get access to the collections."

Within just a few minutes, Giuseppe had gathered up all the materials that he and the Monsignor were reviewing. He strongly encouraged his host to become his guest at the Vatican Library and help them find some fresh clues. Francis was actually eager to stay involved and grateful for the opportunity to try to redeem himself.

Giuseppe and Francis arrived at the steps of the library to join Paul. As soon as the three men entered, the Inspector General made his presence known. In fact, he enlisted the curator who had confronted Paul, along with one of her assistants, and the five of them set out into the main Reading Room with a clear purpose. She led them directly back to the shelf that Paul had been investigating. This time, the curator herself, with a gloved hand, reached for the book in question. She confirmed that it was, in fact, the famous *Decet Romanum*. As she laid the book on a viewing stand, Giuseppe pulled his colleague aside.

"Paul, we really aren't looking for a book. We're looking for a hiding place for the lab sample; or at the very least, we're looking for an indication of the archives of Custodes Tempus."

"Agreed. We should let the library staff go back to their work and give ourselves some room to snoop around." The curator was still eyeing Paul warily, and he was anxious to be rid of her.

When they were alone in the collection, Giuseppe turned to the other men. "We need to look for any indication of the archive for your society, Monsignor. This is a good area to start, given the references to 1521; but we're probably looking for something that's a little out of place—a marker. If we can't find anything here, I propose we move to the Galileo collection, given that the society was founded by Urban VIII."

"Yes, Inspector. I suggest that we fan out."

About twenty minutes later, they had covered sufficient area that they found themselves creeping into adjacent, but unrelated, collections. Giuseppe was motioning to the others, drawing them back to where they began their search, trying not to cause a stir among the employees or those with official reading passes. As Monsignor Hellman approached, he noticed the top shelf for the first time. Only from this new angle did the clock stick out. It was an unusual piece, different from all the standardized timepieces on the walls of the library. They would later discover that it was one of the first examples of a Huygens clock. It was placed there ironically by Innocent X, Pope Urban's successor, who initially built the archives of Custodes Tempus. Christian Huygens had developed the pendulum clock, using the lessons learned from Galileo's experiments on motion.

No sooner had Monsignor Hellman fixated on the clock than Giuseppe Guidice noticed where he was looking and the same thought crossed their minds. He reached up and lifted the device from its perch. There was a click that froze Paul in his tracks. He hadn't made it back to the others and was walking near the wall at the end of the bookcase. The others couldn't hear the click, and because he found nothing particularly unusual about the clock, Giuseppe returned it to its original place.

"There it is again," Paul thought. Then he said, "Inspector, pick up that clock again, please."

The two men looked at him quizzically, but Giuseppe complied. "What are you wondering?"

"I'm not wondering anything. I believe you just opened a door." He located the point nearest the source of the sound and started to rummage around on the bookshelves. It was then that he noticed a small indentation on the flat side of one of the bookcases, just large enough for the tips of his fingers. He pulled and the case moved as though perfectly balanced on massive hinges. "Can you bring the clock here, gentlemen? I believe you found the key to The Time Keepers."

Paul opened the bookcase, now a door, wide enough for the three of them to enter. There was a narrow spiral stairwell in front of them. Each of them flipped on their smart phones, illuminating the stairs in front of them. Giuseppe, still holding the clock, found a small shelf with a receptacle that appeared to just fit the clock's base and set it down. Comfortable that he had found the return keyhole, he closed the door behind them to keep prying eyes away. He chuckled as he thought of the curator wondering where the police had disappeared to.

The trio descended stairs for what seemed to be three stories. They found what appeared to be a little-used reading room, illuminated adequately from some indirect source that wasn't immediately evident. They paused to take in what they were seeing; having been on this journey together, no one needed to tell them. They were inside the secret archives of Custodes Tempus; a collection of documents that told a parallel history of the Catholic Church. This was a history that not every Supreme Pontiff was invited to share. The possibilities were staggering.

They all knew what they were here to find, so they fanned out. There would be time enough later to inspect all the extraneous materials. The only time one of them got sidetracked was when Paul found a volume of King Henry VIII's love letters to Anne Boleyn. These were the kinds of documents that the society used to convince Popes how to act. In this case, these letters gave Pope Clement VII certainty that the young king was nothing more than a randy young man and the Pontiff should deny his annulment.

In the far corner of the room, Giuseppe found a table that appeared to be a staging area. There were a number of items and documents lying next to what appeared to be a catalogue and some index cards. Someone was acting as librarian for the archives and had fallen behind. Right in the middle of the table was a Styrofoam case containing three small vials of blood. It had a sticker with a number, which cross-referenced with the catalogue and indicated that this was a blood sample from Pope John XXIV, taken on the day he fell ill. Giuseppe took the time to gather his accomplices and have them take note of the evidence, should it later be questioned.

He put on a pair of latex gloves that he found in a dispenser on the table, carefully placed the samples in a plastic bag and led the men back to the stairwell. With the clock once again lifted from the shelf, all three men heard the lock click open, and Monsignor Hellman pushed the bookcase open. Fortunately, there was no one around to see them emerge from the wall; Giuseppe was not ready for the world to know about what they had discovered beneath the Vatican Library.

When he had emerged into the sunlight outside the library, Inspector Guidice's phone picked up a cell tower and indicated that he had a voicemail. It was one of his men letting him know that they had Sam Walters in custody and the Roman police had permitted them to bring him back to the Gendarmerie for questioning. The policemen split once more. Paul agreed to take the blood samples to his friends at the Do Good Brothers Hospital on the Tiber; Giuseppe would return Monsignor Hellman to his apartment, where he was placing the cleric under house arrest overnight. They would meet back at Giuseppe's office to jointly question their mystery man.

Paul was extremely careful with the samples and presented them to the laboratory director, Dr. di Alberto, as though they were holy relics. The doctor quickly assembled a team—intake clerk, technician, and Paul's favorite records clerk, Maria—and agreed to expedite whatever tests they could do. Paul requested the broadest spectrum of toxicology exams possible, but before they could even complete the intake paperwork, the technical team concluded that the condition of the samples rendered them impossible to test adequately. Any results would be suspect, and the police had already discussed the issue of the lost chain of custody and the value of any results.

Rather than risk damaging what remained of the blood samples, Paul asked the team to prepare them as best as possible for safe transportation. While they were busying themselves with this task, he made two phone calls. The first was to Deana Cutler, who would make all the preparations with the FBI Laboratory at Quantico. The second was to the FBI attaché to the U.S. embassy in Rome, who would include the samples in a diplomatic pouch that would be flown overnight to Washington DC.

After fighting Rome's famous traffic to the embassy and then back to Vatican City, Paul found his partner waiting less than patiently for the interrogation to begin. Together they entered the room and found young Sam Walters scared out of his wits.

Without introducing Paul or his American credentials, Giuseppe launched into the questioning with the thickest Italian accent Paul had ever heard, all the better to keep the young foreigner off-guard. "Seniore Walters, you are an American citizen, no?"

"Yes," came the timid reply.

"Have you been in Rome long?"

"A little over three years, sir."

311

"Have you ever been to the Vatican?"

The young man swallowed hard. He should have expected this. "Yes, sir."

"Have you ever been a priest?" The Inspector's accent was clearing up.

"No, sir."

Paul jumped in and introduced himself. He laid his FBI credentials on the table in front of young Sam, to ratchet up the seriousness. There was nothing like the bright badge and large "FBI" printed on the identification to create focus in a witness. "Sam, you just tell us everything you know, and we'll compare your story with our notes and score you for accuracy at the end."

"Yes, sir. I received a call a couple of months ago. The man suggested that I could make a sizable amount of money and not have to do anything more dangerous or illegal than to draw someone's blood and pass it off to someone else."

"Did he say why he picked you?"

"No, he didn't. But he seemed to know that I had a criminal record and was having trouble finding a job."

"Had you ever met this man before? Do you know who he is?"

"No, to both questions. He claimed that he was a Bishop and worked at the Vatican."

312

"When you say 'claimed,' did you not believe him?"

"He had the collar and cassock, but he just didn't carry himself like a Bishop. You know, they seem to carry themselves like they're above the fray; but he was nervous and twitchy."

"How much money did he promise you? Did he explain what this was all about?" Paul was on a roll, and Giuseppe knew to leave him well enough alone until he hit a roadblock.

"He gave me some story about how they needed a clean blood sample for a drug test and all I would have to do is pass it off to an accomplice and disappear. He offered me one hundred thousand euros, which is like five years' wages for someone like me."

"Did you know how to draw blood?'

"No, he arranged for some back-alley doctor he knew to train me. I used to do a little drugs, which is how I got myself in trouble with the law, so needles weren't completely new to me. I think he knew that somehow."

"What happened the day of the event?"

"He had me waiting by the phone for his call. That morning he called and gave me instructions. I met him outside my apartment and he gave me everything I would need. He provided me with a map and directions to the Papal Apartments. I started to freak out a little at that point; but he showed me the money, and I was in too deep already. Besides, he told me that I was to pass the blood to the Papal Secretary at his office. That made it all seem on the up-and-up to me. Shouldn't it?"

Giuseppe tried to reassure him. "Sure, I understand now. Tell us what happened next."

"I loitered around until I heard the excitement in the gardens. I waited ten minutes and then followed the directions to the clinic. I walked in and saw Pope John lying there and all these people hurrying around. When the doctor called me in, I was surprised he didn't see my hands shaking and throw me out. But I took the samples and left as quickly as I could. I waited a day and took them to the Papal Secretary's office, along with a sealed note for him. That night, there was a knock on my apartment door, and by the time I opened it, whoever had knocked was gone and my money was sitting in the hallway in a brown bag."

As if on cue, there was a knock on the door of the interrogation room. In came one of Giuseppe's men with a file folder. He handed it to his Inspector General with a wink. "This may be of use to you, sir."

Giuseppe opened the folder and saw a job application, filled out by Sam Walters about six months earlier. It was a standard Vatican form, printed from the master employee database. The original form had been stamped "denied," with a notation about the criminal background check. He paid particular attention to the name of the hiring manager who had reviewed the application, then he handed the file to his partner, letting him in on this key piece of evidence.

"Sam, I only have one final question: if you saw this Bishop again, would you recognize him?"

"Absolutely, sir."

Chapter Nineteen

Late the next morning, Pope John was sitting in his study and wondering why his calendar was so clear. "Oh, yes," he thought to himself, "I fired my secretary. I need to get Monsignor Donatello in here quickly to pick up the slack."

Not long after, Giuseppe Guidice and Paul Regalo arrived. He heard their voices in the hallway and discovered them giving orders to the seminarians on duty. He also noticed that they had a stranger with them, who Special Agent Regalo called Sam.

The Pontiff poked his head out of his office into the hallway and asked, "Gentlemen, when you have a moment, may I have a word?" He watched them position Sam behind one of the desks, out of the way. When they appeared ready to join him, he turned back into the room and positioned himself behind his desk. "May I ask how your investigation is going…and what exactly you're doing out there?"

As was his duty, Giuseppe spoke up and took the lead in answering the Pontiff. "Holy Father, we believe that we have concluded our investigation. We are here to determine if that's the case and to allow you to witness us wrapping it up."

"Really? You know what happened?"

"If you don't mind, we will ask for your indulgence. It would be best for us if you were just as surprised as the others during the course of this morning's conversations."

"What others? What do you have planned?"

"We have invited all those who attended your luncheon the day you became ill. Until they arrive, I will ask you to hold any other questions. It will likely be evident to you when we are ready for you to enter the conversation."

"Very well." Pope John found himself in an unusually subservient position.

"We should also tell you that each of our guests believes that they are here at your request; and so, we will ask you to play host at the beginning of each meeting. I apologize if that's awkward, but we felt that was the best mindset to have them in."

He glanced at each of them, wondering exactly what agenda he was agreeing to. "I can't say that I understand, gentlemen, but I will try to play along."

Each of the guests had been asked to arrive at a slightly different time, for a very specific reason. If they showed the appropriate respect for the Holy Father's invitation, the intrigue should be well underway, even before the final guest arrived.

Monsignor Hellman was the first to arrive; out of necessity, he was the only one of the guests who knew his visit was at the request of the Vatican Police. As a result, he greeted the Pontiff awkwardly. "Holy Father, I am sorry to be here under these circumstances. I can only hope that my assistance to Inspector General Guidice and Special Agent Regalo will help you in some way."

"It sounds as though you are more aware of what's going on here than I am, Monsignor."

As politely and deferentially as he could, he continued. "Holy Father, I called the Inspector General yesterday morning to offer whatever assistance I could. The conversation you and I had the day before struck me deeply, and I wished to make amends for whatever harm I might have caused you, however unintentional."

The four men chatted for the remainder of their ten-minute head start. When a bell in the study indicated that the next guest was arriving, the two policemen positioned themselves so that Cardinal Compeccio would not immediately see them.

"Holy Father, how nice of you to invite me over today." He greeted Francis second. As he still believed Francis to be the Papal Secretary, it did not seem the least bit odd for him to be there. "Monsignor, it's nice to see you again. I hope that I am not too late." Then he noticed the two others in his periphery and turned to greet them as well, although with a bit of fresh discomfort in his voice. The many possible intents of this gathering were now racing through his mind.

"I believe that you are right on time." That was about all the Pontiff could say before turning the meeting over to its true host.

Giuseppe obliged. "I'm sorry if we lured you here under false pretenses, Cardinal Compeccio. Our intent wasn't to deceive you, but simply to manage the conversations that took place prior to this gathering. We have invited everyone who plays a role in our investigation to join us here for another run-through of the events surrounding His Holiness's illness."

"Very well," he agreed, cautiously.

For the remaining fifteen minutes, before their final participant was scheduled to arrive, the investigators ran through the chain of custody of the blood sample. They discussed the fact that the blood sample never made it to a laboratory at all; that it was delivered, first into Monsignor Hellman's custody and then into the Cardinal's hands. Also, a forgery of a legitimate laboratory report had somehow made its way into the hands of the Papal Physician and into the files at the hospital. They asked the Cardinal again to confirm that he destroyed the sample. Paul's role in all of this was to watch the two witnesses' reactions to the news, but it was difficult to ignore Pope John's.

Then Giuseppe asked the question that would signal a great deal. "Cardinal, would it surprise you if we told you we found the blood sample?"

His reaction was stoic, and Paul's one thought was that this was not a man with whom he would like to play poker. "Well, of course it would surprise me." He didn't want to commit to more details, or to repeat the lie, lest they were actually telling the truth.

While Paul observed the Cardinal's reaction, Giuseppe lowered the boom. "Holy Father, with the assistance of Monsignor Hellman, we did recover the original samples of your blood, taken within an hour of when you fell ill in the garden. Paul sent them off to the FBI Laboratory in Washington DC overnight; this morning we spoke to our liaison there. Special Agent Cutler was able to confirm that it was your blood, that it contained a toxin, and that you were, in fact, poisoned."

Pope John couldn't look at them and chose instead to look at the floor. Cardinal Compeccio glared at Monsignor Hellman, who had also decided that the floor was the most interesting feature of the room. The policemen watched everyone very intently.

To everyone's surprise, Monsignor Hellman broke the silence. "Holy Father, I am sorry that this is true and that I had a role in it, even though I knew nothing of the threat to your life. Cardinal, I am sorry to you also. I found myself caught between two competing disloyalties, and all I could think to do was to fall on the side of truth."

The room fell silent for the remaining minute or so, until the bell rang again. The policemen remained concealed against the wall as the door opened. In strode the final member of the fateful luncheon, Mr. Jacques Fournier, Director of the Vatican Museum. He was a bit surprised to see other people present, but he recognized them all as good friends and fell quickly into greetings. The only thing that set him on edge was the somber mood in the room, until Giuseppe stepped forward and into the doorway behind him. Down the hall, seated behind the obscured desk was young Sam Walters. He stood up slightly and nodded to the

Inspector General, who motioned that he should sit back down and then closed the door to the outside world.

"Mr. Fournier, thank you for joining us. Special Agent Regalo and I needed to review the events surrounding the Holy Father's illness one more time, and we wished to speak to all of the lunch guests together."

Somewhat relieved by the bureaucratic tone, Fournier found a chair and agreed. "I am sure that you know all that happened, but I'm happy to speak again, Inspector."

"Very well. If I am correct, the four of you make up the entirety of the guest list for the luncheon, which took place immediately before His Holiness fell ill in the garden." He looked around and received their assent.

Paul took over. They were changing up their interrogation routine, although the conclusion of this one was nearly certain. "And you all knew each other quite well before that day; you know each other quite well, in general?" Again, no one objected, so he continued. "Do any of you know anyone who would wish for the Holy Father's death?"

Cardinal Compeccio jumped from his seat. "Dear Heavenly Father, no!" He looked at the Pontiff directly. "Holy Father, you must know that I would never wish you harm." The biblical parallels to Judas's protests were not lost on anyone in the room.

"Cardinal, I didn't accuse you of anything. I simply asked if any of you—His Holiness's close friends—if you were aware of anyone who might think this way."

Giuseppe took on an apologetic tone. "Mr. Fournier, we should bring you up to speed on some of what we shared with Cardinal Compeccio earlier. Shortly after His Holiness came to the medical clinic in the Papal Apartments, his blood was drawn. That sample disappeared on the way to the hospital for testing. It turned up later in the possession of Monsignor Hellman and was then passed to Cardinal Compeccio. We have been trying to determine how that all happened, however, because they claim no knowledge of why that all occurred."

He paused for effect. "Back to the matters we're here to discuss. Holy Father, was anyone here aware of your plans for the Church?"

The Pontiff thought about this. "Monsignor Hellman knew the great extent of them, obviously. Cardinal Compeccio was part of some deliberative correspondence that I wrote to some senior clerics, but not in tremendous detail." He thought about this some more and hedged his statement. "At least that's all he knew from me."

Giuseppe jumped around from topic to topic, appearing to be filling in the holes in his notes. "Does anyone remember what was served that day? The chef has informed me that it was a relatively simple meal: some fish and pasta. Does that sound correct?"

Pope John added, "I remember a lovely cheesecake for dessert."

Monsignor Hellman thought that didn't sound correct. "Not that this matters, but I don't remember a cheesecake. We had some fruit."

The Inspector helped out. "Well, that's just it, Monsignor. You didn't have cheesecake. You and the others at the luncheon had fruit, prepared by the chef. Mr. Fournier brought Pope John's favorite dessert as a gift for His Holiness." He paused long enough for the others in the room to catch up; again, Paul was watching the guest being discussed. "The chef was instructed—by Mr. Fournier—to only serve this to His Holiness and to save the remainder for later meals."

Paul stepped in for the next phase of discovery. "Holy Father, I received a detailed report from our FBI Laboratory this morning. Your blood contained the botulinum toxin. It is relatively common for contaminated food to cause botulism, or food poisoning, and if the attack on you had been somewhat less successful, it would have certainly been chalked up to such an accident. However, to cause the paralysis symptoms that were misinterpreted as a possible stroke, the dosage had to be extreme. Slightly more and it would have certainly been fatal. As it was, the attack was sufficient to cause dizziness as well as the first signs of descending paralysis. It is quite rare that an infection is severe enough to be determined through a blood sample. If we hadn't found the early blood sample, your body would have certainly dealt with the toxin sufficiently that we couldn't detect it through the blood at this point. The fact that you recovered over several weeks is very consistent with botulism."

Out of respect for what was just laid at the Pontiff's feet, the room was still. Then Fournier could wait no longer. "Gentlemen, are you trying to draw some spurious connection between my dessert and some unfortunate but still mysterious source of food poisoning?"

Again deferential, Giuseppe joined in. "We agree completely, Mr. Fournier, there is no evidence whatsoever that the cheesecake was the vehicle for the toxin."

Frustrated, Cardinal Compeccio rejoined. "Then would you please give us your conclusions? It sounds to me like you are accusing one of my friends of poisoning another."

"Oh, I am. Mr. Fournier delivered a poisoned cheesecake, solely for the Holy Father's consumption, at a time he could be certain it would be consumed. He then decided to implicate you, Cardinal Compeccio, and you, Monsignor Hellman, by having the blood sample pass through your custody. We knew that we couldn't solve this case simply with the blood sample. We also needed to understand the history of the medic and the person behind that whole charade."

"And what did you confirm?" This time it was the Holy Father, in the most pitiful voice.

"When Mr. Fournier arrived, I had the fake medic positioned outside. Holy Father, this was the young man you heard me refer to as Sam, Walters is his name. Sam indicated to me that Mr. Fournier was the impostor Bishop who hired him to take your blood and pass it to the Monsignor and the Cardinal, in turn. He had come across this young man, and his criminal record, when Sam Walters applied for a job some months ago at the Vatican Museum. He bribed him with cash and consoled him with a story that this was all to dodge a simple drug test. This was our triangulating evidence, all pointing to Mr. Fournier as your attacker."

Paul closed the noose further. "I asked the FBI Laboratory to also review the falsified lab results. They confirmed what the hospital already knew: these were not authentic documents. Mr. Fournier, we haven't located your accomplice for this piece of your plan yet, but with your deep experience in the art world, you must have had many to choose from."

"Well, I'm not going to stand here and take these accusations." With that statement, Jacques Fournier turned on his heals with as much indignation as he could muster and opened the door. As soon as he looked up from the door handle, he saw two of Giuseppe's men appear at the end of the hallway in front of him; and he froze in his tracks.

Giuseppe punctuated their appearance. "I don't think you understand; you are under arrest. There is no chance that this case will fail to hold up."

As Jacques turned back into the room, Pope John looked directly into his friend's eyes. "But why?"

"Why? Are you kidding? You were going to decimate the collections of the Vatican. For centuries, Our Lord delivered the most talented artisans in all the world right to our doorstep. We patroned them, nourished their talent, and gave them the most spectacular canvas on which to work—The Eternal City. Since then, we have curated these collections in a manner that no private party, and few governments, could have. Now you want to throw it away? You want to convert the most precious assets of humanity into a fund to spend on a problem that cannot be solved?

Dozens of occupants of the Throne of Saint Peter were smart enough not to squander these gems. In your arrogance, you thought that you could do what you please with them?"

Paul was still filling in his notebook on the case. "How did you come to believe this? What caused you to take action?"

"His Holiness came to me quite some time ago, after we had struck up our friendship, and started asking questions about the true size of the Vatican collections. This wasn't too unusual; it's common knowledge in my job that each Pontiff, at some time or another, wants to know how much it's all worth. But then I started getting questions about the world art market—how big it was, how resilient—and those conversations distressed me. I knew that Cardinal Compeccio was also close to His Holiness, and I assumed that as a member of the Curia he might know more about his administrative intentions. So I asked him, and he confirmed that Pope John had discussed a plan to sell some artifacts. Apparently, he had come to believe that he could sell quite a bit, without deterioration in the world market."

The Cardinal squirmed at the mention of his name and felt a need to defend himself. "Why on earth did you think you should try to implicate Monsignor Hellman and me?"

"Well, if the Inspector found your hiding place, he must be aware of Custodes Tempus. Perhaps Monsignor Hellman gave it up? In any event, the directors of the Vatican Museum have known about The Time Keepers for about three centuries. We have been keeping our own chronicles of the society—shadowing the shadow government, so to speak." Then he began speaking to the larger group again. "When the Cardinal confirmed the Holy Father's plans for me, I knew they wouldn't sit still, but I wasn't sure they would act decisively. Their history is full of delayed action. So to cover my trail, I figured I'd put the evidence in their hands. I guessed, apparently correctly, that Cardinal Compeccio would be too arrogant to destroy the sample. I guessed, incorrectly, that if the trail led to their secret archives, all investigation would be consumed by inquiry into the society…or shut down by them."

Paul had to know the answer to this particular riddle. "Cardinal, why did you act so suspiciously? I understand why Monsignor Hellman, a relatively junior cleric, would feel compelled to pass you the sample when instructed to do so. But I cannot understand why you didn't destroy it when you had the chance."

The Cardinal didn't have the arrogance left in him to defend himself. "I was concerned that one of The Time

Keepers may have actually been involved and felt an obligation to play my role if requested. I suppose that I don't have the courage to be disloyal, even if it's the right thing to do." This last part he directed at Monsignor Hellman.

The Pontiff finally couldn't contain himself any longer. "Who is this Custodes Tempus? Can someone explain to me what's going on here?"

Giuseppe sympathized. "Holy Father, there is a great deal that we will discuss to give you the full picture. The short story is that there is an ancient society, known as Custodes Tempus, which has given itself the responsibility to measure out the pace of change in the Church. They keep a secret archive here in Vatican City, and we discovered that this is where Cardinal Compeccio hid the blood sample. It is not entirely coincidental that we uncovered The Time Keepers in the course of this investigation, because Mr. Fournier suckered your other friends into implicating the society as part of his plan."

PART IV - SEMPER ADELANTE

Chapter Twenty

In the aftermath of the discoveries a weak earlier, Pope John XXIV had some serious business to attend to. Monsignor Antonio Donatello was with him in his study, going over the amazing series of events since their last meeting, two weeks earlier. At that meeting, which now seemed so long ago, they had met to embark on their new mission together. At the time, neither of them could have had any idea what bizarre revelations were about to become public, nor that Antonio would be summoned to replace a disloyal Papal Secretary.

Pope John had to let his new assistant know all the facts they had uncovered about the attempt on his life. They covered the collusion of Cardinal Compeccio and Monsignor Hellman, which obscured the investigation and might have ultimately given a killer a second chance. They discussed the person responsible for the attack, Jacques Fournier, with whom they had both dined numerous times over the years.

And finally, and if it was possible, the most shocking revelation of all: the existence of a secret society of clerics, who for centuries had taken it upon themselves to act as a governor on any evolution of Church thinking.

Then it was time to get down to business. Antonio had quickly come up to speed on the routine of the Papal Household and the requirements of his new office as Papal Secretary. There was a review of the coming week's calendar, which was expected to now return to normal—as normal as a Pontiff's calendar can be. There were many roles that the Church played—both religious and secular—and it had been a couple of months now since everything had been running as it should. As they should have expected, rumors were running wildly through the Church about the events of the previous weeks; as a result, there were dozens of pieces of correspondence from Cardinals and Bishops. These included letters of support, well wishes, and inquiries, depending upon which particular rumor that cleric had heard. Monsignor Donatello had been advised to put together an internal press release of sorts to alert the world's clergy about the facts of the matter…at least *enough* of the facts to get everyone on the same page.

After a couple of hours, Pope John dismissed his new secretary in order to review the letter that had been saved for last. There was a letter, posted from the United States, from Monsignor Francis Hellman. The Pontiff didn't quite know what to expect, and, concerned about his emotions, had asked for some privacy to review the letter and compose a response. He would ring his assistant when he was ready to resume work on their plans for renewal.

Dearest Holy Father,

I am grateful to you, if in fact you are taking the time to read this note. It was imperative, for my own sake, that I communicate my sorrow and regrets that you would have ever had cause to find me disloyal. I must start by saying, not by way of excuse, that I accepted the continued service to Cardinal Welty before I had the chance to know you, and this was certainly before I understood the strength of your mission for the Church. My disloyalty also belies the true affection that I developed as I came to know you personally.

In the course of our last conversations together, and even in your decision to remove me from my role, I have come to understand the blessed gift that you've offered. My sole and consuming passion now is to learn how to be a priest, a true servant of God's people. When I was younger, I took the easy way out when I was recruited out of parish life to a life of administrative cloister. At some point in the future, my prayer is that I will serve your vision for the clergy through my humble service to my parish.

When I returned to the Diocese of Cleveland last week, Bishop Merrick accepted me back into ministry. At my request, he has appointed me as an Associate Pastor in a suburban parish, to intern with a veteran and beloved Pastor with a very successful history of mentoring young priests. Part of my reason for writing is to confirm that I may return to parish ministry with your blessing. I vow to you that I will take every measure to learn the proper way to serve the Lord's people. I believe you would agree that we need clergy who are motivated more than ever to put their entire spirit into their ministry.

In closing, I will share that I have encountered a great deal of murmuring in the clergy—administrative and pastoral. For my part, I have said nothing about my experiences in Rome. However, the Church is a wonderful gossip mill, and I am afraid that many of the events of the last few months are being accurately relayed. Fortunately, the clergy's confidence in your guiding hand is keeping the tone of the conversation very hopeful. Of course, I will do whatever I can over the course of my life to serve the vision you have outlined.

Your humble servant,
Francis Hellman +

Pope John sat with the letter for an hour or so while he had another cup of tea. He read it a few more times, considering the best way to respond. Ultimately, he decided to write a personal letter to Bishop Merrick. While they had never met, he knew the Bishop to be an early mentor of Francis and felt that he would ensure its subject matter reached a wide audience. This may put Francis's humility at risk, but it would also give him a fresh start, without the hint of scandal; he now believed that Francis had earned that fresh start.

He picked up a sheet of his private stationary.

> *My Dear Bishop Merrick,*
> *I have heard recently from our dear friend Monsignor Hellman and thought that I would write you in reply, as his Ordinary. It warms my heart to hear that you have so quickly taken Francis back under your wing and found him an outlet for his pastoral work. As diligently as he pursued his duties in my household, I have no doubt he will apply himself to becoming a faithful tender of a portion of your flock.*
> *Pax,*
> *H.H. John XXIV*

When that task was completed, he rang for Antonio, as it was time to get on with their work. Pope John remained behind his desk, because he knew that Antonio would want a solid writing surface at which to work. When Antonio arrived, the Pope asked, "Monsignor, do you recall our last conversation on the subject of my plans for the Church?"

"Certainly, Holy Father. We had lunch together on the terrace, followed by a short walk through the gardens. We ended up here, and, if I recall correctly, you became quite animated in your descriptions."

The Pontiff was now wishing that his secretary had a somewhat less-precise memory. "Very well, I will accept your characterization, although I may have used the word *passion* myself. And you recall the three elements of our plans?"

Antonio felt privileged that the Pontiff had used the word *our*. "Yes, Holy Father, I do. We need to redirect the focus of the Church toward supporting the laity in their vocations to each other. We need to support that focus by placing the priesthood in direct service of the laity, which can involve removing bureaucracy and moving our Bishops and Cardinals closer to their flocks. Finally, we need to tangibly demonstrate the importance of putting our blessings in the service of others. All of this involves leading by example, and this final element will start with the planned sale of some notable artworks from the Vatican Collection."

"Outstanding, my dear Monsignor. That was the best synopsis yet; I believe that every time we discuss it, our thoughts become crisper, which is a sign of its correctness in my mind."

"Holy Father, I don't want to get too far ahead of ourselves. These are daunting objectives. These are cultural changes."

"I understand."

"What if the laity is already as involved in the mission of the Church as it can handle? In the modern world, the demands on people are extreme, and the distractions are worse."

"Yes, Monsignor, but we must remember the example of other Christian communities and their largely self-governing structures. I don't believe for a minute that the Catholic laity is less capable of leading. We must retrain the clergy to simply stay out of their way. Do you disagree?"

"No, I don't. But at the same time, we're going to put Bishops and Cardinals closer to laity and ask them to get involved more in direct pastoral care. Isn't that going to simply exacerbate the current problem?"

"There, you have identified a real risk. That's why we need to ensure that these are the correct Bishops and Cardinals before we push too fast. I believe that retirement may be an important component of this element."

"Then where do we begin, Holy Father?"

"Excellent question, Antonio, that's what we need to tackle today. I believe that we should tackle these in reverse order. As I believe you'll remember, the last time we spoke, we used a similar approach: it all began with your paper and concluded with the key mission of service *by* and *to* the laity. Similarly, I think we need to begin with what we alone can control and then move to increasingly broader objectives, where we need to lead the change. Beginning with the third element, we need to engage the new director of the Vatican Museum to develop a plan of sales. I want to push her to be aggressive but thoughtful. We need to maximize the value of our decisions."

Antonio was feverishly writing notes for his next steps. "Then we will need to set up a program as a beneficiary of the funds that are raised."

"Correct. However, I don't want this to be hidden away in some corner of the Curia. This should represent the core of a new Department of Missionary Work."

"Very well, Holy Father, I will start putting those plans in place. Is there anything to be done on the second element at this stage?

"Yes, but more cautiously. Ultimately, we need to work toward a list of retirees from the senior clergy, along with a much longer list of replacements to expand the corps of Bishops."

"What about Custodes Tempus, Holy Father? Should they be at the top of the list?"

"No, Monsignor. I don't want to focus on retribution, or be seen to. Remember that they weren't formed as an attack on my pontificate; they are centuries old. It is my belief that they will find a very difficult time recruiting for a generation or two, if they ever succeed again. In the meanwhile, they may choose to redirect their efforts and take a higher road. Ultimately, they may discover a role in the Church that is somewhat less clandestine and arrogant." He paused to reflect. "No, I'm not worried about them."

"I don't know the criteria that you might wish to use. Age is obvious, but not very effective if you are looking to truly create a meritocracy."

"Correct. I will ask you to contact Cardinal Suarez in Los Angeles. He has quite a good handle on the personalities, as he has taken it upon himself to meet as many senior clergy as possible over the last few years. When I was in Los Angeles two years ago, he introduced me to a hand-selected group of progressive senior clerics. He and I have had a meeting of the minds on this topic, and you can trust his judgment."

"Very well, Holy Father, I will reach out to him today."

"As the two of you develop a list for my review, I would like it to include three things: a list of suggested retirees, an indication of the easy decisions that we could make quickly, and a list of those we must enlist to help with the expansion. In other words, we need the most progressive thinkers to help us by deepening the leadership in their own dioceses."

"Can I recommend that this is also the group that will form a Synod to discuss the broader plans? It will be good to create a forum for discussion and inclusion."

"I couldn't agree more. However, it should also include some of the senior clergy who are likely to provide a thoughtful, not belligerent, counterpoint. We can't remake the Church by repeating the insular practices of the past. We must invite dissent. Our singular goal should be to seek assistance on the process of renewal."

"Yes, Holy Father. I will begin to draft an agenda for your review."

"It needs to cover all three elements of our plans. I will make an address at the outset, making clear that we are gathering to discuss *how* to best execute our plans, not *whether we should* execute our plans. By then, the attendees will have certainly witnessed some of the retirements take place; which reminds me, we should open with the elevation of a handful of new Bishops." He thought for a moment, the expression on his face indicating how perfect he thought this idea. "Then I should like one of those new appointees to address the Synod. I should like him to articulate his personal concerns and what he would most like to know about his new role. That should open the dialogue nicely."

"I don't understand."

"One of the things I would like the Synod to address is how we mentor and train our new Bishops in the ways of pastoral care. Some of the attendees will take the lead to build a curriculum fashioned after the old-style clergy—humility, service, and connecting with the lives of the faithful. By having this conversation out in the open, you will also witness some of our doubters coming around to a new appreciation of where we are wishing to take the Church. They will ultimately become the most powerful advocates. The converted are always the most passionate missionaries."

"This is exciting, Holy Father. I cannot wait to get working on this." Antonio hesitated a moment. "But may I ask, what are we to do with the Curia? Certainly, you intend to reform it, but where does that fit in to our plans?"

"Indeed, I agree that reform needs to come to the bureaucracy of the Church, both as a matter of emphasis and to reduce the concentration of clerics in nonpastoral roles. However, I think we can keep that as a relatively low priority right now. In fact, the vast apparatus might turn out to be useful to us in our reforms."

"That makes sense. Have you given much thought to what it should ultimately look like?"

"We can start working on an organizational plan that looks very simplified, certainly compared to its recent forms.

Perhaps one of our many historians can help us to look back to the early days of the Church for some inspiration. Ultimately, the structure that we fashion should support our ministries of service, rather than simply provide oversight and rules. It would seem that the three elements of our plan are a good starting place."

The two continued their discussion through lunch. When it seemed they had developed a robust approach, there was a very large body of work ahead for the new Papal Secretary. Pope John dismissed him with a simple blessing for the work ahead.

Chapter Twenty-One

Pope John started the afternoon reflecting again on the letter he had received from Monsignor Hellman. It was remarkable in its humility and hopefulness—even more remarkable for such a short time having elapsed. The Pontiff quietly said a prayer for him and the journey he was undertaking.

Then his thoughts turned to the others who would have to be influenced in a similar direction. Many of them would be far less impressionable than Francis Hellman and far more intent on hanging on to their power and prestige. It was up to him, however, to convince them to go quietly. He decided that it was time to compose the letter that he would send to those on the short-list of retirees—those who needed to be gone before the Synod convened.

He crafted a letter carefully over two or more hours, in the quiet of his study. It began, as his letters usually do, on a positive note. He thanked them for their answer to their

344

vocation and the decades of service that all of them had given to the Church. Next, he went into a thoughtful explanation of his plans for the Church, leveraging the beautiful summary that Antonio had just shared that morning. He touched on each element of his plans, with scriptural foundations and historical examples to support his rationale. Then he made the somewhat clumsy transition to why they didn't fit, in their current role, within the new Church. There was room in each section for him to customize the letters with personal references; but the message was the same: "We need new blood." He would invite each to a life of private prayer for the future of the Church, perhaps living in community with a religious order. If they were members of the College, their letter would include an explicit clarification that they would cease to be an elector, should a future Conclave be convened in their lifetime. Each would conclude with a sincere blessing for a healthy and happy future for the cleric.

There was no doubt that the minute the letters went out, the recipients would begin calling their peers, carefully inquiring about their state of affairs without hinting at their own firing. The coordination of these letters would have to be handled carefully in order to minimize embarrassment to the recipients, further encouraging them to leave quietly. A few of them could be expected to respond in a very positive manner, expressing their support for the Pontiff and his plans. They would immediately be put on the invitation list for the Synod, where they could support the efforts in a very personal way.

It was time to bring Antonio back to review the letter and discuss logistics. When Antonio arrived, he quickly dove into the letter and then sat quietly. He couldn't quite decide how to give his feedback.

"Come on, Monsignor, tell me what you think. You don't exactly look excited about my work."

"Well, in all honesty, Holy Father, I think it's too much. I think these letters should be more direct and to the point."

"You believe that I am embellishing? Shouldn't they understand the background and my reasoning?"

"With some, all that is required is an expression of your will that they step down. For the others, that will not be sufficient; in their cases, any explanation simply becomes a topic of argumentation."

"Don't they deserve to understand?"

"They do, I agree. With your permission, I would field those questions and insulate you from the complaints and politics. You should be free to plan the Synod and spend your time with those who are focused on the positive future."

Pope John thought about this as he paced around the room. "Okay, then. Please write up what you propose and we can review it tomorrow during our morning meeting."

"Yes, Your Holiness. We must also remember that the final version of these letters will be on file in the Papal Archives. We will keep each letter standardized, so as to keep personalities out of the history books."

By the middle of the following day, each of the letters had been approved for the two dozen senior clerics who would receive the first wave of *Invitations to Retirement*, as they had begun to call them. The list was developed based upon the initial conversation between Monsignor Donatello and Cardinal Suarez. The list for the next wave would take significantly more time to develop.

Within just a few days of the letters having been sent, the responses began to trickle in. Not surprisingly, Cardinal Welty was the first to call. Monsignor Donatello had tried to handle the request personally, as had been discussed earlier with Pope John, but Cardinal Welty had two things going for him. One, he was too stubborn and arrogant to allow any Monsignor to stand in his way. Two, he knew the Pontiff's personal phone number—one of very few, even among the College of Cardinals, to have that privilege.

The conversation began as formally as most do. "Holy Father, thank you for taking the time to answer my call."

"Of course, Your Eminence, what may I do for you?"

"Nothing for me, Your Holiness. I just thought that your letter deserved a personal reply."

"I wasn't aware that it required one; but very well."

"Holy Father, I respectfully decline your invitation to a new ministry. I am certain that the faithful of the Archdiocese of Boston will benefit from some continuity during the 'significant change' that your letter referenced."

Pope John was stunned. He had let the Cardinal know that he was appointing a replacement, and Welty was calling to say what, that he was going to continue to show up to work and challenge the new Bishop for control? "I'm sorry, I don't think I understand."

"My apologies, Your Holiness, I don't mean to be circumspect. I was calling to let you know that you don't need to appoint a Coadjutor; I will stay in the role and continue to lead the faithful through whatever change is coming." It was a bold move.

"You weren't circumspect, John. You were unbelievable." It was the first time that the Pontiff, any Pontiff, had referred to him by his given name. "I don't believe that you understand the intent of my letter to you. I am not appointing a Coadjutor to wait for your retirement. I am appointing a new Archbishop of Boston, who will be sitting at your desk the first day I so chose. I suppose you could choose to wrestle with him for the chair behind the desk, but that would be quite a spectacle. You will be effectively neutered in your role; and everyone will know that I've appointed your successor. Your choice is simply to take the high road and retain some dignity or to become a laughingstock of the history books." He had never been so direct in a conversation such as this.

There was silence on the other end of the line. Pope John was uncertain if the Cardinal Archbishop of Boston had just dropped dead from shock.

When a faint voice returned to the conversation, he could hear the Cardinal ask the question of resignation quite weakly. "Is there any way that I can delay this move?"

"Why exactly?" The Supreme Pontiff of the Roman Catholic Church now had regained his rightful place in the conversation and was going to complete it on his terms.

"Your Holiness, to your point, everyone will know that you control my office when the dust has settled. I would appreciate your indulgence in letting me retain a little dignity. I should like to announce my retirement and have a traditional transition period, rather than have it be so obvious that I was forced out."

Pope John's heart softened along with the softening of Welty's defenses. "I will grant you your request, Your Eminence. You should announce your retirement immediately. This will actually allow some distance in time, between your announcement and the other appointments I will be making. You should also announce that you have requested that I appoint your successor as well as a transition date. What I am most anxious to see is that you and your peers form a body of support around the coming changes. That should significantly defuse any rumor-mongering."

"I understand."

"If you would draft that announcement for Monsignor Donatello to review, we will give you our approval as quickly as practical. Our ability to stick to your suggested timeline will be dictated by our comfort with the amount of support we are receiving from your peers." He had just put Cardinal Welty in charge of the cheerleading squad for the changes he was proposing.

With complete resignation in his voice, he replied, "I understand, Holy Father. Thank you for your kindness and understanding in this regard."

"Very well, Your Eminence. I hope that you know I do wish you well in your retirement and hope for your continued prayers. Good day." With that, the Pontiff rang off. He looked around the room, suddenly feeling very alone.

Later that day, he would receive a visit from his old friend, Cardinal Compeccio. They hadn't spoken since that day, when all was laid on the table before them. Since the Cardinal would never visit unannounced, Pope John had time to arrange the scene the way he wished. He expected an act of contrition, and so he tried to set the mood as politely as possible. When the Cardinal was announced by the young seminarian on duty, the Pontiff invited him to join him at the leather club chairs. Between the chairs was a tea set with a fresh pot of water and a selection of their favorite teas.

In spite of the relative informality of the setting, the Cardinal was somber. "Holy Father, I hope that you understand that in spite of everything that happened, I do have great respect and affection for you. May we discuss the letter I received?"

Pope John ignored the overture and focused on the request. "Of course, Your Eminence, I assumed that was why you wished to visit today. What is on your mind?"

"I understand that a certain amount of retribution is required because of our transgressions, but does it have to be so complete?"

"You of all people, Luigi, should understand that this is not vengeance for its own sake." This time, the use of his given name drove home the point that they had become very close, all the while he was being spied upon. "You were privy to my deliberations over the last couple of years and you know how I have struggled with my own ego in all of this. You also know that I can't leave people in place who are so committed to the destruction of my plans. I can handle forceful debate, but I cannot permit deceitful undermining."

The Cardinal took this incorrectly as an invitation. "How can you be sure, even after your discernment process, that your ideas are the correct ones? They are so foreign to the way Our Lord's Church has evolved."

"I have to trust the way the Spirit has spoken to me."

"And so I become a sacrifice to those ideas?"

"Luigi, you don't have to think of your lot in a negative way. You can think of this change in ministry as an opportunity. This is an opportunity to learn about the real mission of the priesthood."

Cardinal Compeccio grew defensive at this implication. "I have given my life to the Church. I know what the priesthood is about."

"When you took up your vocation, were you entranced by your family's historic role as leaders of the Church, or excited about serving…even if it might be in obscurity?"

The Cardinal wanted Pope John to think well of him, so he listened thoughtfully as the Pontiff described again how important he thought it was to get back to the roots of the Church. He described the importance of Christians serving the world, out of humility and devotion to their Creator. The instruction moved him a great deal.

"Well, Cardinal, the Church is asking you for one additional sacrifice. It wants you to be a regal example of humility and service. It is up to you to decide exactly how you wish to answer that call."

The Cardinal started to see his past behavior as a parallel to all those biblical disciples who would answer the Lord's call, only to be challenged beyond their capacity. Luigi Compeccio began to see this Pope and his mission in a new light.

All that he could think to say in response was a simple apology. "Peter, I'm sorry for not trusting you."

AFTERWARD

Francis Hellman was sitting among a small group of people he had only just met. The dinner was very enjoyable, and the company was friendly, but he couldn't shake the feeling of awkwardness. And then, as if to put an exclamation point on the sensation, Special Agent Paul Regalo approached.

"Monsignor, do you mind if I join you? I thought it might be nice to catch up."

"Of course, Agent Regalo, but please call me Father. I have tried to avoid using my honorific since returning to parish life. It is going out of favor, as are many outward signs that could be misinterpreted as vanity."

Not sure how to respond, Paul could only think to say, "I suppose I have noticed that trend recently."

Father Hellman wanted to change subjects. "You did a wonderful job as best man."

"Thank you. It's nice to blend into the background rather than have all the usual best man pressures. After all, with the Pope officiating at your wedding, even the bride and groom are apt to fade into the background a bit."

"But he also did a wonderful job. He is so close to them and so genuinely happy for them that it came through in the mass."

"And Abrielle looked beautiful, just beaming up there. I don't think that even the Supreme Pontiff could outshine her today."

"Absolutely. They are so happy together; they are a great testament to the Sacrament of Matrimony. I am sure they will be very happy for a very long time." Father Hellman looked around the reception hall. "I must admit that one of the only things I miss about being at the Vatican is seeing Abrielle's lovely demeanor on a daily basis."

The two sat in quiet for a few minutes enjoying the sight of Giuseppe and Abrielle's friends and family on the dance floor. There were so many little cousins running around, it really looked like a normal scene from any wedding reception. The only exception was that it was being held in Vatican City.

"So, Father Hellman, how are things going for you? Someone told me that you had moved back to your home diocese, is that right?"

"Thanks for asking. I am back in a sprawling suburban parish on the outskirts of the Cleveland Diocese. I really love the opportunity, although that may sound as odd to you as it does to most people. My new life is exciting because of the challenge it represents to me. I have to quite literally change the natural tendencies of my personality in order to succeed as a parish priest. Left to my own devices, I suppose that I am a bureaucrat at heart—preferring to hide away in an office, like any other cog in the wheel.

"And what are you finding in your new ministry?"

"People really need me. They need my attention and support; they need me to become a part of their lives. That's not something I'm naturally comfortable with; but I am rejoicing in the simplest duties, like the baptism of a teenage convert that I shared in recently. That is a huge moment in their lives. The old Francis would have looked at that as a half-hour on my calendar, but today I am a part of that family and celebrating with them."

"That's fantastic."

"Now, mind you, I am still a terrible preacher by all accounts. But I think I can learn that skill. The hard part for me was my personality…in all honesty. I needed to get past the title of Priest and just be comfortable getting to know my congregation as people first. In some ways, I am too introverted for this role; and I think I tried to rely on the title and status to carry me through the duties."

"What do you think about being back in the Vatican? Is it hard to be here and not to be an insider?"

"Actually it's reinforcing. Pope John is right about the vocation of the clergy, and he was right to send me packing. I don't really deserve the second chance I'm receiving—I was both a terrible parish priest and a disloyal bureaucrat. But I intend to make the best of my chance. The most interesting thing for me, being back here, is how negative my reaction is to all the regalia. I think that I see the pomp and splendor through the Pope's eyes now."

"It's funny that you say that, Father. I've seen some rather remarkable changes in a relatively short time. Just one year ago, when I returned home from here, my kids wouldn't have thought that a Bishop was a real person. They were, quite literally, the stuff of Sunday school legend. Today, we have a Bishop living in our parish, right alongside the other priests. It really is a great experience; it provides continuity within the Church that I didn't realize was lacking. Now, he's not there all the time, of course; but he covers a much smaller territory than he used to, and he's an active part of our parish."

"It sounds as though your diocese is on the cutting edge of the changes that are coming. If the rumors are true, there

358

will be a lot more Bishops appointed to create that level of intimacy all over the globe."

"You may end up a Bishop before long yourself."

"Not a chance. If I am to be the best priest I can become, that has to be all that I think about for the rest of my vocation. No more titles for me, thanks. I would like, someday, to be qualified to be a pastor. You know, the new kind."

"Our pastor spends most of his homilies talking about the success stories of our small, sharing communities. He connects the scripture more to our life as a community. He really drank the Kool-Aid. It's all about our fellow parishioners and how they are living out their faith. If it's possible, the entire parish feels smaller to me."

Across the reception hall, Pope John was having a conversation with his Papal Secretary. To an outside observer, the scene had the look of two monks, out on the town in their finest cassocks, simply relaxing over a nice glass of wine. They didn't have much opportunity these days to spend time outside of their offices. The Church was beginning a whirlwind of a journey and things were moving more smoothly and successfully than anyone would have ever guessed.

"I am so glad to see you wearing your simple cassock, Antonio. It becomes you."

"Yes, Holy Father. It's not easy in these surroundings to maintain much humility; but I think that it's important that I do what I can. If I'm occasionally mistaken for a slightly graying seminarian, then that would be great."

"Wouldn't that be wonderful if I could be mistaken for a seminarian? Unfortunately, those days are behind me…for a variety of reasons." The Pontiff chuckled, putting Antonio further at ease. "Monsignor, are you happy in your current role?"

A mild look of concern crossed Antonio's face. "Holy Father, I cannot be more grateful that you have allowed me to serve you in such a direct way. And with such important matters at stake, I feel so petty for my earlier grumbling to you about having been kept on the periphery during my first years here in Rome."

"That's good to hear, because I have more to ask of you."

Before he could continue, Antonio jumped in. "Anything, Holy Father. Anything."

"I'm grateful that you have already agreed. I wasn't so sure you would after I told you what I was going to." He let Antonio stew for a few moments before letting him off the hook. "I have decided to appoint you to the College of Cardinals at the next Consistory. I would like to make the

Papal Secretary's role more like that of a Chief Operating Officer of the Church, and I think that person should be a member of the College."

"Well, Holy Father, I can see that you have been reading those business magazines that Cardinal Suarez has been sending you. What brings all this on?"

"As you say, some of my friends have been trying to teach an old dog new tricks. I suppose I invited it on myself with all this crazy talk about remaking the Church. I do think that we need to turn the Curia and the Papal Household more into a meritocracy. Some of the lessons of the secular business world could be highly applicable. After all, we run some very sizable enterprises, not unlike a major corporation or other governments."

"I don't disagree; but then perhaps the role should be filled by someone with more experience than I have."

"Nonsense. We are still the Church; and the primary qualifications must always be dedicated service to Her mission."

"For practical reasons then, we should be very thoughtful about the appearance of nepotism. Everyone knows how close we are and how long we have been friends. This would be the wrong time to give anyone cause for concern about what we are doing."

"Yes, Cardinal Donatello, I have struggled with that a great deal myself. However, I must listen to those I respect; and while you may be blissfully unaware, there are those who are clamoring to have you present at the next Conclave." He let that sink in a little while he took a sip of his port. The implication was that there were Cardinals already lining up behind Antonio to be Pope John's successor. To break the tension, he continued, "Not that they are looking forward to the next Conclave, mind you."

"I don't know what to say, Holy Father."

"You don't need to say anything. What you need to begin to wrap your mind around is that the Church is more of a meritocracy now. At the same time, word has gotten around about your little paper and people can put two and two together. As the improvements take hold for the positive, people see the visionary impact that we've had…together. They see the potential for the new Church."

Antonio was speechless. He was struggling to wrap his mind around the pace with which his life was now changing. He was afraid of what this might do to his resolve to remain a simple part of the apparatus of change; to stay out of the limelight.

"Holy Father?" He paused, not quite sure how to phrase what was going through his mind; but Pope John wanted to give him some space. After a few moments, he continued. "Holy Father, I am concerned. Of course I will play whatever role you would like. However, I have a request, if you will indulge me further."

"Of course. What's on your mind?"

"If you were to give me my heart's desire, it would be to take over the Missionary work of the Curia. That would allow me to spend most of my time in the field, working with regular people and keeping my focus on what matters. Selfishly, it would also allow me to see my paper come to fruition."

"Very well, I was wondering when you would ask. What would your vision be for the ministry?"

"In my mind's eye, I see the Church as an exemplar of the service God expects from each one of us. I don't want us to be seen sitting here, relying on declarations of faith as the end of the story. I want our service to be the proof of our faith; with our faith simply the beginning of the story."

Sometime later that evening, Monsignor Donatello was off visiting with some of Giuseppe's family that he knew from Sardinia. Pope John found himself sitting quietly, watching the thinning crowd and considering saying his final goodbyes to the bride and groom. But all he could think about was the pace of change that he had already witnessed in the Church and considering ways to accelerate that change.

"Perhaps more appointees to the ranks of the Bishops are the answer," he told himself. "That would allow us to have even smaller dioceses." Then he considered the important work ahead of figuring out the selection criteria and process. "I can't go too far too fast. We have been so reliant on the old system of recommendation and dynasties that we don't really know how to build our bench strength. Yes, *bench strength,* that's what the business magazines call it."

He loved watching the happy young families, here supporting their relatives and friends as they professed their vows to each other for the future. There were children running around, although they seemed to be finally running out of steam. There were young loves blossoming, perhaps attending their first wedding together and imagining the same for themselves…inspired by the example, he thought.

"How do I find more like Antonio, those who want nothing more than to serve?" He made a mental note. "I must remember to write him a little note, for after I'm gone, encouraging him to take a fresh name upon election. That would be our final sign that the Church is making a fresh start."

PAPAL ARCHIVE

First Papal Homily of Pope John XXIV

Sisters and Brothers in Christ, I come before you in a very humble state. As you all have no doubt heard, I have had a busy week. I stand before you today as His Holiness, Pope John XXIV, the Vicar of Christ on Earth; but in my heart, I am Father Franco Calliendo, parish priest of Sardinia. I say this, not to diminish the Throne of Saint Peter that I so proudly occupy, but to share with you glimpse of where my heart remains.

I love you all so much that I feel the great weight of being the pastor to the world. Just as back in my home parish, I felt the weight of service to so many families. However, what I learned in those days was that it wasn't me, who was responsible for you; you minister to each other's needs in ways that I could only marvel.

I am asked in my new role to lead Holy Mother Church, to be the primary teacher in the ways of faith. I unite with my local Bishops as guides to the faithful, to instruct and guide you on your journey. What I learned however, first as a pastor and later as a Bishop, is that the laity is a much larger vocation than the religious life. It is very difficult for priests and sisters to touch your lives as deeply and as frequently as we would like, or certainly as you would like us to do. What I also learned however, was that my lay brothers and sisters have the Holy Spirit coursing through their vocations so strongly that I could scarcely keep up with their pace of ministry.

Today however, I am somewhat concerned that we, the clergy, are letting you down. Too often we blame a lack of vocations for an inability to adequately serve you. I see the problem in reverse. If only we could serve more directly and to inspire you in your apostolate, I believe the natural outgrowth would be a blossoming of vocations to religious life as well. Because what I know is that the more we all serve, the more we are rewarded and the more we all search for additional opportunities to serve.

I don't blame the laity for failing to answer the call of God; I blame myself for failing to inspire the laity to hear God's call. We Church Fathers have done so much of late to interfere with the work of our Lord. We heap scandal upon the altar. We bring disrepute to your church and then wonder aloud why you don't wish to associate yourself more closely with it.

The Council Fathers at the Second Vatican Council, carried on the breath of the Holy Spirit, ushered out hundreds of years of a fear of change, by releasing the Church from its belief in its own perfection. By remarking in the Council documents that "Christ summons the church to continual reformation of which it is always in need in so far as it is an institution of human beings here on earth," the Council Fathers freed us to move aggressively to achieve their vision. In some ways we have, but in other ways we have shied away, or even been discouraged away from the vision. Most importantly, the Council reminded us that you are the Church. It is the clergy's job to inspire you to live out your vocation and find your ministry to each other.

And now I come before you today, I come as your chief servant. I pledge my support as you, the imperfect Church called to continual reform, as you seek out your ministries and relearn the lessons of the Early Church. The Early Church was far from perfect; in fact, the Letters of the New Testament are full of corrective statements and encouragement to the faithful toward a better path. But the Apostles knew that they couldn't possibly minister personally to a church that was blossoming so quickly. Any attempt to do so would be an attempt to control the invitation of God to His people. I seek to return to that notion of the Church, where the invitation of God to all people is paramount. We need to encourage His people, whether they know him yet or not, to open their hearts to Him. The clergy needs to serve His people in the way Christ served His disciples and in a way that inspires them to serve each other. Anything that discourages His people or interferes with their ministry should be suspect.

So to be clear, I, like Mary, have chosen the better part, while Martha toils at the work that needs to be done. I have dedicated my life to serving God's people; but that frees me from concerns about my own well-being, from raising children in a most difficult world and from dividing my attention between my service to God's people and other responsibilities. My brothers and sisters with lay vocations don't have that luxury. The Lord asks you to live multiple vocations, including spouse and parent, while serving as His hands in the world as well.

My role as Bishop of Rome, together with my brother Bishops, is to serve you in that most difficult life that the Lord has called you to. I pledge, on behalf of my brother Bishops, that we will continually provide the sacraments as tools for your spiritual strength; we will assist you with guidance as you continually look for that better path; and we will otherwise endeavor to stay out of your way as you serve as the Lord's hands in the world serving each other.

Please continually pray for me and for the Church, as I do for you.

Private Letter from Cardinal Welty to Pope John

XXIV

[Cautionary letter on the First Homily]

Most Holy Father,

It is with great reluctance that I write to share my humble sentiments on the occasion of your first public homily.

Some of the sentiments expressed in that address could be interpreted by some in ways that you certainly do not mean. Precisely, I am concerned about two things: the discouragement of those in religious life, and by extension discouragement of future vocations; and the encouragement of the laity in the belief that the Magisterium of the Church is somehow vested in the laity, rather than the clergy.

In the first instance, some of the language you used could be (incorrectly) construed as directly critical of our brother Bishops, especially in their careful responses to scandal in the Church. I know that you don't intend to suggest that our responses to scandal should further risk the reputation or supremacy of the Church, by failing to defend Her. Our brother Bishops have dealt with a number of grievous issues during the last decade; and in their responses naturally must balance the concerns of individuals against the Church as a whole.

In the second instance, ever since the Second Vatican Council concluded, we have sought to elevate the role of the laity in the life of the liturgy, ministry and the Church as a whole. However, going back to the days of Martin Luther, we have been required to draw a bright line between the role of the clergy and the laity. To do otherwise, is to risk the same continual evolution of disunity that has characterized the non-Roman Christian world. I would ask that you consider carefully the extension of lay leadership roles, in a way that preserves the full teaching authority of the Church in Her clergy.

Once again, it concerns me that you might misconstrue my intent in writing to you. I mean merely to extend the greatest courtesy of one brother to another; to humbly offer a perspective that could help shape a further dialogue.

I have the honor to be, Your Holiness's most devoted and obedient brother,

John +

John Cardinal Welty

Private Letters from Pope John XXIV to his circle of advisors

[Initial letter to a select group of Bishops]

Dear Brothers,

It has been nearly two years since my election to occupy the Throne of Saint Peter; and in that time, I have come to count you among my closest advisors on matters of the Church. You are my most fervent supporters and seem to carry me along on your shoulders as I seek to discern the better path. For this I am more grateful than any of you will ever fully understand.

As you have come to know me so well, you will each expect that this distinction carries with it more demands, instead of accolades. Now, more than ever, Holy Mother Church needs your leadership. I, more than ever, need your clear minds and thoughtful assistance. I have come to the conclusion that we stand at an inflection point, from which the Church can blossom or she can slide into permanent disrepair.

In this regard, I quote from our late brother, Carlo Cardinal Martini. "Our culture has aged, our churches are big and empty and the church bureaucracy rises up. The Church must admit its mistakes and begin a radical change, starting from the Pope and the Bishops. The pedophilia scandals oblige us to take a journey of transformation." For my part, I believe the scandals are only a symptom of the need for change. They are the natural result of an increasingly insular culture, which must finally open up and through which let the fresh breeze blow. Like all such cultures, we have tended to elevate into leadership those who seem most familiar, who in turn believe that a culture that recognizes their contributions must be one worth defending.

We are in a vicious cycle, where our behavior and our lack of inspiration are alienating the People of God. This leads to both a lack of religious vocations and the belief among the faithful that they have no say in the life of the Church. They are the Church and yet we encourage their belief that they are the customers of a monopolistic business venture.

While I believe that all of the scandals contribute to this cycle – financial, sexual and otherwise – I think the pedophilia scandal is the most instructive. What is the laity to think, if we refuse to do everything in our power to protect the Lord's children? Then we compound those horrific mistakes by making every attempt to secure protection for the institutional church, rather than putting all our energy into making amends to the real Church. Amid the ashes of this scandal, it's a wonder that any professed religious remain in their vocations and willingly accept the public scorn, let alone that we should see an unsustainable decline in the health of new vocations.

Where does this leave us? As you know, I believe in the Glory Days of the Catholic Church. Not the days of political and social power that so many of our brothers seem to crave.

I believe that our best days were those closest to our origins, when the family of believers would risk everything to bring more people to the knowledge of their Creator's love, up to and including sacrificing their own lives. Metaphorically, we need to return to that sacrifice. We need to be willing to give up our lives for the People of God – believers and non-believers.

To that end, I believe that we need to up-end the Church, to make the last first and the first last. I believe there are a handful of steps that need to take place:

We must thin out the ranks of Bishops and Cardinals, simply to remove the incessant bureaucratic tendencies. Our idle theologians have, for centuries, found it necessary to produce tomes which add little to the Church's core mission, but rather focus on the institution and its practices.

Among our brother Bishops, only those who wish to be active in pastoral duties are necessary. All others should be allowed to retire to a life of praying for the work of the Church.

We must reduce the size and scope of our brother Bishops' responsibilities. If necessary, we can add new fresh faces to allow more Bishops to serve closer to their people, just as pastors do for a parish.

You are among those whom I believe place pastoral care above all else. Certainly you are not the only; but I believe you are the few who are willing to take the actions necessary to incite real change. Now I need your thoughts on how to put these ideas into practice. Please reflect on what I have written here; and start to formulate your recommendations for how you would execute these ideas. My plan is to continue a dialogue among this group, leading to a Synod of Bishops in

376

one year's time consisting of a slightly larger group, which will be charged with developing the permanent plan.

Thank you again for you constant support and direction.

Pax,
John XXIV +
By my hand alone,
H.H. John XXIV

[Second letter to the same group, six months later]

Dear Brothers,

You do well to chastise me for moving so slowly on these changes we have discussed. I realize that it has already been six months since I first suggested the notion of a Synod to discuss radical changes in Holy Mother Church. In the days since, I had been beset by doubts and insecurities.

While my heart assures me that the ideas are correct and good, my mind nevertheless vexes me about the practicalities of these changes. Can they truly work in a global church? And of course, there is always the concern that the simplification of the Church is, in some way, just my own vanity.

I encourage each of you to continue your own discernment on these matters. Cardinal Suarez, I am delighted to hear of some of the changes you have made already, experimenting with residing within a parish church and recommending numerous additional Bishopric appointments from among your most ardent pastors. Rest assured that We will continue to support these efforts with our sincerest blessings.

Thank you all for allowing the Spirit to move you.

Pax,
John XXIV +
By my hand alone,
H.H. John XXIV

[Final letter, three months before his stroke]

Dear Brothers,

I thought it pragmatic to address you all collectively, although you have each independently done so much over the last few months to further my thinking on this topic.

Largely due to the wonderful confidence that you all espouse in the resilience and adaptability of the Church, I agree that we should accelerate our discussions on the topic of renewal. I am not yet to the point where I believe a Synod is the proper forum for this discussion, but I grant you my blessing to expand this circle of conversation. Each of you have expressed your belief in the genuine attitude of reform among other brother Bishops; and I believe that, in preparation for a possible Synod, we should start to create broad-based enthusiasm for the cause of reform.

Let us agree to more regular communications on this topic and seek the guidance of the Holy Spirit to conform the hearts of those that might choose to oppose this progress.

Pax,
John XXIV +
By my hand alone,
H.H. John XXIV

Invitation to Retirement to Cardinal Welty

[Sample letter inviting retirement of certain Bishops]

Your Eminence, my dear Cardinal Johns,

I am so grateful for your devoted service to Holy Mother Church during the forty-eight years of your vocation. You have helped to lead our Church with your wise counsel and kind heart through joyous times as well as times of extreme trial. Certainly your name will go down in the annals of the New York Archdiocese, as well as the Church itself, as a loyal and fervent servant in Her interests.

I write to you on the occasion of a decision that I have reached; and I am asking you to embrace a new challenge for the good of the Church. It is my decision to appoint a replacement Bishop to the Archdiocese of New York. I wish to free you, along with many other senior members of the clergy, for a life of contemplative prayer for the future of the Church. I will approve your appointment to reside in any parish church that you should choose, or you may choose to reside within a monastic community of your choosing.

I truly pray that this decision causes you no personal discomfort, even as I know that it may come as a surprise. It is my judgment that, as the Lord's Church goes through some significant change, that we will need an army of prayer-partners to see us through. I look forward to corresponding with you and hearing of your progress in this new ministry.

Pax,
John XXIV +
By my hand alone,
H.H. John XXIV

19006029R00211

Made in the USA
Charleston, SC
02 May 2013